P9-BAU-722

firefly cloak

Also by Sheri Reynolds

* * *

Bitterroot Landing

The Rapture of Canaan

A Gracious Plenty

Sheri Reynolds

firefly

cloak

a novel

Three Rivers Press
New York

Published in the United States by Three Rivers Press,
an imprint of the Crown Publishing Group, a division
of Random House, Inc., New York.
www.crownpublishing.com

Three Rivers Press and the tugboat design are registered
trademarks of Random House, Inc.

Published in hardcover in the United States by Shaye Areheart
Books, an imprint of the Crown Publishing Group, a division of
Random House, Inc., New York, in 2006.

Library of Congress Cataloging-in-Publication Data
Reynolds, Sheri.
Firefly cloak : a novel / Sheri Reynolds.—1st ed.
1. Girls—Fiction. 2. Abandoned children—Fiction.
3. Maternal deprivation—Fiction. 4. Mothers and
daughters—Fiction. 5. Grandparent and child—Fiction.
6. Southern States—Fiction. I. Title.
PS3568.E8975F57 2006
813'.54—dc22 2005022444
ISBN: 978-0-307-34183-9

Printed in the United States of America

Design by Lynne Amft

10 9 8 7 6 5 4 3 2 1

First Paperback Edition

For my momma,

Patsy Reynolds

Acknowledgments

When this book was still a swirl of images in my mind, Nora Budzilek helped me sort through and interpret them. I'm so grateful for her wisdom and guidance. Nora died before the book was completed, so I send out this thank you to her spirit and in her memory.

My readers provided insights, suggestions, and question marks on early drafts that helped me shape and reshape this story. Thanks to Christin Lore Weber, Amy Tudor, Janet Peery, Jenean Hall, and Elizabeth Mills.

When everything was finished but the ending, I got great advice from Sammie Jordan, Mary Beth Jordan, Pat Reynolds, and my friends from the Mythic Journey Dreamsharing Circle in Norfolk.

My agent, Candice Fuhrman, has stood by me and my writing for thirteen years now, and I thank her for her expertise and friendship. Shaye Areheart bought this book before I'd even written it, and I'm grateful to her and her colleagues at Shaye Areheart Books for publishing this novel.

And thanks especially to Barbara Brown. She came home each night and listened as I read aloud every word I'd written. Her encouragement and support mean everything to me.

firefly cloak

The night before she lost her momma, Tessa Lee camped out in a two-room tent with her momma, her little brother, Travis, and a crooked-nosed man named Goose. Goose had picked them up that morning at a grocery store in South Hibiscus and loaded their bags into the back of his pickup while her momma gave Tessa Lee a shove into the cab. When Travis was settled beside her, and when her momma had rooted in and slammed the door, Goose said, "Let's skedaddle," and they rattled through the parking lot, waving good-bye to the old men who sat out front on benches and waited for the ice-cream truck.

It was the first time Tessa Lee had ever heard that word *skedaddle,* and she sang it over and over to a tune she made up herself. She sang it to Travis and grabbed at his pudding belly and made him laugh until her momma told her to quit.

"She ain't bothering me," Goose said. But Tessa Lee shut up, anyway.

She couldn't stop singing it in her head, though. As they bumped their way out of town, Tessa Lee studied the rearview mirror and the dusty ghosts poofing up behind them. "Skedaddle, skedaddle," she mouthed to the ghosts.

They'd left behind her bicycle and her Weebles, her Spirograph and her books. Her momma had said she wouldn't need toys while she was on vacation, but as they drove along hot roads that faded into wavy black seas, it seemed strange to Tessa Lee that she'd be going on vacation with a man she'd never met before. He was friendly enough and let her steer for a long time in Alabama, but while Travis was steering, she turned around and saw that the wind had blown over a bag of her clothes. Her winter coat had spilled out, and the furry hood shivered like a kitten against the tailgate.

Tessa Lee shivered, too, in spite of the thick heat, and said to her momma, "Must be going on vacation in the North Pole if I'm gonna need my fur coat when I get there," and Tessa Lee's momma shook her head and lit another smoke.

"Smart girl," Goose said.

"If she's smart, she'll quit sassing," her momma replied. But Tessa Lee could tell she wasn't mad. Just worried. She could see worry in the way her momma tapped that cigarette at the edge of the windowsill, trying to keep the ashes neat and short and manageable. Not a bit like laid-back Goose who let his ashes grow long and fade to white, then drop down warm onto his hairy belly.

Goose listened to country and sang with all the yodelers and told stories about going on alligator hunts when he was a boy. After a while, Travis fell asleep, and when they stopped for gas somewhere in Tennessee, Tessa Lee's momma was left holding him while Tessa Lee went in the store to help Goose tote out the Yoo-hoos. When the man behind the counter said, "Your little girl's gonna be a heartbreaker," Goose said, "Already is," and winked at Tessa Lee, and she trotted out proud with the drinks and decided it wouldn't be so bad to have a daddy named after a bird.

"Gotta gear down," Goose said as they went up a hill, and

by then they were in the mountains and gearing down a lot. Tessa Lee adjusted her legs so that he could work the gearshift. The backs of her thighs sweated against the vinyl seat, and when she tried to move them, a little bit of her skin got pinched in a place where the seat had cracked and the foam poked through. Goose jiggled gears against the insides of her knees, and Tessa Lee looked at her momma, who took tiny quiet gasps of air and twiddled her fingers through Travis's curls until his head looked like a hundred black fins.

They stopped again at a truck stop off a busy highway, a bright yellow building where they sold ponchos and fireworks and bumper stickers that Tessa Lee wasn't allowed to read. Her momma yanked her away from the stickers and paid for their bags of barbecue potato chips, along with some Handi Wipes for the truck. When they got back out, Goose had moved the truck to the rear of the building, behind three big metal Dumpsters that sat there like a row of rhinoceroses, minus their horns. He was changing the license plates.

"What do we need new license plates for?" Tessa Lee asked.

"Shhh," he said, then whispered, "We're in a new state, gotta have new plates." Then he looked at her momma and said, "Load 'em up, Sheila."

"Come on," her momma said, but Tessa Lee was already hunched down next to Goose.

"These plates aren't new," she said.

"Sure they are," Goose answered, looking over his shoulder and then giving all four screws another quick twist. "They're new to us. Hop on in the truck, now. We gotta scoot."

So Tessa Lee climbed inside and soon they were on the road, the red line of the speedometer climbing up to the middle, then pointing all the way to her momma's bony knees.

She thought about those license plates as she ate her chips, then while she sucked the barbecue powder off her fingers and nibbled the orange outlines from the edges of her nails. She thought about those plates all splattered up with bug bits, little flecks of bugs from faraway places. Finally she asked, "What did you do with the old license plates?"

Her momma sighed and said, "Honey, Goose just swapped plates with somebody headed for where we came from. Now their license plates will match where they're going, and ours'll match where we're going."

"We going to Massachusetts?" Tessa Lee asked.

"Absolutely," said Goose.

THAT NIGHT at the state park campground, they built a fire and had hot dogs without buns, and then marshmallows, and her momma said, "Isn't this fun?" and Travis laughed and ran around spitting on ant beds. He had marshmallow on his face, and the dirt stuck to it and gave him a little gritty beard. When Tessa Lee pointed it out, everybody laughed, even the couple at the next campsite with just a one-room tent.

Goose dug through a cooler and handed her momma a beer. Tessa Lee cut her eyes and said, "You promised," but her momma looked away and said, "We're on vacation." Then she popped the tab and made the beer hiss. Even after Tessa Lee and Travis were inside the tent, trying to sleep with a mess of mosquitoes and no-see-ums, Tessa Lee listened for the hissing of beers, one after the other.

And then it was late, but too hot to sleep. Travis was asleep, but not Tessa Lee. His diaper needed changing, but the diapers were out in the truck, and Tessa Lee's momma and Goose were whispering and laughing in a way that let her know that she shouldn't go out there. Then they moved to the tent, and Tessa Lee thought she should go get a diaper. But Goose and her momma were rustling the walls, so she decided to be still and keep her eyes closed. She'd never been in a tent before, much less a two-room tent, but she wished the walls were thicker and didn't flutter so much.

She kept her eyes closed tight and listened to the swishing walls and the smacky mouth noises, wet and sticky, and she told herself that Goose was just eating blueberries. It sounded like blueberries popping into his mouth, squishy as he sucked on them, and she wondered where they'd gotten blueberries from and why nobody had offered her any.

THE NEXT DAY when she woke up, her momma was gone, and Goose was gone, and the truck was gone. She thought at first that Travis was gone, too, but then she saw him wandering around a couple of campsites over, and when she got there, he was licking a pine tree.

"Get your mouth off that tree," she said and slapped him easy like her momma would do.

"I like how trees taste," Travis said and kept on licking.

He was wearing gray shorts over his diaper—a clean one—but no shirt. Somebody had written a phone number on his back, in big black Magic Marker letters. Tessa Lee looked at the number and didn't know at first what it meant. She took his hand and led him back to the tent and found a box of Cheerios beside their bags of clothes.

"Is that your phone number?" asked the woman at the next campsite. "Whose number is that?"

"I don't know," Tessa Lee said. "Maybe it's the place where Momma and Goose went for breakfast. Probably wanted me to call when we woke up."

But she knew they weren't coming back. They'd skedaddled without her. The clothes in the bags belonged to her and to Travis. Her momma's clothes weren't there. Her momma's clothes had been packed in a duffel bag with the word *Foxy* written in rhinestones on the side, and the duffel bag was gone. The only thing she'd left behind was the two-room tent and her firefly cloak, which Tessa Lee and Travis had used for covers the night before. Tessa Lee put it on over her pajamas and didn't worry too much about dragging it through the dirt.

A security guard sat with them at a picnic table and waited, and then a police officer came, and a nice woman who drew hopscotch squares on the ground for nobody to jump in. Travis went inside the tent and cried until the policeman let him blow the siren on his car. Tessa Lee just paced around the campsite, looking for a note that might have blown away in the wind. There wasn't any wind to speak of, but she thought maybe it had been windy before she woke up, and she checked the back of a BB-bat wrapper she found in the grass, and she studied a receipt half-burned in the fire pit, but there were no words from her momma.

Finally her grandparents drove up in a white van, but

since Tessa Lee didn't know yet who they were, she most certainly did not go hug their necks or try to pet the little dog who hung his head out the window and yowled. She wrapped the cloak tight around her and sucked on a strand of her hair, and when the woman who turned out to be her granny asked if she knew where her momma was headed, she didn't mention anything about Massachusetts.

Seven years later, when she finally found her momma, she wasn't in New England after all. She'd been living two hours away, all that time, up the beach just two hours and never coming to a single dance recital or ball game. Not sending the first birthday card or even calling when she got her tonsils taken out and had to spend the night in the hospital.

All those years, Tessa Lee made up stories for Travis. She told him their momma was a dancer with long legs who wore glitter on her eyelids and white costumes with transparent wings that glowed in the dark. She told Travis that their momma had fingers like feathers, and then he remembered how softly she'd held him, and he cried a little until Tessa Lee whispered that she'd be coming back some day soon.

Secretly, she thought that when her momma *did* come back, she'd punch her in the guts for leaving Travis. Tessa Lee was strong enough to take care of herself, but Travis was still really little. She could have waited until he was four.

Tessa Lee told Travis their momma smiled all the time and knew more songs than anybody, and she sang him the one about the itsy-bitsy spider and also the one about shoofly pie.

She told Travis that whenever their momma laughed, her laugh was as strong as cheese. Then they both tried to laugh that way, practicing to sound like their momma. They ate cheese slices on the back doorsteps, in case that would help them get the sound right, and Travis would say, "Like this?" and he'd eat some cheese and whinny like a mule, and Tessa Lee would say, "No, more like this," and then she'd call up a laugh from the lowest part of her throat.

But it never sounded quite right, and Tessa Lee knew it was partly her fault that Travis never got to hear their momma laugh. If she hadn't nagged her so much, she probably wouldn't have left.

Their granny, who was no fan of nonsense, would say, "Quit filling his head with dreams. Your momma's a drunk. I'm sorry to say it, 'cause I raised her better. But she's a drunk."

And Tessa Lee knew it was true, but she couldn't stand for Travis to think that. "She only drank wines from foreign lands," she insisted. "High-class wines. And one time, she met a prince in the cabernet section of the grocery store, and he offered to take us all back to his country."

"Why didn't you go with him, then?" her granny asked.

"'Cause in some countries, they treat women like slaves," Tessa Lee explained. "And here, women have opportunities."

WHEN TESSA LEE found her momma, she was working in a wax museum on the boardwalk strip. It was the hottest part of summer, and she'd walked a long time down High-Seas Avenue, past beachwear shops and sunglasses huts, past dingy motels built of cinder blocks and motels that jutted up twenty stories and blocked out the waves breaking just over the dunes. She'd been walking for ages when she stopped for a sno-cone and asked the girl behind the counter how much farther it was to Fantasies of the Boardwalk, and it turned out she had a long way left to go.

She walked through air thick and sweet with cotton candy, then suntan lotion, chili, hot garbage. In the next block, there were diesel fumes, pizza spices, and incense wafting through a beaded doorway where a man with barely a mustache at all smiled at her and tried to wave her inside.

She walked over cracked sidewalks, around orange highway cones where workers replaced pipes beneath the concrete. Sometimes she walked faster than the cars could cruise, and she ignored the boys who shouted at her and invited her to ride. Her granny had warned her about boys like that.

She hoped her granny was all right and not too worried, not lying on the couch with her head hanging off the side, swallowing bits of crushed ice like she did when Travis died and her heart wouldn't quit banging. Tessa Lee's own heart slammed against her ribs, thinking about her granny, so she cleared her head and kept walking.

Finally, she could see the sign up ahead, a black sign with neon letters—FANTASIES OF THE BOARDWALK—and a row of white lights flashing all around the edges. Her breath came fast, like those lights, electricity jumping from one bulb to the next. What if her momma had been transferred to another wax museum somewhere far away?

Tessa Lee stopped, took off her backpack, and fished around in it for the flyer, a full-color brochure advertising the place where her momma supposedly worked. The wax museum boasted life-sized replicas of famous celebrities and monsters. It promised freaks of nature, like the "Amazing Three-Legged Ballerina and Other Wonders."

She'd taken the flyer from the inside cover of her granny's bible the day before. She'd memorized the directions. She'd memorized everything on that flyer, including the code for a dollar-off coupon she knew she'd never use. Almost every day since her granny's cousin had delivered the flyer to them, Tessa Lee had visited it, tried to charm the meaning out of it. She'd folded and refolded it, sniffed it, rubbed its edges along her face. The cousin claimed he'd seen her momma working there when he was at a medical-supply conference, and he'd picked up the brochure from his hotel lobby.

As soon as he mentioned her momma's name, her granny had sent Tessa Lee outside and told her to water the gardenias. But she'd turned on the hose and then hung out beneath the kitchen window, listening. Her granny asked the man if he was certain it was Sheila, and he was 99 percent sure, so she put the flyer in her bible, right next to their season passes for the water park. Afterward, whenever her granny went to the recreation center to teach a craft class or over to Rosie Jo's to play a hand of rummy, Tessa Lee visited the flyer, studying all the pictures, imagining her momma and the Amazing Three-Legged Ballerina twirling together across a stage.

The flyer described Fantasies of the Boardwalk as "dazzling" and "out of this world," so Tessa Lee was surprised to see a sick-looking bum leaning against the side of the building next to some garbage bins. She was surprised by the mildew that stained the white paint green where the gutter was broken and the rain had dripped down. Those weren't things she associated with her momma or things she'd imagined as she left home early that morning.

Just that morning, she'd tiptoed in her bare feet down the hall past her granny's room, where her granny snored softly beneath the buzz of her window unit. She was careful with the door and didn't let it squeak or slam, and she didn't put on her sandals until she was off the deck. She'd walked the mile out to the highway, then down the roadside in the dewy beggar-lice, her thumb pointing north, and about the time the sun got hot on her head, a trucker stopped, a nice trucker who bought her a breakfast biscuit. She'd heard stories about the dangers of hitchhiking, but the man who picked her up was a part-time evangelist, and all he wanted in return for the miles was to hold her hand in his while he prayed for her safe journey.

So she said "Amen" and then "thank you." She hopped out of the truck at the edge of town and took off again on foot.

When she found the place where her momma worked, it wasn't much past lunchtime. But what if her momma was off that day? Her heart kicked hard, and a part of her wanted to run back to Hully Sanders's Mobile City where her granny was probably worried sick.

She hoped her granny wasn't crying and that Rosie Jo was with her. She'd waited for Rosie Jo to get back from her Caribbean cruise before she took off.

Tessa Lee was sweaty, and she didn't want her momma to see her like that, so she went inside a dark arcade, where boys in loose T-shirts watched other boys shoot targets on a screen. The boy working behind the counter had safety pins through his ears and green hair that stood straight up, and Tessa Lee was a little afraid to talk to him. Boys didn't look like that where she came from. There was a sign that said NO PUBLIC RESTROOMS right there on the counter next to the cash register, but when she asked the green-haired boy if she could use the bathroom, he nodded and pointed her to a hallway, where she wedged between cardboard boxes and stepped around a bucket of water and an old moldy mop to get through the door.

The toilet was broken, but she used it just the same. She splashed water on her face and hoped her sunburn wouldn't keep her momma from recognizing her.

It was too hot for makeup, but she put it on anyway: eye-liner, mascara, lip gloss. She powdered her face even though she knew it would dew right back up and combed out her ponytail and redid it high up on her head.

On the way out of the arcade, she thanked the boy behind the counter, who gave her a nod. Then she cleared her throat and said, "I'm looking for a woman named Sheila Birch. I heard she works at Fantasies of the Boardwalk. Do you know her?"

But the guy just shrugged and scratched at a bite on his arm.

IT WAS HER momma, all right. Tessa Lee recognized her right away. She had long dark hair with loose waves, like Tessa

Lee's hair, and very round hazel eyes, like Tessa Lee's eyes. But she was really skinny, with collarbones that scooped in and made moats around her neck. Tessa Lee put her face up close to the glass and stared until a breathy voice said, "Welcome to Fantasies of the Boardwalk. Buy your ticket at the booth to your left."

Her voice didn't sound quite real. It sounded like a bird imitating her momma.

Her momma was dressed like a mermaid, reclining in a conch shell, but she was shrunken, not full size. The conch shell itself was just a little larger than a baby's cradle, and her momma was small enough to fit inside it. She didn't look much bigger than a baby or a doll. Tessa Lee wondered what it would feel like to hold her.

"Welcome to Fantasies of the Boardwalk," her momma repeated. "Buy your ticket at the booth to your left."

Tessa Lee watched her mouth move and saw that she was actually speaking. It wasn't a recording. But there was something wrong with her teeth. They didn't fit. They were too big for her mouth. They pushed her lips out a smidgen too far to be her momma's lips. Her momma's long legs were missing, too, hidden somewhere beneath the blue-green tail that draped over the side of the conch shell and arched gracefully into a perfectly useless fin.

Her bra was made of shells, maybe cockleshells, and Tessa Lee stared at her small breasts, her tanned skin, her long brown arms, at the slight wrinkles at the base of her neck.

Her momma sighed and said: "Girl, are you gonna buy a ticket or just stare at me all day? You act like you've never seen a mermaid before." It was the same voice that might have said, "Girl, are you gonna pick up those blocks or leave them scattered all over the floor?" and something in Tessa Lee's chest broke open and spread out warm.

"I'm sorry," she said. "I haven't had a lot of experience— with mermaids."

She could tell now that the conch shell was made of plastic, that it was like a bed, like the spaceship bed Travis had looked at over and over in the mail-order catalogue. Pop-Pop wouldn't buy it because there wasn't enough room in the mobile home for a bed with a pointy nose.

A man in flip-flops carrying a little girl on his shoulders edged up to the window. The child pointed and laughed, and while her momma told them where to buy their tickets, Tessa Lee noticed that there were crabs crawling around the bottom of the fake conch shell. She couldn't tell if they were real. They looked real, but it was hard to be sure. They might be windup crabs, like bathtub toys.

She went to the ticket counter where a man, eyes closed, was bobbing his head to music only he could hear. Tessa Lee knocked on the glass, startling him, and she bought a ticket and strolled through the museum. She was the only patron in those stuffy, dark halls. She looked for an inside view of her momma while she worked up the nerve to tell her who she was.

She saw wax renditions of a famous clown, and some old movie stars, and she saw the characters from a cartoon she used to watch with Travis. She could see rough edges on every figure, like nobody'd bothered to scrape off the extra wax when the figure came out of its mold. Tessa Lee had made candles with her granny to sell at craft fairs, and she knew how important small details could be. Here, nobody seemed to care. And on top of that, there was no sign of her momma.

So she went back to the picture window, where the mermaid said, "Welcome to Fantasies of the Boardwalk. Buy your ticket at the booth to your left," like she'd never seen Tessa Lee before in her life.

Tessa Lee looked around, and since nobody else was there, she said, "Momma, it's me, Tessa Lee."

The mermaid peered out from her conch shell with empty round eyes while the crabs clicked around on the floor.

Tessa Lee held her breath and tried to swallow past her heart, which had made it up as far as her throat. "Remember? You left me and Travis seven years ago?" she said. "You left with Goose?"

"I don't know nobody named Goose," the mermaid said, sharply now.

But she looked like she might cry, like her mouth was about to crumple. Her teeth nudged out past her pout, her all-wrong teeth. Tessa Lee studied her about-to-crumple face, and her hair, which sat cock-sided on her head.

Her momma was wearing a wig.

"Sheila Birch?" Tessa Lee asked. "That's your name, right?"

"I don't go by that name," the mermaid whispered. "I'm on the clock," she said. "You gotta go." She looked confused, her eyes darting every which way.

"You gotta come home," Tessa Lee said. "Something bad's happened." She wanted to tell her about Travis and how he'd died, but she couldn't. Not when her momma was wearing a costume.

"Shhh," the mermaid shushed. "I don't know you." She adjusted her shoulders and jabbed at one of the shells of her bra, and Tessa Lee wondered if she had anything underneath that shell at all. Maybe the mermaid wasn't her momma. Maybe she wasn't real.

The mermaid composed her face, sat up taller, and gave her shoulders a wiggle. "I can't have children," she said. "All my children are fish." And then she laughed a startling laugh, too loud for someone so shrunken, too rich.

The sound was completely familiar, and Tessa Lee could feel her face get hot. She touched her cheeks and touched her nose, and she could feel tiny blisters from the sunburn breaking, damp on her fingers as she rubbed them away. Her whole face was wet with sweat and blisters, and she couldn't breathe.

"Momma," she said. "Please," and then she took off her backpack and pulled out the firefly cloak, hoping it would help her remember. Because maybe her momma'd been in an accident and had amnesia, and that's why she'd never come back. Tessa Lee held it up for her momma to see. "Look," she said, and she put on the firefly cloak, which fit her perfectly by then.

It was a faded navy blue velvety robe, with tiny gold fireflies glowing all over. Some of them were so gold they almost looked green, and when she held up her arms, the fabric made wings. Just putting it on made Tessa Lee feel stronger, gave her something to cloak herself with and made her feel safe.

But her momma sucked in a deep gasp, and when she let it out, she cried, "Nooooo," long and hard. It was almost a shriek, almost a wailing. In an instant, there were people around Tessa Lee on the boardwalk, tourists and shopkeepers and the guy from the hot dog cart across the street, watching the mermaid, who kept crying. She put both hands on her face and wiped backward from her eyes until she'd pushed the wig far enough for everyone to see her bleached hair frizzing yellow beneath it. She smeared her mascara in thick swoops, and Tessa Lee was ashamed to see her like that.

People swarmed around the window, and one woman tapped on the glass and said, "Easy, honey," and tried to calm her momma down as Tessa Lee backed to the edges of the crowd.

Then a door opened from the side of the wax museum, and a man with thick gold chains around his neck and hair like a rusty Brillo pad sauntered up to the window and said, "What the hell's the matter with you?" He looked official. He had a cell phone on his belt and a knife in a little holster with a swinging golden chain.

Her momma was gasping, like she was choking. She looked a little like her granny right after Travis died, when she got too worked up and Rosie Jo had to put a paper bag over her nose to keep her from hyperventilating. Her momma kept shaking her head, wheezing "No, no," her voice already hoarse.

The guy from the hot dog cart pointed to Tessa Lee and said, "That gal right there's the one who riled her up, Reggie."

"Her?" the man asked, and Tessa Lee looked away and started stuffing the firefly cloak back into her backpack. She wanted to run, but she hadn't even told her momma about Travis.

"Yeah," the hot dog guy said. "I saw her. She was doing some kinda voodoo or something, whispering and putting on a robe."

The zipper on her backpack got caught in the fabric, and Tessa Lee forced it, blushing, trying not to look at all the people who were looking at her, puzzled and accusing.

"What are you harassing my employees for?" Reggie asked. "Get outta here, you little punk," and he took a step toward Tessa Lee, like he was running her off, like she was a raccoon in his garbage. But before Tessa Lee had a chance to bolt, her momma let out another big cry, and she couldn't just leave with her momma crying.

"Holy shit," the guy from the hot dog cart said and laughed, and Reggie shook his head like nothing in the whole world made sense. He grabbed Tessa Lee by the arm, and when he did, her momma howled again.

She tried to yank her arm away. She almost yelled out "Travis got killed," but that seemed like the wrong way to break the news, especially when her momma was already so upset, and besides that, she didn't want to say Travis's name out loud if her momma was just going to deny she knew him.

Before she had a chance to do anything, Reggie shouted back to the mermaid, "Straighten up in there! Cut off the light and go clean up your face. I mean it!"

And in a flash, just that fast, the picture window went dark inside. The mermaid disappeared, and Tessa Lee'd missed her opportunity. People on the boardwalk oohed and laughed and began to disperse.

Tessa Lee tried to wiggle her arm away, but the man grabbed her tighter.

"You're hurting me," she said, not quietly.

"You shut up," he said under his breath, and he pulled her down the block, his fingers tight on her arm.

"Let me go," Tessa Lee demanded. "That's my momma. I've gotta talk to her."

Reggie paused, looked down at her, and laughed. He had on sunshades, so she wasn't sure where he was looking, but she thought he might be looking at her breasts.

"You can't talk to her right now," he replied, but he relaxed his grip a little. They turned the corner and moved toward an amusement park. "I got a business to run," he said. "Can't have any whacked-out mermaids screaming at the customers, you understand?"

"But she's my momma," Tessa Lee insisted. There was bile in her throat. Her heart was rising, fluttering. She needed some crushed ice.

"Whether she is or whether she ain't, she's on the job right now," the man said.

Tessa Lee clenched her teeth to keep from crying. "I've waited a long time to see her," she whispered. Then she tightened every muscle and pulled herself into the darkness at her center, where none of it could touch her, where there was no need to give up because there was nothing else to lose.

The man with his fingers still clamping her arm said, "She gets off at 11:00, and you can talk to her then. But I don't wanna see you back on that block before. You hear me?"

When Tessa Lee didn't reply, he grabbed her chin and held it up, and he pulled his face down close to her, so close she could see the clogged black pores on his nose.

"You hear me?" he repeated. "If I see your face again before 11:00, I'll call somebody to come get you. Or better yet, I might put you to work for me." He leaned down and kissed her on the mouth, then swatted her hard on her bottom. "You mark my word," he said.

He left her next to a trailer stand where girls dressed up as belly dancers made jewelry out of gold chains. The chains were on spools that they pulled out like thread. They said, "Hey, Reggie," and he said, "Hey, ladies," and walked away.

Tessa Lee started walking in the other direction. She didn't have anywhere to go, but that didn't stop her. She wiped her mouth off hard with the back of her hand and marched on.

SHE FOUND a library and read the Bible for a while, but it didn't help. God hadn't said anything new in so long, hadn't written a gospel for her generation or named a single new prophet in two thousand years. So she studied atlases instead and ran her fingers along meridians and flipped through changing terrains until the library closed and she had to leave. After that, she wandered back to the amusement park and walked among the rides. She listened to the merry-go-round music and longed for Travis.

There was a little boy who reminded her of Travis, waiting to ride the kiddie bumper cars. He was wearing red swim trunks, no shirt, and he was plump like Travis. His little brown boobies jiggled as he ran to get a car. She watched him laugh and ram his car into the others, then get stuck at the side, unable to back out, frustrated, hollering for help. He looked a lot like Travis looked when he was five or six. He had black hair that curled all over, but his eyes were brown, and Travis's were green.

Some sidewalk performers put on a show, so Tessa Lee

sat down and watched, admiring their backflips and the way they balanced on each other's shoulders. She nibbled a candy apple and tried to make it last a long time.

She walked past the trailer where the jewelry makers were dressed as belly dancers and looked at the bracelets and necklaces on display. One of the girls had chains around her waist, and whenever she moved her hips the least little bit, the chains tinkled and laughed against one another. There were three girls there, all about her same age. They weren't very old at all.

She wanted to be at the museum by 10:45, in case her momma got off early, or in case her watch didn't match the time clock at Fantasies of the Boardwalk. But she was scared Reggie might be there. She could still feel his fingerprints on her arm.

So she went to the arcade instead and moved between video games and people and streams of smoke. The green-haired boy wasn't there anymore. She breathed the music in and out as it screeched and beat inside her blood vessels, and she wandered spirals through the room. She pictured her fear behind her, trailing like a vapor. As long as she kept moving, she'd stay ahead of it. Whenever it came close, she concentrated on her feet, on her red sandals with their thick soles, and she took another step.

Finally, it was late enough to return to the wax museum.

But her momma wasn't there. There was a new mermaid in the conch shell, a chubby one with red hair and a bright pink clam-shell bra. She told Tessa Lee she didn't know anybody named Sheila Birch.

"But she was just here," Tessa Lee insisted. "I saw her this afternoon."

"No," said the new mermaid. "That was just an illusion. This is a town of illusions, honey. You better go on home, get back to wherever you came from before you forget who you are."

Three older boys wearing tight jeans and muscle shirts and matching bandannas on their heads clustered up around the window and asked the new mermaid if they could get inside her shell. The leader, whose jeans were white, rubbed himself between his pockets, and Tessa Lee looked away fast. The mermaid cackled and told them to buy a ticket at the booth to their left.

One boy invited Tessa Lee to come with them. He dallied his tongue around his bottom lip and said he'd buy her a ticket.

"Yeah," another one called back. "We'll have us a party," and when Tessa Lee declined, they called her a tease and a bitch, and then they walked away.

"See here," the new mermaid told her. "You better go. Hanging 'round here by yourself this time of night, somebody'll make you their bride."

"But I gotta find my momma," Tessa Lee said. "Her name's Sheila Birch, and she works here."

"Baby," the new mermaid said, "your momma ain't here. There's only room enough for one mermaid in this town, and I'm it. Now get outta here."

So Tessa Lee went.

Sheila Birch had eighty-one dollars in her pocket when she flagged down a taxi on the highway at 10:45. She'd left work early, even before Sophie'd arrived to take her place. She'd crawled out of her room full of mirrors, mirrors angled in a thousand directions to make her look tiny and frame her in a shell. She'd loosened the corset of the mermaid's tail on her own and thrown it over a chair in the dressing room, then changed clothes quickly and left through the back without even clocking out. She didn't want Reggie to know. Not until she'd had time to get away.

She cut through the alley and across the parking lot of the pancake house. She didn't want to be seen, and she didn't want to be found.

"Where to?" the cab driver asked her.

"Anywhere," she said and laughed. "Loop the city, and tie a knot in it," she said. "A strong knot so it can't wiggle out."

"I'm gonna need a deposit," the driver said, so Sheila tossed him a twenty and stretched out in the back.

She watched the lights pass by, neon and halogen streetlights, traffic lights, the spotlight outside a dance club, a sea of lights. Sheila was underneath them, in the backseat of the cab, at the bottom of that sea. Somewhere out there she had a daughter. A fish-child in a firefly cloak. She was high and she was drowning. It felt good for a while, and then it didn't.

"Take me home," she said to the cabbie.

"Lady, I don't know where that is. Why don't you sit up and tell me?"

"I can't," Sheila answered. She burrowed into the vinyl of the seat's back and closed her eyes tightly so it would be dark for a minute. But when she looked at the dark, she saw fireflies, lighting up and flickering, sneaking up on her and glowing. The fireflies mocked her and made her feel sick.

"I better sit up," she said, and she did. Something was clotting inside her mouth, so she went through her bag looking for gum. But then the light caught her eyes again. She looked up at the light, then down in her bag, and all she could see were fireflies, so she gave up on the gum and tried to rest.

Sheila was drowning in the lights, but she was a mermaid, so she knew it'd be okay. All she had to do was swim away. The cabbie's voice kept calling her back: "Lady, you're not OD'ing, are you? You want me to take you to the hospital?"

"No," she insisted. In her ears, her voice sounded far away and small.

"I need more money," the cabbie said, "or I'll have to put you out."

Sheila wadded a twenty into a loose ball and threw it over the seat.

"I need an address," he added.

Sheila tried to remember where she wanted to go. Not back to the wax museum. She couldn't go there anymore. The girl would keep looking.

Not to the apartment. Reggie would find her there.

"Where do you live at?" the cabbie asked.

"Way out of town," Sheila said. "Take a left. Buy a ticket at the booth to your left."

The driver threw up both hands and said, "Aiee, why are you doing this to me, lady?"

"I'm sorry," Sheila said, and she tried to reach over and put her hand on the driver's shoulder to give him a squeeze,

but she missed and squeezed his headrest. "T
there. See that road, right up there?" She pulle
from her pocket and tossed it toward the driver. This one fluttered gently, then caught a current from the AC vent and blew over to the passenger seat.

The driver turned west and kept going.

Sheila threw her last dollar into the air to watch it fly. "I used to live in a swaybacked house," she said and settled against the seat. It pleased her to remember that. It sounded perfect, the perfect answer to every question, though she wasn't sure what it meant.

"You are one messed-up chick," the cabbie said. "You got a driver's license? Show me your ID."

But Sheila ignored him. She was following the lights to the swaybacked house that she could picture in her mind. She knew if she could get back there, everything would be okay. Nothing would turn out the way it had, if she could just get back to the swaybacked house. She could undo it all once she got there.

Then she was crying at the memory of that house. The roof was sunken in the middle, arched in from the weight of something—snow that didn't melt for a long time, the awful weight of winter. She always expected the roof to collapse, to fall in on her, but something kept it intact.

A vine grew inside that house, twining up from the ground and supporting the whole thing. It was dark inside and damp, and ferns grew in the corners, and all the walls were soft, so soft you could leave your fingerprints there.

It didn't collapse. The vine held it up, and from the outside, at the very front where the rafters met in a perfect A, the vine burst forth—green, with soft red tubular flowers.

"Take me to the swaybacked house," Sheila muttered. "I used to live in a swaybacked house, but now I can't find it."

"Lady, sit up," the driver said.

"I used to live in a swaybacked house," she sang, and then she was rocking in the backseat of the cab, or maybe they were going down a dirt road, a bumpy road. They were out in the country, on the way home.

When she got home, she'd be safe, like a fern, protected by dense, cool shade. The lights were already gone. No more lights, just a serene darkness. She was going to the place before fireflies.

And then she got sick. The great wash of her mistakes, all of them came rushing out, sour years and decisions dripping from the seat and running in the grooves of the floor mats.

"Damnit," the cabbie said, "you old crackhead," and he hit the brakes. "I try to be good to you and look what I get. I shoulda took you to the police. Now *get* out."

"I'm sorry," Sheila said. She wiped her mouth hard with the back of her hand. "But you got me home. Thank you."

They were nowhere at all. There was nothing around but some woods and a ditch. The driver said, "You know, I'm doing you a favor, leaving you here. If I took you to the police station, they'd throw you in the can."

"This is exactly where I wanted to go. Do I owe you more money?" she asked.

"Nah," he said. "You're paid up."

"Good," she said. "'Cause I'm out of money," and she laughed.

The driver shook his head. "Listen," he said. "The road's not too far back thataway," and he pointed from where they'd come. "Sleep it off, and somebody'll give you a lift tomorrow."

"I'll do that," Sheila said. "I'll just sleep it off." She stepped out into darkness and stumbled just once. Then she set off looking for her swaybacked house.

It was nearly midnight when Lil convinced Rosie Jo to go on home.

"You sure?" Rosie Jo asked. "'Cause I can stay right here and sleep on the couch."

"I'll be all right," Lil told her. "Go get in your own bed. I'll holler if I need you."

Lil walked her to the door and held it open. Rosie Jo patted her shoulder and said, "Call me if you hear anything."

"I will," Lil said. She stepped onto the deck so the bugs congregating around the outside light wouldn't fly in, and she watched Rosie Jo cross the yard, cross the street, and walk up her own little driveway lined with the conch shells they'd picked up when they'd taken a shelling excursion the summer before.

"Night," Rosie Jo called from across the way.

Lil waved, went back inside her trailer, and shut the door.

She cut off the overhead so Rosie Jo wouldn't see her

shadow pacing back and forth from the kitchen to the den, but she couldn't stand the darkness. It felt like the darkness might erase her, dissolve her, so she turned a lamp back on.

She sat down at the kitchen table, where the cards were still spread out from the game she'd been playing with Rosie Jo. They'd stopped the game at some point, when Lil forgot to draw or discard, forgot how to count, and so she picked up the cards, stacked them neatly, and put them back in their box.

It wasn't like Tessa Lee to just leave. Tessa Lee was a good girl. She didn't drink or stay out late. There wasn't a boyfriend for her to run off with. She'd told the policeman that. It didn't make any sense.

What if Tessa Lee'd been kidnapped and the police just didn't know it? They'd hardly even investigated. What if she was like those little children out in California or Utah, taken from their beds? And nobody even looking for her! They should have put together a search party. Lil went to Tessa Lee's window to make sure the screen hadn't been cut in some unusual way, in some place they hadn't seen, but the screen was fine. Besides that, the window was too small for anybody to get through. That's what the policeman had said, anyway. He'd dismissed the possibility as soon as he saw that the window cranked open from the inside.

Why did the police just assume she'd run away? She wasn't even considered a "Missing Person" yet. Lil put on her garden shoes and went out with her flashlight to look again for footprints outside Tessa Lee's bedroom window.

She didn't know exactly how long Tessa Lee'd been gone. They'd watched a TV program the night before, and then Tessa Lee went to bed. When she didn't come out for breakfast, Lil just assumed she was sleeping late and didn't bother

her until nearly ten o'clock, when she had to leave for the recreation center. Lil was scheduled to teach a class on making seashell wreaths at 10:30. So she knocked on Tessa Lee's door, then pushed it open, but found no one inside.

At first, she figured Tessa Lee'd gone to the pool, but since she didn't ordinarily get out early, it niggled at her all the way to the center, all the time she was unloading boxes of shells and bows. She asked the kids at the paddleboats if they'd seen her, but they hadn't.

Lil started her class late, hoping Tessa Lee'd be back home by the time she returned, hoping she'd just gone to the store or something. But her suspicions made her careless. She burned herself three times with the hot-glue gun and stuck the demo bow on crooked before a group of eleven ladies from four different states. When she got back to the trailer that afternoon and there was no sign of Tessa Lee, no flashing light on the answering machine, no note, that's when she knew for sure something was wrong.

Tessa Lee's friend Amber swore up and down that she didn't have any idea where Tessa Lee might be. Lil spoke with her on the phone, twice, and Amber was a good Christian girl, so Lil was inclined to believe her.

That afternoon when the rec center girls rode around on their golf cart with the megaphone to advertise bingo, they announced Tessa Lee's disappearance all over Hully Sanders's Mobile City so that by the time they ate their supper, the permanent residents and the transients alike all knew that Tessa Lee Birch was missing.

By nightfall, Hully Sanders himself was out stapling Tessa Lee's tenth-grade school picture to telephone poles, HAVE YOU SEEN THIS CHILD? in bold letters across the top.

There was a picture of Tessa Lee on the light pole right out in front of their house. Lil went and stood beneath it, put her hand on the pole and touched Tessa Lee's paper cheek. The dew had already fallen, and she was damp.

Where *was* she?

It was unbearable, not knowing where she was, not knowing if she was alive or dead. Lil's heart shook her body, and she pictured Tessa Lee locked up somewhere, in some crazy man's dungeon, her fists around bars, shaking them, trying to get out. Her love for Tessa Lee shook her heart like that. It was almost electric, the way her heart shook.

And then what was that *roar*? Was it coming from inside her? As Lil listened, it got louder and louder, and it took her a while to figure out she was hearing the light, high up on the pole, humming. It sounded loud enough to wake the whole neighborhood.

She stayed outside by Tessa Lee's picture for a while. She leaned her head against Tessa Lee's head and said a prayer for her safety.

And when her prayer was over, she intended to go to bed. But on the way inside, she stopped to deadhead the pansies in the pot just outside the front door. Tessa Lee had planted them, had insisted on pink and purple even though the yellow and white would have looked so much better with their color scheme. Lil picked all the dead flowers away, and with each dead flower, she said *please Lord*. She plucked through the droopy ones and into the live ones. She plucked until there wasn't a pansy left.

Tessa Lee had plenty of money for a motel room. She and Travis had both been saving up for bus tickets to Massachusetts. When she left, she took all the money, and she hadn't spent ten dollars all day long. But the signs along the strip flashed, NO VACANCY or sometimes N AC NCY. A woman outside a tattoo parlor told her that happened a lot in the summer, especially when there was a convention. She pointed Tessa Lee to a little place two blocks inland where she might find an efficiency. But when she got there, the man at the desk wouldn't give it to her without an ID. She told him she'd lost her wallet, and he said, "Uh-huh," and he picked up a phone and started punching in numbers, so Tessa Lee took off.

She was old enough to get her driver's license and already had her learner's permit, but her granny hadn't had a chance to take her back to the highway department for the driving portion of the test. Since Travis died things had been hectic.

Her only other ID was an old Girl Scout card with her name typed on it and her signature below. At least she'd had the good sense not to use either of those at the motel. It pleased her and also scared her that nobody knew her name.

When she couldn't run any farther, she crossed over to the beach, took off her sandals, and walked along in the dark. There were shadows of people huddled up together on the sand, teenagers splashing out in the water, laughing and calling to one another, surfing on their bellies to shore.

She wished Amber were there. If Amber were with her,

she wouldn't be so nervous. They might even go swimming in the ocean.

Farther down, some men speaking Spanish and all wearing suits circled around, laughing and teasing, trying to get her to tango. One of them stuck a red cup in her hand, and she moved along with them for a while without intending to, and after she'd broken away from what must have been a wedding party, she drank what was left of the watery honey in the cup.

From the balconies of hotel rooms, people cheered and whooped and held up their drinks, and she could hear the horns from High-Seas Avenue, the whistles and calls and sirens. She walked along the beach back toward the wax museum, in case her momma had come down to the beach after work.

For a while, she paced that part of the beach, and then she gave up and sat down near the dunes where the sea grasses grew. It was after midnight. She rubbed her throbbing arches. Her face was tight from sunburn, and she was burned behind her knees. Her shoulders ached from carrying the backpack all day long.

A couple walked by, fussing with each other. They stopped and pointed fingers and shouted, then one walked ahead, and the other threw keys, hitting the crying one in the shoulder. She was glad when they were gone.

But soon a mob of kids with a boom box passed too close, and one of them was setting off firecrackers, lighting them with a cigarette lighter and throwing them over his shoulder. One almost hit Tessa Lee, and the kids all laughed when she jumped.

So she scooted up the sand, until she was in the dunes

and hidden by sea oats. She pulled off her backpack to use as a pillow and buried her face in her hands and cried.

After a while, her tears ran out. She couldn't force any more out, even when she thought of how scary her momma had looked, pushing back her wig, yowling like crazy, or even when she remembered how Reggie had kissed her.

She hoped her granny was all right.

She put the firefly cloak back on and clenched herself up into a tight ball so that the fabric could cover her feet and keep the biting flies off her ankles. She pulled the hood up over her head and over her face, leaving just her nose out for air, and she said her prayers.

She slept for a while, but then from somewhere nearby she heard moaning, quiet at first, then heavier, and more and more high-pitched. For a moment, she thought that she was back in the church, trying to pull her granny away from Travis's coffin, but there was something different about this sound, and as her head cleared, she remembered that she was far from home, and Travis had already been buried a solid month. So she lifted her head, carefully, and peeked out from behind grasses, and there on the beach, a woman was bent over, holding her own ankles, while a man behind her, his hands on her hips, butted against her, goatlike and forceful.

He looked like he was trying to bust her in two, and her cries climbed higher and higher. Tessa Lee didn't know if she should go get help or not, but then the woman laughed and said something, and she walked her hands out into the sand, making a tent of her body for the man to break into again and again.

It went on that way for a while, and Tessa Lee couldn't sleep through it. She'd never done what they were doing, and now she knew that she didn't want to, ever. Sex was for married couples, that's what her granny said, and she wasn't allowed to do it until after her wedding. She decided not to get married for a long time.

Then she got a horrible feeling. What if the woman on the beach was her momma? She had long legs like her momma, and long hair falling down into the sand and sweeping the shells as the man pushed and pushed and pushed against her.

He was doing to her what waves do to sandcastles.

Tessa Lee prayed that it wasn't her momma making such a ruckus on the beach, and she prayed that it *was* her momma, so maybe she'd get a chance to see her again.

Then a voice shouted out, and the beam from a spotlight followed, and Tessa Lee ducked down, before the light found her. But she'd seen the woman's face in the flashlight beam when she turned and straightened her skirt, and it wasn't her momma. It was a girl with braces on her teeth, probably not even out of high school, probably not a Girl Scout. The security guard with the spotlight ran them off the beach, told them they'd go to jail if he saw them again. Tessa Lee lay very still and very flat. The light spanned out across the dunes, but she held her breath and finally the light passed.

Thunder came before morning, but the rain held off awhile. In her sleep, Sheila felt the thunder inside her, shifting in her bones, stretching in her bowels or maybe her womb. Just as day was breaking, she woke to thunder mumbling in her ears and thunder in her head, a horrible pounding behind one eye. The sky above her was dark, and she wasn't sure if the darkness was leftover from the night or if the rumbling she felt was a storm on the outside as well.

She'd been sleeping under bushes growing wild, under honeysuckle so sweet it made the ants too drunk to bite her. The leaves above her head were dense and green, greener than anything she'd known before. The sky, still dark but with light behind it, was starting out purple gray, and the winds that blew the clouds were perfect sieves of purple, until everything was gray, and then the drops fell, big thick rain, as hard as ticks.

She was at the edge of a yard in the middle of a field. There were woods behind her, and she must have come through them to get to this place. There were fields on her left and fields on her right, none of them planted or tended, and straight ahead, an old abandoned house. She must have been headed for the house when her memory left her. The yard was overgrown, with weeds knee-high, growing up around rusted-out cars on blocks, and thick oak trees turning gray beneath their kudzu canopy.

The rain came harder, pecking at her head, and since there was a lean-to for garden tools, she ran there and crouched down with old corroded shovels and a snaggle-toothed rake. The thunder rumbled and cracked as she sat listening to the rain hit the old tin roof.

Her boy had worried about storms, even before he was old enough to talk, always pointing at the sky like he knew some secret about what hid up there, something nobody else understood. His chin would crinkle up when it thundered, and he'd come crawling to Sheila. She took him with her to work and fixed him a pallet in the corner, and he played there while she cut hair and teased out permanent waves. Such a good boy. He didn't cry unless it stormed, but when it did, he left his blanket and crawled through all that leftover hair on the floor, pulling himself up against her pants until she put down her curling iron and held him, a hairy little monkey of a boy.

Sometimes she'd hear him whimper when the next-door neighbor cranked his truck. Mistaking it for thunder, he'd hurry to his momma. Silly boy with that black hair and all those curls. Her customers would say, "Make my hair look like that, Sheila," as though you could get that heartbreaking beauty from a box.

The girl was a different story. She was never, ever afraid, too saucy and defiant for fear to stick to her. Sheila didn't have to worry about her. She'd be fine with rain on her head. She could sleep right through it.

She faded into rain, into the sounds and the spray on her face from the empty doorway, and she let it wash the pounding around behind her eyes.

When she woke again, the pounding floated all through her head, and she saw that the house was a patchwork of all kinds of houses, a quilt of a house. She was shivering and wanted to go inside and be wrapped by it. The back wall had plywood sides, but part of the wood was covered with siding, and part was covered with guinea brick. There were strips of tar paper half-nailed, half-dangling and a section of old white clapboard.

The lowest windows were boarded over, but up higher, she could almost see into the glass. Through the rain, she thought she could see something moving in those windows. She strained her eyes and blinked a few times to clear them.

There were birds in the windows, looking out at her. Birds inside that house, dry as could be, looking down at Sheila so wet, so wet all over.

Or maybe it was all in her head. She couldn't remember what she'd taken, whether she had smoked or snorted or swallowed it. The day before was a soft red tunnel, a tubular flower at the end of a vine, and she climbed into the flower and went backward in her memory, backward and down the long path that ended at the museum, where the girl outside in her firefly cloak called her "Momma," recognized her, just like that.

Damn her.

Wrapped in that cloak like the night that Sheila left her.

Goose had whispered, "We gotta go," but there was a mosquito still with them in the tent, and she wanted to kill it before it bit the children to pieces. She'd written her momma's phone number over the bites on Travis's back, black on red. Sheila'd counted no less than ten red welts on Tessa Lee's face when she bent down to kiss her good-bye. She could still hear it buzzing, that mosquito, as she backed out of the tent. All the way down the highway that morning, puffing one cigarette after the next and wiping her nose against her shoulder, she pictured her two babies swatting in their sleep.

Over and over, Sheila's hand had flown up to swat at her

children, but they just kept coming back for more. Just like a damned mosquito.

She wasn't fit for children. When she left them, she swore off everything with wings, even that man named Goose who waited for her outside a truck-stop bathroom while she hitched a ride the other way.

She'd made a whole new life, and then the girl had come back, looking like Sheila from another time, before she went under, before she drowned. And now there were birds watching her from inside windows, looking down on Sheila, who was gulping air like she didn't know how to survive on it, a mermaid who'd lost her gills.

Tessa Lee was in and out of sleep all that night, sand in her mouth and eyes, bugs on her face. Amber would be impressed. She wasn't as brave as Tessa Lee. She'd never sleep on the beach by herself, without a tent.

A siren woke her once, and then another time she was startled by a dog who came by, sniffed her, and moved on.

She tossed around in the sand and longed for her bed back home, her floppy pillow that would mold into any shape beneath her arm and head. She'd complained a lot about her tiny bedroom in Granny and Pop-Pop's trailer, but it seemed a whole lot more appealing after a night in the sand. Granny and Pop-Pop hadn't been expecting another batch of children on the day Social Services called and told them Tessa Lee and Travis had been abandoned at the campground not ten miles from their door. They'd just retired to Hully Sanders's Mobile City, where they could play bingo with the neighbors and square-dance all night if they wanted. They only had one spare room.

So Pop-Pop went to Sears and came back with bunk beds, and Tessa Lee and Travis shared that room for a while.

Then when Travis was older, they got a shed out back and put the washing machine and dryer inside it. They took the bunk beds apart and moved one of them into the washroom for Travis. It always smelled like bleach in there, even after Travis had been sleeping there for years.

Tessa Lee was still awake when the seagulls began circling and squawking, the laughing gulls first, and then the dumb ones the color of tea. But she couldn't move her body yet. Her arms and legs felt stiff, like her joints had rusted up in the salt air. So she watched the seagulls flying and diving into the ocean for breakfast.

Fantasies of the Boardwalk opened at eleven. Maybe her momma would be there again, and maybe Tessa Lee would have another chance, but she had to be careful about what she said. She had to say just the right thing, and she couldn't do anything that would make her momma scream.

Her momma didn't even know that Pop-Pop had died, and that'd been more than three years. His tombstone had already turned green inside the letters, LEWIS BIRCH, but Tessa Lee had scrubbed them out with a toothbrush and bleach until they were shiny gray again. Granny said her momma and Pop-Pop fought like tigers, so maybe having him dead would help.

There were fishermen coming up the beach, holding a giant-sized net on two long poles. They walked almost as far as she was, then stopped. They couldn't see her. The tide was out, and she was high between two dunes, in a soft dip with not too many bugs. They were down close to the water, while she was up in powdery sand, where the tide never reached.

Two of the fishermen stayed on the beach, a big-bellied one holding the pole and a short one sloshing around in a cooler. The other two waded far out with their pole and net. They went straight out, then swung the net wide and began to pull in, and Tessa Lee thought of all the things that might be in that water between the shore and the net. Fish and crabs. Little snails on sea grasses. Plankton. Maybe there was even a mermaid out there. They were sneaking up on the sea and everything that lived in it, forcing themselves in.

Just the winter before, she'd kissed a boy on the church hayride, and it wasn't bad. His mouth was wet and smushy, but she'd given him the benefit of the doubt. He was a big-eared boy who played the violin, a sweet-enough boy. Amber said he was cute.

The next time they were together, he'd asked her if she wanted to do it.

"No way," she said. "I took the abstinence pledge."

"Bummer," he replied.

"You're not a virgin?" she asked quietly. It seemed like the sort of thing that should be whispered.

"Nah," he said. "I had a girl at Thanksgiving when I went skiing with my stepdad."

And Tessa Lee felt young and silly, but she said, "Well, I'm not like that." Then she added, "I'm gonna be a virgin when I get married. I signed the pledge at camp," and she was just about to leave when he tugged on her sleeve.

"Wait," he said.

"What?" she asked.

"It's nice that you're a good girl. You'll make somebody a real good wife."

Tessa Lee wasn't sure exactly what that meant.

"But nice girls do it, too," he assured her. "There are other ways. . . . You can still be a virgin and do it."

"How?" she asked. She was surprised to be having this conversation before Sunday School, surprised to be having it with this boy. He wasn't like her cousin Drandy, who made Vs with his fingers and wiggled his tongue through to make girls feel trashy. This was a boy who played the violin.

"If you stick it in the back hole," he said, "then you're still a virgin. That's how all the nice girls do it. You just can't put it in the place where the babies come through."

TESSA LEE'S granny had warned her that men just wanted to stick their things everywhere. She'd said they couldn't help it, that if they saw a hole, well, in it went. She didn't seem to worry much about Pop-Pop, so maybe his private parts had dried up by then. But whenever Granny's youngest brother would come to visit, she'd say, "Mind your cooter, now. Your uncle Howard'll be here directly," and Tessa Lee knew to keep her distance from him.

What Granny said had to be true—because once she'd even caught Travis playing with his pecker. He'd poured all his BBs out of their container, leaving five hundred pellets on his pillow. And he'd stuck his thing in that yellow and black cylinder and was pointing it this way and that way when Tessa Lee walked in to collect his dirty clothes.

These fellows on the beach were exactly the same, with their poles and their net, laying claim to anything they wanted. They'd get the whole ocean if they could.

As they got closer to the beach, the two in the water started jogging, then running with the net, pulling it through the breakers, and the net swayed back behind them, pregnant with all they'd caught. They ran onto the beach whooping, just like little boys, and yah-hawed as a hundred crabs scuttled desperate through the sand and up toward the dunes.

If she were a crab, she'd be running, too.

They pulled fish from the net and tossed them in the cooler, pulled crabs from the net and sent them sailing toward the waves. The crabs that didn't get away on their own flew and splatted onto the beach. One hard landing after the next.

Tessa Lee was watching crabs fly when the boy with green hair approached. She wasn't sure how many boys sported bright green hair, but she figured he was the boy from the arcade. As he got closer, she could see the glint from his ears. He had a plastic grocery bag over his arm, and he was smoking a cigarette.

"Great God almighty, it's the Jolly Green Giant," one of the fishermen said.

"Catch anything?" the green-haired boy called out as he walked up to the men and tried to start a conversation that Tessa Lee couldn't hear.

But the men were already rolling up their net, closing

their cooler, preparing to move on. "Get outta here, freak," one of them hollered.

The boy shrugged and walked back toward the dunes. Tessa Lee felt bad for him and wanted to defend him, but she was scared to get up.

"See there, fellows, that little faggie's got pincushions for ears," the big-bellied pole-man called from behind him. "Looks to me like he *likes* to be poked."

"Looks like the Jolly Green Fag to me," another one yelled, and Tessa Lee's anger rose up the way it came on her when boys mocked Travis for stuttering or being too sissy. Once she even got in a fistfight with a boy who spit on Travis. She was suspended from riding the school bus for a week.

The green-headed boy picked up his pace, muttering to himself, not looking back, and he might have walked right past Tessa Lee without noticing her if she hadn't sat up and said, "Hey."

He leaped a little, almost like a deer. "Hey," he said. Then, "Oh, it's you."

Tessa Lee pushed herself up with her hands.

"Huh," he said. "I guess you're new in town?"

And Tessa Lee said that she was and dusted the sand from her backside. "I recognized you from the arcade," she said.

"Oh," he said. "Well, hi."

"Hi," she repeated and felt dumb. She pulled her cloak around her and fiddled with the place where the clasp had been. She'd lost the big gold button that held it together at the neck.

"I come out here every morning," he told her. "'Cause I don't sleep too good."

Tessa Lee smiled at him, then realized she still had the hood up on her cloak and pushed it back.

"That's nice," he said. "Your beach cover-up . . ."

"It's a cloak," she told him. "I'm Tessa Lee."

He smiled and said, "I go by Rash. That's my nickname, anyway—'cause I used to grow poison ivy. But now I'm turned on to sandspurs. You think I should change my name?"

And Tessa Lee shrugged.

"I come out here every morning and collect 'em, see?" He opened his grocery bag to show her the greenish yellow shoots with the sharp prickles at the tips. "There are lots of them here. You stepped on any?"

"I don't think so," she said.

"Oh, you'd know it if you had. They're terrible. In another month, when they turn brown, they'll be lethal."

"Why are you collecting them, then?" she asked.

"'Cause you never know when you'll need an unconventional weapon," he told her. "You wanna get breakfast?"

And Tessa Lee was starving, so she said, "I do."

SINCE RASH had to be at work by nine, they went to a café near the arcade, on the ocean side of High-Seas Avenue. Tessa Lee had walked past the place several times the day before and never noticed it. From the outside, it didn't even look like a restaurant. It just looked like a cloudy glass door in an unmarked building, sandwiched between two flashier places. But on the inside, there were simple wooden booths painted sea-foam green with tiny vases of flowers on each table and a checkerboard floor. The music was soft, flutes and little bells—not a thing like the arcade music—and Rash said, "Come on. Let's sit up front." He led her deep into the restaurant, to what Tessa Lee ordinarily would have considered the back.

"I like to look at the water," he said. "But I bet you've seen enough of it for a while."

"I like the water," Tessa Lee said and yawned.

They stared at the ocean for a while, and Tessa Lee was so tired that it hypnotized her. She watched the waves rise up too soon and break before they made shore. Then they rolled up and crashed again, second-try waves. She hoped the clouds brewing darker didn't break. She didn't have a raincoat in her pack.

"Order whatever you want," Rash said. "I've got an account here."

Tessa Lee assured him that she had money, but she could tell he didn't believe her.

He took the tiny flowers out of the vase and sat them on some napkins at the side of the table. Then he pulled a spray of sandspurs from his plastic bag and arranged them in the vase. "Gorgeous, aren't they?" he said. And he was serious.

She laughed. "I never thought of them that way," she said. "Granny makes me squirt 'em with Roundup."

"Ahhh," Rash winced. "You gotta be kidding. They're like stars. Doesn't your granny like stars?"

Tessa Lee didn't know how her granny felt about stars, if she had any opinion about stars at all.

"I like weeds," Rash said. "Sometimes it seems so random—what people try to grow and what they try to get rid of. Like, what makes a rosebush more lovable than a clump of sandspurs? Roses have thorns. But nobody sprays Roundup on *them*."

"It's true," she said. She could tell it upset him that her granny killed the sandspurs. He was sensitive, like Travis, and she wished she hadn't mentioned it.

It would upset her granny to think of Tessa Lee with a green-headed boy with safety pins through his ears. But Rash was much safer than the violin player from her Sunday School class. It didn't take long to see that.

He rested his chin in his hand and said, "A couple of years ago when I was living with my mom in Florida, I found this old baby pool, and I put it in the backyard and filled it up with dirt. Then I went door-to-door, asking the neighbors if they had any poison ivy they needed dug up."

Tessa Lee raised her eyebrows at him and toyed with the saltshaker, wiping the top and then tapping it so that all the little holes were cleared for easy sprinkling.

"They thought I was crazy," he said.

"I guess so," Tessa Lee replied and went to work on the pepper. She wondered how long his hair had been green, if it'd been green when he'd lived in Florida.

"Anyway, a lot of them would let me into their yards, and poison ivy is *great*. I mean, it hangs out at the very edges, behind sheds and stuff. It grows in shade, and it grows in sun. And it's pretty. You have to admire a plant like that. It's tenacious."

"I know," Tessa Lee said. "We spray Roundup on that, too."

"Don't tell me that," Rash said, with mock seriousness. "I'm gonna have a talk with your granny."

Tessa Lee couldn't picture that at all. "So what'd you do with the poison ivy?" she asked.

"Replanted it," he said. "In the baby pool. Some of it died, but some of it lived. Some of it was downright lush."

"Aren't you allergic?"

"Sure, but I probably got some immunity from handling it so much. I might not even be allergic now."

"Is there poison ivy here?" Tessa Lee asked.

"A little," he said. "But not much. I live at the Sand-Dollar. Do you know that motel? About six blocks down and three in? Anyway, my dad owns it, and he's got every inch of land paved so people can park, so we don't get much poison ivy. Not nearly as much as I could find in Florida."

"So you're into sandspurs now . . ."

"Yeah," he said, and he pulled another stalk of sandspurs out of his bag and waved it around like a magic wand, flicking it once at Tessa Lee. "I like what other people don't."

Their food came—a great table full of food—eggs on one plate and pancakes on another, sides of hash browns and bacon for each of them, and when the waiter looked for space to set down the syrup, Tessa Lee pulled the plastic bag of sandspurs to the seat beside her.

They ate with relish; the food was good. Tessa Lee wanted to lick the plates, hers and Rash's both. She could have eaten another stack of pancakes. When she was done, she was wiped out, but in the most satisfying way.

"You mind if I smoke?" Rash asked, and when Tessa Lee said no, he went behind the counter and got an ashtray and lit up. "So did you find that woman you were looking for yesterday? The one who works at Fantasies?" he asked.

"Oh," Tessa Lee said, and suddenly her stomach felt too full, like she had a fist in her belly. "No," she said, but she choked on the word and sipped her water. "Well, I thought I did," she admitted. "But I didn't. I might try again today."

"What'd you say her name is?"

"Sheila Birch," Tessa Lee said hopefully. "Do you know her?"

Rash fingered one of the safety pins in his ear, sliding it through his skin back and forth. "Don't know anybody named Sheila Birch," he said. "But if she works at Fantasies I probably know her. Nobody uses their real names there."

"Why not?"

Rash shrugged and looked away. "So what does she look like?"

"She's really thin," Tessa Lee said. "Her eyes are sometimes green and sometimes hazel, sort of medium sized and round. She's got bleached hair . . ."

"With dark roots," Rash said. "She's one of the mermaids, right? She goes by Juana."

Tessa Lee had her fingers around a sandspur, rolling it and feeling the sharp points pricking at her skin, and she pressed in to feel it pierce her.

She'd given her momma that name. Her momma called her "Saly," which was short for "Salamander," so she called her momma "Juana," which she'd thought was short for "Iguana" when she was just six. They were silly names, names they borrowed from her lizard book. They both called Travis "La-La," which was short for "Monkey-La-La," a tropical lizard with a reputation for walking on water.

"Juana," she repeated. "Yeah, that's probably her." Her stomach hurt, and she hoped they had a bathroom.

"But you didn't find her," Rash said. "Did you look hard?"

"Yeah," Tessa Lee said, and then she couldn't talk anymore, so she kept her face down. She was holding Rash's plastic grocery bag of sandspurs, and a tear fell out and plonked there.

"Those don't really need watering," Rash said. And then he added, "Hey, it's okay. You'll have another chance to see her."

Tessa Lee was shaking her head so hard that she could feel her ponytail swiping at her back. And her belly was rumbling inside, rumbling fierce. "She doesn't want to come home," Tessa Lee said. "Maybe if I see her today, and call her Juana, maybe she'll recognize me then. I don't think she recognized me yesterday."

"Has it been a long time?" Rash asked.

"A real long time," she said. "I gotta find the bathroom." And she jumped up and ran to the back, which ordinarily would have seemed like the front.

But she didn't throw up after all. She talked herself out of getting sick, reminding herself that she'd handled hard things before. She washed her face and went back out to Rash, who was waiting.

"So Juana—" he said. "Or Sheila—if you wanna call her that—she's a real nice lady."

And Tessa Lee relaxed when she heard him say that. "She is?"

"Yeah," he said. "I mean, we all got our problems . . ."

"Of course," Tessa Lee said quickly.

"But she's always been nice to me. I don't know her very much," he said. "But I talk to the mermaids when I go by. And if they know you, they'll shoot the breeze."

"Where does she live?" Tessa Lee asked.

"I can't tell you that," Rash said, and Tessa Lee wondered

what he meant by it, whether he knew where she lived and wouldn't say, or whether he didn't know.

"She has a red bicycle with fenders," he told her. "One of those new old-fashioned ones. And she rides around on the sidewalks even though you're not supposed to do that, according to the cops, but they ride their bikes on the sidewalks, so nobody listens."

Tessa Lee laughed.

"I know she likes to read," he said. "'Cause sometimes in the off-season, when people don't walk down the strip that much, she reads in the conch shell."

"She used to read to me a lot," Tessa Lee said. "We had a lot of books."

"I've seen her sitting on the beach sometimes in the early morning," Rash said. "One morning she helped me collect mermaid's purses. You know what those are? The little black bags that hold skate eggs, or stingray eggs? They've got little wings on them, just like rays?"—but Tessa Lee didn't know what he was talking about. "Anyway, I like mermaid's purses. And Juana helped me pick some up one morning, and then a few days later, she came into the arcade and dropped off a whole bunch more."

"Huh," Tessa Lee said.

"But I'm pretty sure she's a user," Rash said.

"Oh," Tessa Lee said. "You mean drugs?"

He nodded.

"Why do you figure that?" Tessa Lee asked, even though it made sense when she thought of the way her momma looked at her, so empty, and how she screamed, so sudden . . . If she was on drugs, then she probably didn't keep up with birthdays or think to send gifts.

"A lot of people there are users," he said. "They don't make their money from the product they advertise, if you know what I mean."

"How do they make their money?" she asked, but Rash wouldn't say any more about it.

"Do you think she takes *addictive* drugs?" Tessa Lee asked.

"I don't know," Rash said. "None of them are that good for you. I've only popped pills myself, and they made me itch, so I quit."

"I don't do drugs," Tessa Lee said. "And I'm a virgin." Then she blushed, because he hadn't asked.

"That's cool," he said. "But you know what? I don't think you should stay around here much longer."

"I have some money," she said. "I could get a motel room—if I could find one where they don't need an ID."

"Do what you need to do," Rash said. "And if you decide to stay, then come to the Sand-Dollar. We don't need an ID there and we'll have rooms." He wrote the address down on a napkin, drew a sandspur at the bottom, and wrote a note: "Dad, she's my friend. No cops. Phillip."

"Phillip?" Tessa Lee asked.

"Just to my dad," Rash said. "There's a crackdown on runaways around here. Desperate kids get pulled into some not-too-good shit, you know?"

"But my momma," she said, and then she flinched, because she hadn't told Rash before who Sheila-Juana was.

"You don't want to turn out like her," he said. "She's a nice lady, but you can do better than this. Stay around here, and you might be dressing like a mermaid, too."

"I like costumes," Tessa Lee said.

"That's not what I mean," Rash told her.

"I wish you could help me find her," she admitted.

But Rash just smiled and said, "I gotta go to work." He reached up to his ear, unhooked one of the biggest pins, and slipped it out. Then he leaned across the table, over the sandspur arrangement, and pinned her firefly cloak across the top, where the button had come undone.

"There's a pay phone right out back," he said. "Call your granny and tell her to pick you up from the arcade."

But Tessa Lee wasn't sure she was ready.

"Your mom recognized you," he told her. "She knew it was you. But if she ever comes back, she'll have to do it in *her* time," he said. "You can't force it."

Off and on, all through that morning, Sheila told herself that when the rain let up, she'd know what to do. When her head stopped throbbing, she'd get back on her feet, and then her mind would follow. It would wake up and know where to go.

She had a pain beneath her armpit, against her side, and she tried to remember if someone had kicked her. She couldn't remember being kicked. If she could just move her head, she'd be able to look to see how badly she was bruised. Maybe she'd slept funny.

Her head felt big and swollen, a monstrous thing about to break, an egg with a dinosaur inside it. She kept her eyes closed, but there was light behind them, and she could almost see through her eyelids, two eyes looking at her.

She thought it must be the birds staring, but instead she found a frog in her face, sitting on a bucket right by the tip of her nose, a big slime-colored frog that didn't even hop away.

What was that story about the frog? A woman kissed it, and then the frog turned into a prince. For a long time, Sheila'd wished for a prince, but now she just envied the frog. If it was real, maybe it would kiss her and she'd turn into a frog, too. Seemed like an easy life. She lifted her hand and poked the frog, but instead of kissing her, it leaped away. Watching it go made her pulse beat harder in her temples, so she closed her eyes again. She might be dying.

Water. That was what she needed. That was all in the world that she needed. Her tongue was stuck to the bottom of her mouth, behind her teeth, and she had to peel it up to dislodge it. She needed water in her mouth, so she reached her hand into the rain, and water fell on her fingers. But her head hurt too much to pull the fingers back to her mouth, so she left them there in the rain.

She slipped into the deep redness of her mind, pulled into herself, cocooned and safe and tight.

Until the face of the girl outside the wax museum appeared.

The girl had grown tall, but she had the same face. A big face—but Sheila could picture it tiny—with the same expression as the day the nurse first handed her to Sheila. The baby's eyes had popped open and stayed open like they couldn't believe what they saw. Sheila had laughed at her baby girl, newborn and blinking, those round eyes taking in everything. She'd come into the world looking surprised, and Sheila had the feeling that even before she was born, she'd been looking around, peering right through her belly at all that awaited, and finally swimming free with her eyes wide open, little tadpole of a girl.

If she'd just kept her mouth shut, if she'd just looked without speaking, it wouldn't seem so awful. But she'd called her "Momma," and she really shouldn't have done that.

The girl said that something bad had happened, and Sheila didn't want to hear it. She couldn't fix any of the things that went wrong. She'd never been able to do that.

When Tessa Lee was a baby, she'd been on the road. Later, once she settled down, she hadn't been able to work enough hours to buy food and clothes and pay the rent, too, and when she tried, she couldn't help it that Tessa Lee had to stay at a nursery where the owner lined them up against a wall and whipped them with a belt, or so the girl claimed. "She whips us once a day," Tessa Lee tattled. "Whether we're bad or not."

But Tessa Lee made things up. Sheila knew that.

It was the only place Sheila could afford. Then when she picked her up, the owner scolded her for always being late.

She was glad when Tessa Lee was old enough for school, but then she had Travis. She took him with her to work and gave him medicine to keep him quiet on days when he was fussy, and she hated it, but what choice did she have?

She knew she shouldn't leave them in the car when she went to bars, and she only did it sometimes. Sometimes she had to. Tessa Lee was old enough to watch her brother, and Sheila told them to go to sleep, and Travis usually did. But Tessa Lee stayed awake and played with Weebles half the night. Tessa Lee wasn't scared. Sheila went out to check on her, and when she asked if she was scared, Tessa Lee always said no.

They got colds that didn't get better, both of them. The snot poured from their noses, green and yellow, everywhere. They didn't have insurance, but finally she had to take them to the doctor. The baby had pneumonia. One more day, the doctor said, and he'd have been dead. He threatened to call Child Protective Services if he ever saw them in that shape again.

She had to pay the doctor's bill, somehow. She had to pay for the medicine. So she left the children at night, after she'd put them to bed. She was only around the corner, dancing in a go-go bar—not far from them at all.

She saved most of the money for the doctor's bill and the rent. She didn't go to bars then, but she bought herself a bottle. Because didn't she deserve at least that—a shot every once in a while? Sheila couldn't stand herself without it.

When she'd finally come home, in the middle of the night, Tessa Lee would be awake, sitting on the floor with her crayons. She was six or seven by then.

"What are you doing up?" Sheila'd ask.

"Coloring," Tessa Lee would say, and she'd follow her down the hall and into the bathroom. While Sheila ran a tub of water and soaked and steamed her thoughts away, Tessa Lee would sit on the toilet and watch her.

"Do you have to go to your other job tomorrow night, too?" Tessa Lee would ask.

"Yes, baby," Sheila'd tell her. She tried to be patient, she really did. "But if you just go to sleep before I leave, then you won't even know I'm gone. And I'm not far. Right down the block. I work at night when you're asleep so I can be home more when you're awake."

"You're not home then, either," Tessa Lee whined.

Almost every night, Tessa Lee was there to hand her the velvety blue robe when she got out of the tub.

"I don't like it when you leave at night," Tessa Lee complained.

"But I always come back," Sheila said. "Just like the fireflies," and she led Tessa Lee to bed and kissed her. "The lights go out, and then they flash back on. You don't know where they'll be when they flash again, but sooner or later, they always light back up."

Tessa Lee hugged her and said, "Please quit your night job," and Sheila said, "Maybe soon."

But she couldn't quit. And over the next year, Tessa Lee hardened her face like a scab. Some nights she still stayed awake, and some nights Sheila'd find her crashed out in the middle of the floor, and after a while, she didn't have the energy to carry her back to bed, so Tessa Lee just slept there.

Tessa Lee found Sheila's bottle and poured it down the drain, and then she had the nerve to admit it. When Sheila slapped her face, she didn't even cry.

And Sheila couldn't fix any of it. She went to the welfare office, and they helped her get a job cleaning rooms in a nice hotel, and that worked out for a month or two. Then her transmission blew up, and she couldn't get to work. She lived too far out of town to take the bus and didn't have the money to move. Then her welfare checks got sanctioned, because she wasn't working, and without a paycheck, she couldn't pay the phone bill. So the phone got cut off, and then they couldn't call her back from the temp agency where she'd scored really high on the typing test, seventy words a minute even though her fingers shook.

They moved from place to place, from town to town as the rent came due.

They moved in with a nice man who cried on the day he kicked them out and gave them $300 to help make a new start. They moved in with another man who yanked Travis's arm out of the socket, which meant another bill, another move.

As soon as she could, Sheila found them a safe place, but in the end, it wasn't enough.

She couldn't stand the memories, one failure after the next, and all the accusations.

But suddenly there was another voice:

"You gonna stay in here all day?"

And where did that one come from? It wasn't a girl's voice. It was a voice Sheila didn't know, and she shook her head to clear it, thinking, *please don't let it be that frog.*

"You been in here all morning long," the voice said. "And I left you alone, but now you gotta help me."

Sheila wiped her eyes to find an old man in overalls, his cheek swollen with a wad of tobacco. He was stout and piggish, and he wore an old dress hat on his head with a feather in the brim. He spit over his shoulder, then said, "Come on. It's safe 'til it quits raining, but then they'll be back."

"Who?" Sheila asked.

"You know," he said. "Hurry up."

So she pulled herself to her feet, then pulled her wet clothes away from her body and followed him through the drizzle.

"I thought you might be the enemy," he said. "But I

checked you out, and my sources say you're here to help." He led her through deep weeds up to the old house, and they paused at some cinder-block steps while he searched through keys to open a padlock.

"I have to lock it up when I step out," he said. "Even for just a minute."

"You live here?" Sheila asked.

"Yeah," he said. "It's no wonder you didn't know that before. I've got it camouflaged," and he unhooked the lock. Then he pulled a pair of binoculars out of his pocket and held them to his eyes, surveying the landscape from left to right. Satisfied, he pushed in the door, and said, "After you." So Sheila entered.

There were seventeen locks on the back door: bolt locks that slid and others that clicked, chains, hooks and eyes, several that needed different keys, which the man produced quickly and turned with a practiced hand. When he'd locked all the locks, he barred the door with a two by four.

"Can I have some water?" Sheila asked.

"Hold your horses," the man replied. "I gotta set the alarm," and he proceeded to rig a system of ropes and pulleys and an anvil, which Sheila supposed would somehow work to knock any intruders in the head if they managed to get through the door.

"Now then," he said. "Let's get your water."

He led her through the house, and Sheila was so amazed at the clutter and disorganization that she halfway forgot about her headache and the pain beneath her arm. There were mounds of papers everywhere, disheveled and yellow, and birdcages with the doors flung open, and bird seed spraying across every surface. There were empty bottles, paint cans gone rusty and stacked against a wall, and disconnected light fixtures, wires spraggling askew, old chandeliers and lamps tilted and teetering.

There were clothes and blankets thrown across chairs, and machine parts and bicycle tires and a pogo stick and a silver baton. Sheila thought she must be hallucinating. She'd crashed before and seen crazy things.

They crossed into the kitchen, where the table was covered with a sheet. Hammers and screwdrivers and tacks and nails and a big toaster took up every inch of space. "My toaster's broke," the man said. "But if you want some toast, I can make it in the frying pan." Then he leaned over his own shoulder and spit onto the linoleum. "You want some toast?"

"No, just water," Sheila said.

"Why don't you sit?" he suggested.

So Sheila pulled out a chair and placed the empty cereal boxes situated there on the floor beside her.

"No, no," the man said frantically. "Put those back," and so Sheila replaced the boxes.

"Sit on this one," he said and offered her a different chair, with just some green tomatoes in a cardboard box on the seat. He took the box of tomatoes and examined each one, then sat them in the boarded-up window, as if they might pinken there anyway.

He pulled a silver tumbler from the kitchen cabinet and filled it with water from the sink. Then he looked inside the cup before handing it to Sheila.

She drank deeply, tasting rust and minerals in the water, but when she was finished, she asked for more, and the man obliged.

The water traveled slow through her body. It was thicker than water she'd tasted before. As she swallowed, she pictured it diluting her headache and the deep throbbing sting beneath her arm.

"The CIA broke into my house three times last week," he said. "They're after me again. I don't know what I'm gonna do."

"Why are they after you?" Sheila asked. "Did you do something wrong?"

"No," he maintained. "I live a good honest life. But my wife was a spy for the Russians." He snorted hard and shook his head like he hated to admit it. "They come and got her and took her away, and now they think I have information."

"Oh," Sheila said.

"They'll be back," he insisted. "And I've gotta transform this toaster into a bomb before they get here. Do you know how to make a bomb?"

"No," she said.

"Shoot," he replied. "I thought that was why you come." He settled down at the table and began taking the toaster apart. He got the metal housing off, and then showed her the coils inside. "See there?" he said. "That's where you have to put the explosive powder, in those coils."

"Oh," Sheila said again.

"You know how to make explosive powder, don't you?"

And Sheila thought back to the science experiment she did with Tessa Lee at their kitchen table in South Hibiscus. They were making a volcano, and they put together baking powder and something else, something that foamed up. Maybe vinegar?

"Yeah," Sheila said.

"I knew it!" the old man said, and he smiled a huge smile, and Sheila could see that his teeth had all turned black.

Some of her own teeth had turned black, in one short year, and she'd had them pulled and relied on false ones that cut into her gums, but she didn't care. She didn't eat that much, and when they hurt her, she just took them out. Reggie liked how her mouth felt without teeth.

When Sheila saw that the old man's teeth were gone to rot, something inside her lurched up. "You got a rock?" she asked the man. She was joyous. It was the happiest she'd ever been. "Give me some. I'll pay you."

"A rock?" he asked. "What kinda rock you mean?"

"You know," she said.

"No, I don't," he told her.

"I'll pay you," she said, and she went to where he was sitting and put her head against his knee and reached up for the buttons of his fly. The floor was sticky with tobacco spit, but she didn't care. "Give me some," she begged.

But the old man shied away.

"I'll do it for you right now," she said, "but show me that rock."

"I ain't got no rock," the man told her, guarding his lap. "I know a song about a rock," and he started singing "Rock-a-bye Baby."

"Listen," she said, standing up. "You got anything? Weed? Tequila?"

"No," he told her. "But I got some Gatorade."

"Shit," she said, but she drank the Gatorade, and it seemed to help her headache. It didn't do a thing for the pain beneath her arm, though.

"I gotta get this bomb ready before they come back," the man explained. "But you can make the explosives, right?"

"Yeah," she replied. "I shouldn't mix them until the CIA gets here, though. If we mix them too soon, they won't be any good."

"Oh," the man said. "I reckon so."

"You got somewhere I can lay down?" she asked.

"Yeah," he said. "You can stay in my wife's room. I had to tear the stairs down, but I got a ladder."

The ladder was propped up in a downstairs bathroom, in a closet, behind the hot water heater. The old man got the ladder and then led Sheila to the place where stairs used to be, where the stairwell remained, though the steps had collapsed into a heap of boards and faded pink carpet.

"Did the CIA try to get up here?" Sheila asked him, while he extended his ladder.

"They did," the man said. "But I stopped them." He winked at her and smiled.

She climbed the ladder behind him, then waited for him to pull it up. They went down a little hall and entered a woman's room. It wasn't messy like the downstairs part of the house. It was dusty but not too cluttered, and Sheila realized that this old crazy man had once had a wife, and she wondered where she'd gone, and if she left him because he spit on the floor.

"You can sleep in here," he said. "I'll be on lookout downstairs, and you can do lookout duty later on."

"Okay," she said.

"I'll get you up if they come," the man said. "'Bout how much time do you need to make a bomb?"

"Five minutes," Sheila said, and the old fellow said, "You

must be good at it!" and extended his ladder downward, climbed to the first floor, and then took the ladder away.

THERE WAS A bathroom next to the bedroom, and Sheila locked herself inside it, using all six locks, and then she stripped off her clothes and looked in every pocket for a pill or a nub of a joint. Anything. She dumped the contents of her bag and sifted through the dirt that came from the bottom, hoping there'd be something—enough powder to snort or a crumb. But there wasn't.

She'd gone off cold turkey before. She didn't want to think about it: the chills and tremors, headaches and nausea, the itching and wanting, goddamn, she could feel every cell of her body contracting, pleading. She could feel it in her gums, tingling, twinging. She could feel her ear bones vibrate. *Please, please, God,* she begged, but she wasn't sure what she was asking for.

Like when she'd given birth that first time. They'd said the baby was full-grown, viable, ready to live outside her body at the moment her labor'd begun. But as the pain darkened around her, and quickened, she knew that the baby was being made right then, at her birth. Maybe her body'd been there before, but her soul came into being during those last hours, when she was demanding Sheila's cells, tearing half of them away for herself, one by one, pinching and gnashing her way through Sheila, a sacrifice so wide that there was no way to describe it, a tornado inside her.

In the medicine cabinet, she found a headache powder, so she snorted that, and she found cough medicine with a sleep aid, and so she drank what was left of it, and then she ran herself a tub of rusty water, and she soaked there until she dozed off, not even waking up when the hot turned cold.

Lil took solace in guardian angels. She'd been wearing a guardian angel pin on her clothes for years. Rosie Jo had given her the first pin when Lewis died, saying it was just a reminder that there was always somebody looking after her, and she'd picked up another one for herself when she was stuck in the checkout line at the grocery store and had nothing better to do.

And guardian angels must have come into vogue that year, because she got a third one from her Secret Santa at the recreation center.

Travis even made one out of colored felt and clothespins at Vacation Bible School, and while it was way too big to pin on her jacket, it dangled just fine from the rearview mirror in the van. She hadn't had any wrecks since then—not even a speeding ticket.

But she'd never before seen a guardian angel with bright green spiky hair.

"Lord have mercy," she muttered to herself as she pulled up at the address Tessa Lee'd given her. Tessa Lee waved from the sidewalk, then held up a finger to say just a minute, so Lil put on her flashers as the horns behind her honked.

Tessa Lee threw her arms around the green-headed boy

and hugged him, and that fellow hugged her back until Lil rolled down the window and hollered, "You better *get* in this van."

The sports car behind her blared the horn some more, and though Lil considered herself a Christian, she shot the driver the bird.

Finally Tessa Lee opened the door and leaped straight into her granny's arms, and Lil wrapped her tight, and sniffed her head like honeysuckle, and said, "Where the hell have you been?"

ALL NIGHT she'd been up worrying. She'd pruned the roses and transplanted a little azalea that was lost beneath a bigger one. Then in the backyard, she'd staked up her tomato plants, all the time praying to Jesus to bring Tessa Lee back home.

At one point, she made herself go to bed, but she couldn't stay there. Her sheets were too cold, colder than they'd ever been, and she couldn't get warm, even though it was summer. She couldn't stand to just lie there and be so still. Never before had she spent a night alone, never in her life.

She considered taking a pill to help her sleep, but what if she fell out hard and didn't hear the phone ring? Finally, she got up and played Solitaire, red on black on red until daylight.

By morning, the local news station had picked up the story—because Tessa Lee's disappearance just weeks after Travis's death was almost too much to believe. They'd interviewed Lil right in her trailer, while neighbors stood in the kitchen as they'd done a few weeks before and asked one another how much one soul could bear.

Then the phone call came, just before lunchtime. Rosie Jo had answered for Lil, and when Tessa Lee said, "Granny?" she'd shouted out, "She's alive! She's alive!" and Lil could hardly hear what Tessa Lee was saying for all the commotion.

"I'm gonna whip her ass when I see her," Lil said as she found her sunglasses and checked her pocketbook to be sure her wallet was in it.

"I don't blame you a bit," Rosie Jo agreed. She escorted Lil to the van and leaned against the door. "If my granddaughter scared me that way, I'd do the same thing."

She offered to ride with Lil up the coast and to the city, but Lil declined. She needed the time to clear her head.

"Has your blood pressure gone down?" Rosie Jo asked.

"Yes," Lil assured her.

"Has your heart slowed down any?"

But Lil was already pulling away. She had to get to Tessa Lee before she changed her mind.

And Lil did a lot of thinking on that drive. A lot of thinking and a whole lot of praying. Tessa Lee might have run away, but in twenty-four hours' time, she wanted to come back home. Lil was more determined than ever to make home the best place Tessa Lee'd ever seen.

"I'M SORRY, Granny," Tessa Lee said, and Lil hit the gas, leaving the green-headed boy coughing in her exhaust.

But as soon as they turned the corner and rounded onto High-Seas Avenue, they were stuck in traffic, a bumper-to-bumper mess. "Must be a wreck up there somewhere," Lil said.

"It's always like this in the summer," Tessa Lee replied. "You should see it at night."

"Well, aren't you the expert?" Lil said, more sharply than she intended, and Tessa Lee looked away. They didn't say anything for at least two or three car-lengths. Then they were directly in front of Fantasies of the Boardwalk and stalled again.

"She works right there," Tessa Lee told Lil and pointed.

Lil looked at the place and felt a funeral in her heart. "That's too bad," Lil replied.

"She works in that window," Tessa Lee said and pointed to a dark window with words above it: LUSTY YOUNG MERMAID, CAPTURED BY PIRATES. "Momma's the mermaid, but she didn't come in today."

"Is she sick, you reckon?"

"Maybe," Tessa Lee said. "I hear she's using drugs, so it's hard to say."

And Lil nodded. "Did you get to talk to her at all? Did you tell her about Travis?"

Tessa Lee shook her head. She leaned over the wide seat and buried her face in Lil's thigh. Lil kept one hand on the wheel, and one hand on Tessa Lee's back, rubbing and rubbing on that lightning bug housecoat.

"Poor child," Lil said. "Poor sweet child."

Sheila shivered for the longest time, there in the bathtub, looking down at her feet in the water. Her feet looked too white, like dead catfish bobbing at the water's edge, and she thought maybe she'd died, and maybe she was being preserved in melted ice.

Her hands floated beside her, and no matter how hard she tried, she couldn't sink them. Her hands were lily pads, floating beside her hip bones.

She was dead. She was a surface, an island in a frozen sea.

She was marooned.

From far beneath the water, she could hear her own voice bubbling up, but she couldn't understand it. She didn't know what she was saying. It was hard to hear over the birds.

Then she heard herself instruct her toes to pull the plug and drain the water. Her voice was cold inside her, swimming in slush. Her voice made it through her ears, but her toes were frozen, so they couldn't hear to drain the water.

They couldn't hear because there was a thicket overhead, screeching birds, peeping and clawing and scurrying around. It was a frozen thicket. The birds were trying to stay warm but they had ice on their wings, and that's why they were screeching.

So she shivered in the bathtub a long time more. She could see that the ceiling was weak, stained from rain, buckling above her. She imagined the birds with ice on their wings falling down and landing on her lily pads, her island, like winter loons at low tide, leaving track marks on her belly.

Lil never went anywhere without her scissors, and they came in handy just outside the city limits, where she stopped at a roadside nursery and bought an aloe vera plant for Tessa Lee's sunburn.

Tessa Lee didn't even protest when Lil told her to get in the back and strip to her underclothes.

Lil snipped the speckled green arms right off the plant, pressed the slippery juices out, and doctored Tessa Lee's face and arms and legs. The fluid oozed and spread across her sunburn, thick as egg whites, smearing over blisters.

"Sure does stink," Tessa Lee said, groggy.

"That little plant just sacrificed its life for you," Lil replied, squeezing the sticky fluid into the scorched part of Tessa Lee's head. "Least you could do is appreciate it."

"I appreciate it," Tessa Lee said and yawned, "but it still stinks."

There was no backseat in the van because Lil'd taken it out so she could haul her supplies and products to craft fairs. But she had an old sleeping bag back there, so Tessa Lee stretched out and went to sleep.

She'd been sunburned just that bad on the day when Lil first saw her. She was eight years old with stringy brown hair cut into a long shag, and her freckled cheeks looked like somebody'd rubbed strawberries all over them. Her nose was as hard as a little shrimp shell from all that sun. And she was wearing that ridiculous housecoat even then, looked like she was playing dress-up. She wouldn't take it off for the longest time, until she dragged it through a pile of poop left in the yard.

"Let me wash it," Lil'd said, but Tessa Lee wouldn't take it off. "Your lightning bugs got stinky all over 'em. You don't wanna smell like stinky, do you?"

Then Lewis had jumped in and said, "Take off that housecoat, girl. You gotta mind your granny."

"It's not a housecoat. It's a cloak!" Tessa Lee'd insisted. "And they're fireflies, not lightning bugs!"

"Okay, then, but they're shitty little fireflies," Lil'd said, and Tessa Lee'd laughed, suddenly, and peeled the housecoat off.

When it was clean and folded up, she'd asked for a clothes hanger, saying she thought they better put it in the closet, in case her momma needed to wear it when she came to get them.

A few days later, she asked Lil for a pillowcase and stuffed the lightning bug housecoat inside it. That's where it had been ever since, on Tessa Lee's bed. Not the pillow she rested her head on, but the one she kept under her arm. And Lil could see in the rearview mirror that she was using it for a pillow again.

While Tessa Lee slept, Lil passed through town after town, little fishing villages and mini resorts, singing a song in her head:

Lost in the forest of sin, despair, and shame,
I faltered and stumbled, then called on Jesus' name.
And yea, through the shadows, a light was cast o'er me.
He led me through the thorns and snares.
Praise God, He set me free.

It was an old song from when she was a girl. Back then she went to the country church with her aunt and girl cousins, and with the boys before they reached their teenage years and quit. That church didn't have electricity. Just fans provided by the funeral home to wave in front of your face while the preacher paced and banged on his pulpit and called on sinners to repent. They didn't sing that song in her new church, but it still ran through Lil's head during troubled times.

Sinking in the quagmire, my burdens weighed me down.
I struggled through that dark bog, but found no solid ground.
At last I called on Jesus. He heard my humble plea.
He took my hand and heaved me up. Praise God, He set me free.

The problem with that song was that the person who wrote it was already out of the forest, up from the quagmire. It was harder to praise God when you were in the middle of a mess.

Still, she had Tessa Lee with her, and that was a lot to be thankful for. Sometimes singing that song could remind her that she'd get out of the mud one day, and that was enough.

Lil passed the place where she and Lewis had gone to a bluegrass festival the year before the children came to live with them, and she passed the road that led to a park where they had an annual craft show. For the past five years, she'd sold her wreaths and painted napkin holders there. The toilet-paper dolls didn't do so well at that fair, but they were a big hit in North Carolina, where she and Lewis had lived before they moved to Hully Sanders's Mobile City.

From time to time, Lil's emotions threatened her, like a

gang, hiding around the corner. They stepped out one at a time, each individual feeling, until there were too many of them to manage and they backed her against the wall. When she crouched down, they crouched down, too. They breathed up all her air.

Over the years, she'd learned how to handle them. To keep them away, she had to concentrate on what was right in front of her. She had to name it: billboard for gas station, silo, big field, woods, blue Honda, dead possum, watermelon stand. As long as she concentrated on the facts, the feelings couldn't touch her. She had to be disciplined about it, though. She couldn't indulge any of the feelings or else she might get swamped with them all.

She was naming the details along the highway when she noticed a body of water she'd never seen before, a new sea on that familiar road. But really, it was just a field of tomato beds, covered in sheets of polyethylene, shiny and the palest blue. A sea on her left, then a sea on her right, one after the other, and the highway became a bridge as she passed over seas in the middle of fields.

How could she name the facts when nothing was what it seemed?

Maybe that was why Sheila used drugs. Because nothing was the way it seemed, anyway.

She hadn't slept the night before, and now the whole world seemed strange. She kept picturing red tomatoes beneath the sea, and then she pictured Sheila as a mermaid, swimming among them.

Sheila'd been a sweet little girl, a loving child who rode on her daddy's tractor and waved as they pulled up at the barn.

She'd been a hardworking girl. She'd fill her shirttails with tomatoes: some of them pink and some of them ripe, and it never mattered, anyway, because Lil loved them red and Lewis loved them green, so no matter what Sheila picked, somebody'd always eat it.

Stewed tomatoes, tomatoes for canning—they used them for that, too—and Sheila just a little girl standing on a stool, her arms buried past the elbows in tomatoes, squishing them up, tomato seeds in her hair, splatters of tomatoes in her eyebrows, working all day long without the first complaint.

When she was a little girl, she could do no wrong, but when she was a teenager . . . Lord God.

Now Lil had Tessa Lee to worry about. Tessa Lee still had a chance, and Lil had to concentrate on her. It was just as well that Sheila wasn't around.

Still, Lil had wanted to send word when Lewis died. She wrote a letter, but there was nowhere to mail it.

But Sheila knew where *she* was. Somehow. Somehow she knew their phone number, too—even though they'd moved out of the state by then—and she'd written it on Travis's back. Lil'd scrubbed and scrubbed to get that number off. Even after she'd bathed Travis for a month, she could see Sheila's handwriting coming up through his skin. She'd made a line through her 7 so nobody would mistake it for a 1. And as mad as Lil was about what Sheila had done, she still found it touching, that Sheila'd go to so much trouble. She knew that deep down, Sheila must love those children if she cared about where they wound up. And Sheila must love *her* a little, if she wanted her to raise them.

If Lil had been a really horrible mother, then Sheila might have written somebody else's phone number on Travis's back.

After Sheila ran away, Lewis wanted to sell the farm and start over somewhere else, but it took Lil a long time to give it up. She kept thinking Sheila might come home, and she wanted to be there if she did.

The last time she saw Sheila, they'd argued. Lil was knitting a skirt for a toilet-paper doll, green and white, she remembered, and Sheila pranced into the room with an attitude, telling Lil she was going out. Not even asking.

"Not on a school night," Lil'd said.

"Yes, I am," Sheila replied. She had both hands on her hips, and Lil remembered seeing her that way and realizing that she actually *had* hips. It made her mad that Sheila had hips, even though she couldn't help it.

"Go to your room," Lil told her.

But Sheila just stood there, defying her.

Lil kept right on knitting, making the doll's skirt. When she was done, the skinny doll's legs would slide into the toilet-paper roll, and the skirt would billow out wide over the toilet tissue, covering up what was private. Her needles hit hard against each other. "I know who you've been running with," she said. "And I won't have it. Now go to your room."

"Momma, I'm going out," Sheila repeated.

Lil's stitches were way too tight. She felt her mouth pull in like those stitches, tense. "I won't have it," she said. She didn't look at Sheila. "You're not allowed to see him. I mean it. Not never again." By then, her voice was raised.

And by then, Sheila was crying. "But I *love* him," she said.

"You do *not* love him," Lil shouted. "You're a child and you don't know the first thing about love."

Sheila walked over to the door but didn't step outside it.

She stood there with her forehead against the screen, the tears sliding down her cheeks.

"Do you want to kill your daddy?" Lil continued. "Do you want him to have a heart attack and die? 'Cause he'll die if I tell him who you're seeing."

"Don't you say that," Sheila said, her tears turning to sobs.

"It's the truth," Lil said. Her needles clicked furiously. "It'll kill him."

"But I love him," Sheila wailed.

"Then go be with him," Lil spit. "But if you do, don't you *ever* come back here again. You hear me? If you leave here right now, I don't never want to see you again."

And when the screen door slammed, Lil shouted, "You better get back in this house, Sheila Birch! You better get back right now." But her voice was weak and croaky, like an old woman's voice.

The sound of Sheila's sobbing stayed with her as she knitted, sobs ratcheting up, then fading out as Sheila ran down the drive. Lil sat there with her toilet-paper doll until she finished the skirt. She concentrated on the green yarn and the white. She counted stitches. She even made a matching hat, and when she was finished she was an old lady and her daughter was gone. Too much emotion at one time could do that—could catapult anybody right over midlife and into old age.

She could still conjure Sheila's crying. It was a sound that transcended time, and just thinking of it made the goose pimples rise on her arms. So she had to concentrate on concrete things: cinder-block beauty shop, Baptist church, cornfield, cornfield, grammar school.

It was late afternoon when Lil got to the turnoff for Hully Sanders's Mobile City, but she drove right past it. She drove another half an hour before she called Rosie Jo on her cell phone.

"I'm taking the long way home," she told her.

"How come?" Rosie Jo asked.

"Can't get my foot off this gas pedal," she said. "Feed the fish for me. We'll be home tomorrow."

When Tessa Lee woke up, Lil'd just tell her they were lost, and they'd get a motel room somewhere. She'd give Tessa Lee the map and let her find the way home.

Lil wasn't ready for company. She knew Rosie Jo'd have a cake made. Might even string up balloons. And Lil was thrilled to pieces to have Tessa Lee back, but she didn't feel like celebrating. And what if the newscasters came back? Rosie Jo could deal with them. Lil needed concrete details passing by: dead raccoon, Georgia pines, bridge over dried-up creek bed. She could drive for as long as Tessa Lee could sleep.

It'd taken Lil a long time to admit that Lewis wouldn't have cared who Sheila loved. Sheila could have married a sheepdog, and eventually Lewis would have called him "son."

She was the one whose heart seized up. *She* was the one who felt like dying.

So she ran Sheila off, and she shut her out. She concentrated on concrete things: an empty bedroom, an empty mailbox, white paint, white paint, white paint. She painted the whole house, top to bottom, inside and out, and when she was done, she sold it.

It was dark outside, and then it was light. Sheila woke up sweating in a Russian spy's bed. The birds overhead were rioting, scratching and chattering, babies begging for worms.

The pain in her head had lessened, but the pain beneath her arm was worse. She lifted her arm and studied her side, but nothing was there, no purpling, no yellowing, no bruising at all.

She was naked. Not a stitch of clothes on.

So she wrapped herself in a sheet and went to the bathroom, where she was sure she'd undressed. But her clothes weren't there, either.

She yelled down for the old man, and when he didn't come, she sat down in her sheet shroud and dangled her legs over the landing, where stairs should have been.

She was ravenous. If the old man didn't come soon, she'd have to jump. With a running start, she might clear the debris, or miss most of it. And what was the worst that could happen? If she broke her legs, she'd drag herself to the refrigerator.

She could get by without legs.

For years, she'd worked as the mermaid. Day after day, she'd climbed into the tail, and Reggie had laced it behind her, tightening the strings of the corset snug over her thighs and her hips. Then she pulled herself into the closet. She was strong as a seal. She hoisted herself into the bed that became her conch shell—when the lights were turned on and the mirrors did their work. Each time she arranged her tail so that it flipped perfectly, the ends curling just so, and then she waited for her legs to fall asleep.

The edge of the bed cut into her thighs, but soon she couldn't feel her legs at all, just the tingling when she moved.

By the time she got off work each night, her legs felt like they belonged on someone else's body, her narrow thighs lonely for each other when she pulled them apart.

Reggie laughed to see her pulling herself around with her arms. "You'll never be able to run away from me," he joked.

Then, years later, when Sophie came to work there and Sheila was showing her around the dressing room, she'd lifted the heavy sequined tail and asked, "Why do we wear this stupid thing?"

It had seemed obvious to Sheila. "We have to create the illusion," she said. But she noticed how tattered the tail had become. Some of the sequins were missing and the bottom was badly scratched.

"Well my God," Sophie replied. "Think about what they can do with mirrors. They can make us look like we're a foot tall. They can make us look like we're in a conch shell instead of on a nasty old stained-up mattress. You think it'd be that hard to make us look like we're wearing a tail?"

Sheila hadn't thought about that. Her legs had been numb for so long.

"Or why not give us a tail like an apron?" Sophie went on. "We can bury our legs under the covers, and throw the fake tail over the side of the bed."

All those years, and she hadn't even asked.

But Reggie said no.

"I like the authenticity of the mermaid tail," he said. He fiddled through the seashell bras, examining Sophie's chest and then holding up each bra as if to size her. "The tail's part of the costume. You're wearing it."

"But *why*?" Sophie asked.

Reggie threw a bra in her direction, and when she leaned in to catch it, he backhanded her so hard that Sheila winced, even though she was half a room away.

"How bad do you need this job?" he asked Sophie.

She kept her eyes down and said, "Real bad."

"Then put on the fucking tail."

He gave Sophie the late shift five nights a week and moved Sheila to the day shift, except for the two nights that Sophie didn't work. Those nights were weeknights anyway, Mondays and Tuesdays, and that made a lot of difference. It was the biggest promotion of her life, in a way. The early shift in the conch shell was nothing like the late shift.

Mostly Sheila was grateful to have a better schedule. She could keep regular hours, maybe even clean up. But part of her worried that she was getting ugly and that Reggie worked the new girl nights because she was prettier than Sheila and younger. He paid her better money, too. She had bigger boobs and no wrinkles. Whenever Sheila tried to get clean, her fears got in the way and she ended up smoking her paycheck.

She was a backslider. That's what her daddy called Christians who stopped attending church, took little vacations on the wild side. Her daddy had made backsliding seem shameful, but it looked better than his old boring life. Backsliders could always come back to God, any time, any day, whenever they were ready.

She wondered who Reggie'd hire next to replace her. A girl with meat on her bones, most likely. He thought Sheila was too skinny.

. .

NOW SHEILA needed food and lots of it. She was empty as a straw. So she called again from the landing, "Hello. Anybody down there?"

After a long time, the old man came scuffling in, rubbing his eyes. "Good morning," he said. He'd lost his hat, but he still had the dent in his hair from where the hat had been.

"Did you take my clothes?" Sheila asked.

"Oh no," he said. "The CIA got in. I must have drifted off, and they were here. They got your clothes."

"Oh," she said.

"They took the toaster, too," the old man said. "I got instructions from my sources. I hope you're feeling better, because I've got to put you to work. We've been infiltrated."

"I need my clothes," Sheila told him.

"You'll have to borrow some clothes, I reckon," he said. He went away and came back with a pair of overalls and a white T-shirt exactly like his own, and he bundled them up and threw them to Sheila, who caught them from the landing.

His overalls were too short. She adjusted the straps to make them as long as possible, and when she came out of the bathroom, he said, "They look real good on you!" But he still didn't have his ladder.

He looked up at her apologetically and shook his head. "I can't let you come down," he said.

"Why not?" she asked.

"You don't know how to be careful," the man said. "You don't know how dangerous it can get."

"I'm starving," she said.

"I knew you'd be hungry. So I'm gonna fix you some toast in the frying pan."

"But how will I eat it?" Sheila asked.

"I'll bring it to you and give you a chance to prove yourself."

She was trapped on the second floor of his house. Now that she had legs, what she needed was wings.

Through a window in her sleep, Tessa Lee could hear her granny's humming. Sometimes she was asleep, and sometimes she wasn't. Sometimes she remembered that she was in the back of her granny's van, and sometimes she forgot, blacked right through it in her mind, like the big black X she had made on her calendar the day that Travis died. She'd never have that day again. Never again. Sometimes she blacked out just that thick, and then she'd feel the bumps as the tires went through potholes. She'd jerk—just like the tires—and she'd remember.

She turned over on the sleeping bag. It was the flattest sleeping bag in the world, hardly any stuffing in it at all. A sleeping bag with a flannel lining that smelled like Travis, a sweaty boy smell, hot and like peppers, like Travis's head always smelled when he'd been playing basketball or wrestling with the dog.

Tessa Lee breathed it deep. The sleeping bag smelled a

lot like dog, too, even though they'd given Travis's dog away, sent him off to Iowa with Hully Sanders's grandson because it made her granny sad to see the dog scratching at Travis's bedroom door.

Stupid dog. She hated how he slept with his head on Travis's shoes, one paw stretched out long and one pulled in close to his brown belly.

She sniffed the sleeping bag and wondered what they'd done with Travis's shoes, with his brown Hush Puppies and his black rain boots.

Through a window in her sleep, she heard her granny's humming and saw Travis's shoes walking, walking, step-by-step, all the way to Iowa to get his dog. No body in his shoes, just his shoes going down the side of the road, through grasses and weeds, then on the broken sidewalk along High-Seas Avenue, walking to the wax museum to find his momma, brown Hush Puppies and black rain boots.

One foot went one way; one foot went another. One foot turned upside down and walked in a direction that was sure to split the two feet apart. "Keep your legs together," she tried to tell him, but there were no legs. Just shoes.

Tessa Lee remembered that Travis was dead—a bump in her dream, a pothole in her chest, big enough to fall right into. Her body remembered, too, but separate from her mind: a flat thudding, a jolt, a terrible awakening.

The old man leaned his ladder against the landing and began his slow climb. Every step jerked and vibrated. Sheila could feel him climbing in her teeth. She didn't see any toast, though. She debated pushing him off, pushing the ladder down to the floor with the old man on it.

But if the ladder fell, she'd still be stuck.

She offered her hand as he approached the top, and he took it. For a moment, Sheila thought of letting go. Maybe she could hold the ladder with her foot, so that while he lay there unconscious, she could slip away.

But she didn't really want to hurt him, and besides that, where would she go?

"Here's your toast," he said, and he pulled a greasy paper towel out of his pocket. Wrapped inside were four pieces of bread, soggy with too much butter and crumpled up, but still warm.

She shoved a whole slice into her mouth at once as the old man pulled up his ladder and led her down the hall.

He stopped beneath a small ceiling panel that opened to the attic. There were no stairs there, either, but it didn't look like the attic had ever had stairs. When he stretched to push the panel away, there was just a hole gaping into darkness.

"I can't get up there," the old man said. "Hole ain't big enough. But I know you can fit, a bony little thing like you. That's why you're here, I reckon."

Sheila licked her lips and tore another piece of toast in half. Chewing made her temples throb, but she ate it anyway. "What's up there?" she asked.

"The enemy," the old man replied. "Your job is to go up there and locate the enemy." He grabbed Sheila's wrist and said, "Up, up," pushing her toward the metal rungs.

"Wait," she said and shoved another section of toast into her mouth.

"It's urgent," he told her. "Something bad's happened."

Sheila flashed again to Tessa Lee in her firefly cloak: *Something bad's happened.*

"Let me get some water," she said and went into the bathroom and drank from her cupped hands. What sort of situation could Tessa Lee think *she* could improve? Maybe her momma'd had a stroke—or even died. Maybe there'd been a wreck.

The old man stood in the bathroom door and pleaded with his eyes. "They came in and raped a nest of grackles," he said. "They planted surveillance cameras in all the baby birds. Now we gotta kill 'em, bless their hearts."

She wiped her mouth on her shoulder. "You want me to go up there and kill baby birds?" she asked.

"Well, first you gotta find them," the old man replied.

"What if I say no?" Sheila asked.

"You can't say no," he told her. "You gotta do what I say."

She looked at him for a long minute, then climbed up into darkness and pulled herself through the hole. It was easier to go along with him than to argue. There were windows up there, two at each end of the house, and they weren't boarded up. Light slanted through them, light that looked a hundred years old.

She dusted herself off and prowled deeper. There were birds in the rafters—not many, but a few. She could see them in the shadows. Some of them sat very still, and one flew squawking across rays of dusty light and out through a gap between the floorboards and a soffit.

It was too hot to breathe. There were feathers and dander, and from what she could see, the whole attic was painted white with droppings.

She went back to the hole to catch her breath and panicked when she saw that the ladder was gone. The old man was gone, too, and she yelled, "Hey! You come back here with that ladder."

What if none of it was real? What if she was tripping, and there was no old man, no house with birds inside, no daughter in a firefly cloak?

She'd dropped bad acid, but it would end. It always ended eventually.

Or maybe there was an old man, and his house went up one stairless level at a time. She couldn't let him trick her into rising floor by floor with no way to ever come down.

Each level would be hotter. She'd always been taught that heaven was up above and hell was down below. But it'd be just like God to twist it all around.

Maybe the old man was God. Maybe she was dead, and this was the afterlife.

"Hey," she called again. "Hey, you asshole! Where'd you go?"

The old man scurried over from somewhere nearby and said, "Now you listen to me, young lady. I won't be called names." He explained that he needed the ladder because he had to take down a ceiling panel where the baby birds were nesting. "They're between the ceiling and the attic floor," he said. "And between the two of us, we'll trap 'em, and then we'll kill 'em."

"I'm not killing any baby birds," Sheila said. She was dizzy. She thought she might pass out.

"Think of them as the enemy," he said.

"I can't do this," she said. "It's too hot."

"You need some water?" he asked. "I'll get you some. You need a flashlight? You need some goggles?"

Sheila said those things would help, and the old man said he'd be right back. "But I'll have to take the ladder," he told her. "Don't call me names while I'm gone."

PART OF THE attic floor was covered in plywood, and part of it wasn't covered at all. Sheila had to step from beam to beam to get around.

The white droppings on the old boards looked powdery in places, and she couldn't help wishing it was coke. She'd done a lot of things to get high before. Even chopped up the little orange crabs from inside oysters, chopped them fine and cut them with hash to smoke.

She'd gone pretty low before, but she'd never snorted dried bird shit. It was time to get cleaned up. She was already on her way.

She was doing fine. She was handling it fine.

She crawled to a window and banged until it opened. From up there, she could see field after field, with patches of woods in between, a dirt road curving around, packed down from rain. She wondered where the dirt road led, if it led to the ocean or away from it.

And she wondered where Tessa Lee had gone.

After Reggie ran Tessa Lee off, he came back in to talk with Sheila.

He'd put on his eye patch and bandanna, picked up a machete, and crawled into the closet of mirrors. He played pirate whenever he broke into her conch shell. The tourists loved it.

"Brought you a little something to calm your nerves," he said, and he passed her a joint. "Some juana for Juana. Keep it down, now, in case there's anybody undercover on the strip."

But Sheila knew to do that already, and Reggie knew she knew. He just liked giving instructions.

So she smoked the joint, which was too hard to distinguish from a cigarette outside the picture window, anyway.

"Why didn't you tell me you had a daughter?" he asked.

"She's not my daughter," Sheila had sworn.

"Bullshit," Reggie said. "She looks just like you. Bigger tits, though."

Sheila squirmed inside her fish tail. She wiggled her toes to keep them from dying. "Coincidence," she said.

"Well, good," Reggie replied. "Then you don't care if I fuck her."

And Sheila tensed and said, "Don't you dare."

"I knew it," Reggie said. He laughed hard and waved his machete around. "I'll be damned," he said. "A grown daughter. You think she wants a job?"

"She's not grown," Sheila said. "She just looks it. Listen, I can't talk about this."

"I told her you get off at eleven."

"Reggie, no."

"She wants to see you. Said it's been too long."

"No," Sheila repeated.

"Come on, now, baby," he teased. "How long's it been since you've seen her? She's a pretty little thing. I can give her a job."

"No," Sheila said again. "Don't do this."

"*What* am I doing?" Reggie goaded. "Am I doing something to you?"

Sheila couldn't get a good breath, so she toked hard and toked again. She closed her eyes and held the smoke inside her for as long as she could.

"She'll be here when you get off," Reggie said. "You bring her to the office and introduce her to me. I need to apologize for being rough."

"You were rough with her?"

"Just a little bit," Reggie said. "But I can be sweet, too. I want her to see my sweet side."

She was a horrible mother. She'd run off again and left Tessa Lee outside the wax museum with Reggie waiting. He was a fucking shark. He'd fuck her daughter. She knew it. He'd put her in the mermaid shell after hours and open the inside window where men paid to watch the mermaid blow the pirate.

She could see the line growing outside the wax museum when the lights in the picture window went off. Teenagers with erections they couldn't even manage and old bums with their bottles, lining up for the show. She tried to clear her head but the image came right back: Reggie unlacing the back of the fish tail and fucking the mermaid from behind.

She didn't deserve to be a mother. She didn't deserve to be alive.

She leaned out the window, stretched out far, only her

hips and her long legs left inside. If she weren't so scared of heights, she could just dive and be done with it. "Dive," she told herself.

But there was another voice inside her that said, "Don't." And maybe she didn't need to dive. Maybe she was just tripping. Reggie'd given her a joint laced with something, got her all fucked up so she couldn't move. Her body was still in the conch shell, and she was tripping.

Then she heard a banging, felt the beams beneath her vibrate, and Sheila realized that the old man was throwing things into the attic: goggles, a flashlight.

She swallowed hard and pulled herself back in.

"If you want the water, you gotta lean down and get it," the old man hollered. "I put it in a pickle jar, and if I throw it, it'll break."

So Sheila climbed back and looked down at the old man.

He reached up to hand her the jar, and she reached down to get it. "You're gonna make a real good helper," he said and smiled at her with his mouth full of blackened teeth.

Tessa Lee's mind twirled on its toes. She kept trying to steady her thoughts, reminding herself she was in the back of her granny's van, headed home. But then she'd forget again as her dreams spun by in dazzling pink tutus.

The Three-Legged Ballerina named Reggie pirouetted over and did three quick pliés. He lifted up his middle leg, strong and muscled, extended it toward her, his toes pointed directly at her face.

She knew she was supposed to clasp it and hold on. She knew she needed to stand on her tiptoes, so he could spin her around, faster than she'd ever been spun before, until she churned to butter inside.

He'd spin her like the lady in her jewelry box, her arms above her head. Once Travis wound her up too tight, and the tiny lady had spun so hard her spring popped and she flew across the room, her last dance ever.

"No," Tessa Lee said in her dream. But the Three-Legged Ballerina wouldn't take no for an answer. He wouldn't pull his third leg back.

"No," Tessa Lee said, and then her granny hit another bump, a deep one, and the man in tights bounced out the passenger window.

Travis was dead.

When Tessa Lee remembered, suddenly, just how dead he was, she woke up all the way. He'd never be able to break her things again, and it was her fault. She wished he could break a hundred jewelry box dancers. She was wide awake, but she kept her eyes shut so her granny wouldn't ask her any questions.

Once she'd had a doll that peed her pants and another one made out of stockings. Travis scribbled on their faces with a pen and gave them around-the-ear haircuts while Tessa Lee was at school.

Her granny scolded Travis, but he was still really little and didn't even know what he'd done wrong. Then her granny went into the closet and came back with one of her momma's old dolls, a porcelain doll with cheekbones and a painted-on mouth, soft brown pincurls close to her head.

Tessa Lee and Travis both loved that doll until one Sunday, their older cousins Drandy and Eric visited, and they pulled off the doll's head and used it for a softball after they lost their real ball in the lake. Tessa Lee was pushing Travis in the swing when Drandy hit the doll's head. She flew right past them with her eyelids blinking and her head all dented in.

Travis leaped out of the swing and chased after it. He gathered it up in his hands and cried, and when Drandy and Eric made fun of him, Tessa Lee started punching them both, swinging and stomping and biting, not even knowing who she was hitting or where, not even sure which adult pulled her off the boys.

Later, Pop-Pop did some reconstruction and put the doll's head back on. But she never looked right after that. One of her eyelids drooped and she always seemed confused.

That's how her momma'd looked, too. Like somebody'd whacked her in the head and knocked out all her good sense.

Tessa Lee was glad her momma hadn't recognized her. She was glad she hadn't told her about Travis. Her momma wasn't even real. Tessa Lee didn't need her anymore. She was lucky to get away before her momma had a chance to *really* hurt her.

Sheila shined her flashlight around and toed her way through nesting material, bits of sticks and moss. She kicked toward the sound below of the old man's banging. He worked beneath her to take down drywall from the ceiling.

She leaned over ductwork, dipped her hands beneath drooping fiberglass, and shined her light through a hole where she could see the old man's flashlight, pointing up.

"Somewhere in here," he said.

Suddenly, a grown bird flew straight at Sheila's face. She leaped backward as the bird grazed her cheek with one wing, squawking as it flew through the rotten soffit.

"I knew that would happen when we got close," the old man shouted.

"I see how the birds are getting into your house," Sheila told him. "We can block off that rotten place when we're done if you want to keep them out."

"Nah, I don't wanna keep 'em out," the old man said. "These birds don't know it ain't their house. They think they own it; I think I own it. I don't mind sharing with the birds, but I ain't sharing with the government."

"They're making a mess up here," Sheila told him.

"And I'm making a mess down here," the old man said, and he laughed.

The baby birds kept peeping, but the scurrying had stopped. The old man coughed and rattled and loosened boards, finally pulling the ceiling down.

"I can hear 'em, but I can't see 'em. You see 'em?" he asked.

But Sheila didn't.

"I know they're in here, 'cause their nest fell on my head.

They must've got scared and left that nest," the old man claimed.

Sheila looked everywhere, trying to track down their cries in the dark. Their momma was gone. They didn't stand a chance.

"Be careful, now," the old man said. "They might have hypodermic needles attached to their beaks. The CIA does that sometimes. They do it with dolphins and with baby birds both."

Sheila climbed over the duct and crouched in the tiniest place. Her eyes were protected by goggles, but bits of insulation got in her mouth, and the soot and the grime streaked her filthy. Splintered wood stuck to her sweat and pricked her. She coughed and held her breath, listening for the birds. At last, she realized that they'd gone into the wall, between drywall and studs, probably when the old man had taken down the ceiling.

She twisted herself toward the sound and reached into a place she couldn't see. When she felt them, she jerked her hand back, then returned it. They scurried around and cried against her fingers.

"You want me to hand them to you?" she asked the old man. She hoped they were old enough to fly. She could let them go in the attic if they had any feathers.

"Yeah," he said. "I got a box."

They ran around and squawked beneath her hand. She could barely reach them, and each time she almost grabbed one, she'd get squeamish and let go.

Finally, when she got a grip on one, she squeezed too hard. It felt like testicles in her hand at first, and then there were bones.

She bit her lip and pulled her hand up.

But with her hand around the bird, made into a fist, she couldn't get it out of the pocket in the wall. The space was too narrow. When she opened her hand enough to lift it, the bird fell out, thudding gently somewhere below.

"It's not working," she said. "They're down too deep. Can you get me a stick or something to dig them up?"

"Yeah, I'll be right back," he said. "Be careful, now. Don't let them cameras take pictures of your face."

WHILE SHE WAITED, Sheila began to hum something soft, as if she could sing the birds to sleep. If they could just go to sleep, it'd be better. They'd die without even knowing it.

She'd done that all her life, hummed her way through her most frantic moments. When she had Travis on her hip and Tessa Lee by the hand, and they needed to cross a street where cars came too fast, Sheila hummed a song and hurried them across, praying the notes would transport them to the other side before they got slammed by an eighteen-wheeler.

On days when she was drunk and not sure she could fix them something to eat before she passed out, she sang a lullaby to soften her fears, to pace her as she heated the water, put in the spaghetti, watched the pot bubble. She repeated the song as she drained it, spread it out on a plate to cool before giving it to her babies. She sang as she watched them eat it, and she didn't pass out.

And once, when she had a gun to her head, when an angry man put the cold metal tip to her temple, twisting a moon into her skin, when there was shouting all around, the man saying, "I'll do it. I'll kill her," and Reggie saying, "Go ahead, motherfucker. Shoot her," Sheila had hummed to herself, a tune she'd made up when Tessa Lee was new to the world. She hypnotized herself with it, sang it inside her head until it was over.

Even the next day, when she woke up safe in her own bed, she was still humming that song.

THE OLD MAN returned with a yardstick and passed it up to Sheila. She hummed as she shoved the stick into the pocket, rammed the baby birds against one side and hoisted the first one high enough to grab it.

The old man had his flashlight shining up at her, so when she pulled the bird out, she could see it. There were no feathers, just quills. It was bluish gray and downy, almost dead already, not strong enough to be lifted by the wing. It was tearing at the place where the wing attached to the body.

Everything was so delicate. New skin so tender. You had to be careful with newborn skin. Travis couldn't stand a Band-Aid until he was almost a year old. Every time she'd peel one off, it'd take his skin, leaving a red streak, a new wound.

She held the bird in her hand, but it didn't really look like a bird. It looked like molding fruit, gone soft at the place where the wing attached to the body.

In her head she hummed.

"Give it here," the old man said. "That's one."

But there were others, frantic, peeping. Sheila chased them with the yardstick again to the edge of the pocket, maneuvering until she could grab another, this one by the throat, her knuckles locked around the tiny neck.

It had its eyes closed when it came up, golden beak wide and only the softest squeak escaping the tiny constricted throat.

Sheila hummed as she pinched. She gritted her teeth and hummed against her shuddering, and hummed as she felt the slight bones crack.

Keep it quiet. Make it be quiet. The sooner the quiet came, the sooner it would be over for everybody.

"You're doing real good," the old man said. "It looks like a baby bird, but it's the enemy."

She hummed in her head, but it wasn't in her head. The old man said, "That's a pretty song. You could be a singer, you know. What's the name of that song?"

Sheila didn't reply. There was another one to get. Another lumpy little mound of life, still living but as good as dead.

Even if she left the baby there, the mother wouldn't come back. The mother would take care of herself. She'd make another nest, lay other eggs. Start over.

If Sheila quit, the last bird would die another way. It would starve to death, terrified and waiting and alone.

There were no good outcomes.

A lot of bad things had happened.

"Don't cry," the old man said. "You've done a great thing today. You saved the whole wide world."

He held the ladder while Sheila climbed down, filthy nasty, caked with grime and feathers, her hair full of sticks and dust, her hands sticky with birds.

"Don't cry no more," he said. "Them birds were the enemy. You did a great service by getting them birds."

"But they were just babies," Sheila said.

"They were the enemy," the old man consoled.

She tried to keep humming, but there was something in her throat: dust, fiberglass, particles of down. Her hum turned to a cough.

"You need a shower," the old man said. "I'll take care of the rest. You get a shower. You've been a good help, and you've saved the world today."

Something vague peeped inside the cardboard box, just once or twice. A bird that was barely a bird, hardly a bird, not a bird for long.

She coughed but couldn't bring it up, what hid inside her throat. She couldn't swallow past it. It choked her, crouching there in darkness, lump of flesh and chirping. Her mouth became its mouth. It lodged there in her throat, beak wide open, begging.

Lil was almost on empty when she stopped for gas at a run-down station that doubled as a sewing machine repair shop. She'd left the highway a long while back, driving without direction or intent. Now it was going on dusk, and she couldn't decide whether to wake up Tessa Lee or let her sleep.

The gas pumps were the old-fashioned kind, not digital, with numbers that rolled into one another, sixes turning to sevens turning to eights, quicker than you could count. They went too fast, those numbers, and she turned her face away from them and away from the thickening fumes.

She'd married at seventeen, miscarried at nineteen, had Sheila at twenty-one, then two more dead babies before her emergency hysterectomy at twenty-seven. It made her dizzy to think of how fast it had happened, how fast a life passes by. She'd been thirty-eight when Sheila left to be with a colored man, and forty-nine when she'd inherited her grandchildren, who somehow turned out to be white. When she was fifty-three Lewis had died; when she was fifty-six Travis had followed. Now she was two months shy of fifty-seven, in the middle of nowhere, with Tessa Lee passed out in the back and Sheila off somewhere on drugs.

At least her gas tank was full.

"Tessa Lee," she called. "You need to use the bathroom?"

Tessa Lee mumbled something and rolled over, so Lil left the windows rolled down in the van and went inside the station to pay for the gas and get the bathroom key.

The bathroom was just as nasty as she'd expected: stained up concrete floors, overflowing trashcan, spiderwebs crusty with carcasses in all the corners. She held herself off the toilet seat and flushed with the toe of her shoe. Then she stood before the mirror, washing her hands and patting down her always-frizzy hair.

The day she'd married Lewis, she'd had him stop at a gas station bathroom so she could prepare herself the best she could, tucking and softening her curls, digging the dirt from around her fingernails so she wouldn't be too ashamed before the justice of the peace.

They'd been fishing that afternoon, though it was windy

and they hadn't caught much. Lil'd helped Lewis load his boat onto his trailer, cranked the wench to hoist the boat up high and tight.

"You gonna marry me or not?" Lewis had asked her as he checked the motor. He didn't even look up.

"Reckon so," Lil said.

Out in the dark river, a fish jumped up, and invisible birds whistled from the limbs of scrub oaks and cypresses that lined the river banks.

"Well then," he said. "Let's do it."

They stopped at the gas station so Lil could do her primping, then drove directly to the courthouse, with Lil stealing glimpses of Lewis out the side of her eye. He was just back from Vietnam, already back when boys her own age were being drafted left and right. Lil liked him because he'd survived. He'd been shot three times in the shoulder and arm, and he'd already healed up, this quiet older fellow with dark eyes and a flattop haircut. Their courtship was just shy of a week when she promised to love, honor, and obey him for the rest of her days.

They were back in the truck before the water stopped dripping from the boat—husband and wife.

LIL FOLLOWED THE directions from a billboard on the highway to Deep and Wide Cabin Rentals, family owned and family operated, the sign had said. She turned onto a road paved with coquina shells, blinding white in the last bits of sun.

It was the first time since Lewis had died that she'd been on a long trip. The road crunched beneath her tires, and suddenly Lil worried that her tires might not be up to snuff. She hadn't thought of her tires before, not ever. Maybe her treads were gone and she didn't even know. Lewis had taken care of the tires, and now here she was, on a crunchy shell road headed for a river she'd never heard of with a name she couldn't pronounce.

She'd always been able to trust that Lewis would take care of things. From the first day of their marriage, he'd handled the details.

"Stay put," he'd told her as he drove up to the big house that first time. It was a farmhouse, but not the sort that Lil was used to. This one was painted white, and had columns and a brick walkway. As soon as Lil saw it, she realized that the Birchs must be high-class farmers, farmers who owned their own land. Lewis turned off the ignition and got out, and Lil's stomach did flip-flops until he came over, opened her door, and threw her right over his shoulder.

He didn't just carry her across the threshold. He carried her across the yard and up the porch steps, too, and Lil couldn't help laughing. She was a big girl, not fat, but strong and taller than most. No man had ever lifted her up before. But Lewis was accustomed to heaving things around: bags of fertilizer, bales of hay, bodies of soldiers the color of pinecones. He'd told her about them out on the boat. And he wasn't even panting when he kicked the screen door open and hollered, "Momma, I want you to meet my bride."

He carried Lil into the room where his momma rested in a hospital bed, her white hair in swirls all over her pillow, her sunken eyes hazy as taffy. Lil was still cradled in Lewis's arms when the attending nurse got up and left them there to visit.

Lewis's momma shook her head. "My Blessed Redeemer," she crooned, "out of all the women in the world, you've married that worm woman from Foggy Swamp." She sighed one time, and then she was dead. Didn't even have time to close her mouth before the Good Lord took her.

So Lil inherited another woman's house. She cleaned it for the first time in preparation for the wake, acquainting herself with the broom and the mop and all the secretly dusty corners of the Birch homestead.

As the relatives came and went, Lil served up tea and cooked biscuits to go with the ham somebody'd brought by. Twice at the wake, Lewis made an announcement that Lil was his new wife, and his sisters hugged Lil cautiously, and his brother-in-law and uncle said, "Here here," and held up their whiskey in a toast. But it wasn't the right time to celebrate, so the announcements faded into quiet sobs, and Lil stayed busy washing up glasses and watching the wind blow the tall pine trees just outside the kitchen window.

They didn't have a chance to consummate the marriage those next few days. There were siblings and cousins and great-aunts in all the beds, and they stayed even after the funeral to clean out the closets and claim the heirlooms before Lil had a chance to want them.

But Lil didn't have her eye on knickknacks or sapphire rings. It didn't bother her one iota that Lewis's sister took the china. She didn't need fine things. What she needed was more practical: a house, a husband, a chair to sink her bones in at the end of a long day.

THERE WERE TWO chairs on the cramped front porch of Cabin F, both of them plastic, both of them mildewed. Tessa Lee threw her backpack down in one and collapsed into the other while Lil fought to open the door.

"Where *is* this place?" Tessa Lee asked.

"Deep and Wide Cabin Rentals," Lil told her.

"Am I still dreaming?" Tessa Lee asked.

"Maybe," Lil said. She worked the key into the lock, but even after it turned she couldn't open the door. It was swollen from the heat, and she had to push and push and finally bang it with her hip before it gave.

There was a dusty box fan in the window, so she turned it on. The sheets on the bed seemed clean enough, though the blanket had black moles from cigarettes. When she sat down on the toilet, her knees bumped into the pipes beneath the sink.

She was so tired. She sat on the toilet and looked at her reflection in the dappled metal S-trap, and her face stretched wide like a piece of fruit, something exotic. Maybe a pomegranate. She hoped she wasn't hallucinating.

Tessa Lee came into the bathroom and said, "I'm gonna take a shower," and Lil just sat there and watched her undress, watched the sand pour out of the cuffs of her shorts as she slipped them off.

"Try not to touch the shower curtain," Lil warned.

But Tessa Lee'd turned on the water by then and didn't hear her.

IT SEEMED like Tessa Lee showered for a year. Lil unpacked the boxes of chicken and potato wedges she'd bought at the gas station. The potatoes were already limp and cold. She pulled out the soft drinks and set the table with plastic forks and paper towels, and Tessa Lee kept on showering.

Lil took the little cup of coleslaw with her to the TV and nibbled at it as she adjusted the rabbit ears. She fiddled with the TV awhile, but nothing tuned in past the static.

Tessa Lee and Travis had grown up with cable, more channels than anybody could ever need. Travis loved all the animal shows—especially the ones where they train dogs to weave through obstacles and jump through hoops. But he never watched for more than thirty minutes before he took the dog outside to practice tricks.

Tessa Lee loved the exercise programs. After school, while Lil cooked or made bows for wreaths, Tessa Lee would stand before the television, the volume turned low, telling Lil all about her day. She could follow along with the exercise instructor, stepping up and down on a little stool, stretching to the right or the left, never missing a turn, and all the time filling Lil in on how the Fellowship of Christian Athletes planned to raise money for the annual rafting trip.

Before he died, Lewis loved the History Channel. Anything about the military and he wanted to watch it. He was an expert on wars and knew what pivotal decisions and battles each documentary left out.

Lil didn't have a program she watched regularly. She watched what everybody else watched. So it didn't matter much that the TV in Cabin F had bad reception. A news anchor came in on one channel just faintly, but her head scrolled up and ran off the screen, reappearing at the bottom and climbing over again, like a scene from a dream that repeats itself or a memory that won't go away.

A screen door slamming a hundred times, a daughter's cry, a heart monitor flatlining.

"You want the breast or the short thigh?" Tessa Lee asked her, and Lil realized the shower had stopped and Tessa Lee was there at the dinette, fixing her plate. She hadn't even heard the water cut off.

OVER SUPPER, Lil tried to talk with Tessa Lee, but everything she said came out funny. She meant to ask, "Why didn't you leave me a note?" but what she said was, "Why didn't you leave me a coat?" and she didn't even know she'd *said* coat—or rather, she knew, but the word *coat* suddenly *meant* note right then.

Her mind was tangled. At least it gave Tessa Lee something to tease about. "I didn't know you wanted a coat," Tessa Lee said.

"You know what I mean," Lil insisted.

Tessa Lee laughed and said, "No, I don't."

Tessa Lee didn't make much better sense, though. She kept talking about IDs, and how you couldn't rent motel rooms without them, how she needed to get her driver's license so she'd have one, like having an ID would make her an instant grown-up.

"You've got no business renting motel rooms," Lil said.

"Beats sleeping on the beach," Tessa Lee said. "And next year I'm going to Junior/Senior weekend. Me and Amber are sharing a room."

"No, you're not," Lil said. "You're grounded. For the whole year."

• • •

SHE HADN'T EVEN thought about grounding Tessa Lee until just that minute. She hadn't intended to punish her at all. But the words had come out, and now she was stuck with them. She didn't back down when Tessa Lee protested or when she went to bed and cried onto her knees while Lil cleaned the table and threw out the greasy leftovers.

Like Tessa Lee had any business running around the beach on Junior/Senior weekend! Lil knew what happened after the prom. They drank wine coolers and went off with boys. She hadn't let Sheila go when she was in high school, and she wouldn't let Tessa Lee go, either, no matter how much she begged. She was lucky Lil hadn't blistered her ass right there at the arcade, right in front of her green-headed friend! Tessa Lee didn't know how good she had it.

LIL HAD GROWN up on the banks of a different river, in a shotgun house with spare bedrooms built onto either side. She lived with her aunt and uncle, and all their children, and a few other cousins who, like Lil, had lost their parents along the way. She was never exactly sure how many people were living in the house, but there were so many children that they didn't even bother with assigning them each to a bed. They just packed into bed as many as could fit, and throughout the night, as another one came to sleep, the one on the farthest side got up to find another space, so that all night long they switched beds, wishing for a bit of pillow and respite from kicks and fingers.

Her uncle was a waterman, and all the boys worked with

him out on the river, tending the nets, setting hooks, bringing home brim and spot and trout.

Lil and the other girls cleaned the fish and kept them on ice. They sold them out by the highway, tying and sewing old nets in their spare time.

The aunt and the uncle were good to Lil, but she knew they didn't have much—and she wasn't really entitled to anything of theirs. So she worked hard to earn her keep.

She was best at digging earthworms. Early every morning and again at dusk, she'd run down to the riverbank and turn the earth and dig the worms, pulling them up carefully so she wouldn't break them and packing them into little cups to sell to fishermen.

That's where Lewis met her when he was just back from Vietnam, and that's where he came again to get more worms the following day. On the third day, when he invited her fishing, she leaped into his truck and left her cousins behind to sell the bait.

She intended to say "I do" from the very beginning. Lewis drove a Chevy truck with hips, a recent model, and though his boat was small and battered, his motor was brand-new.

The farmhouse had lots of rooms, and every room had lots of air. There were embroidered curtains already up in the windows. What more could she want?

It seemed wrong to be so happy when Lewis was grieving for his dead mother, wrong to feel so joyous as she rode by Lewis's side in the car that followed the hearse to the graveyard on the hill. But Lil had plans.

"I'm sorry you're still sleeping on the couch," Lewis told her on the way home from the funeral.

"It's a comfortable couch," Lil said.

"They're never gonna leave," he worried.

"Yes, they will," Lil assured him. "Soon as they get her things packed up, they'll go."

"I wanted to give you a sweet honeymoon," he told her, and she moved over to sit closer to him, beneath his waiting arm.

"It's okay," she said.

"No, it's not," he said. "I've a good mind to pull off the road right here. I'd do it, too, if Uncle Bart wasn't driving right behind me. Tonight we'll go out walking after supper."

When they were back at the house, Lil slipped up to Old Ms. Birch's room before the sisters returned. She found some nail polish in a vanity drawer, and she sat in front of the mirror, her fingers splayed, and she covered her stained nails with the richest color pink she'd ever seen.

SHE'D FELT so lucky to find that nail polish, like polish could make her a lady. She was seventeen then, the same age as Sheila when she ran away from home. Sheila'd never been to Junior/Senior weekend, never had a chance to drink a wine cooler that Lil knew of, but she ran away just the same and never came back. Tessa Lee wasn't much younger, not even two years younger.

Lil climbed into the bed next to Tessa Lee, and Tessa Lee rolled over, so her back was facing Lil. She kept making miserable little hiccups, and left a wet welt in the pillow where her head had been. Tessa Lee was still such a child. Her early years had exposed her to adult things too soon, and in some ways it seemed like she was making up for not getting her fair turn at being a baby. But maybe she was crying about more than being grounded.

"Have you and Amber discussed a chaperone?" Lil asked her.

"What?" Tessa Lee said.

"For Junior/Senior? 'Cause I can't let you go without a chaperone, a Christian chaperone," Lil said.

Tessa Lee rolled over on her back. "Really?" she asked. "We can go?"

"With a chaperone," Lil repeated. "Maybe one of the young marrieds from the church."

"Cool," Tessa Lee said, and she didn't pull away when Lil stroked her head. "Am I still grounded?"

"I reckon not," Lil replied.

Lil watched their shadows against the paneling, watched the slow movement of her hand over Tessa Lee's head. She could almost feel it. She could almost remember what it felt like to have her own head stroked.

"Did that boy, the green-headed one, did he stay with you on the beach?" Lil asked.

"No," Tessa Lee said.

And Lil didn't know whether to be glad or not. She didn't know if that had made Tessa Lee safer or not.

"He seems like somebody out of a dream," Tessa Lee said and yawned. "Not like somebody who bought me breakfast."

Lil wondered if Sheila'd had breakfast, if anybody'd been kind enough to scramble her some eggs, runny, the way she liked them.

"Let me put some more of this aloe on you before you go to sleep," Lil said, and Tessa Lee didn't argue. In the lamplight, Lil broke and squeezed the aloe, rubbed it slippery onto Tessa Lee's burned skin.

Tessa Lee fell asleep before she finished and Lil shined

her burns with the oils, left it thick so her skin could soak it up all night.

SHE MISSED LEWIS most when the lights were out. That's when she felt most alone. She missed the companionship—understanding him, and being understood. She missed the time at night when they'd finished talking, when they were almost asleep, the way he rolled up against her back. She missed the soft, familiar weight of his hand on her hip.

Sometimes she missed the lovemaking, too. There'd been times, of course, when she was busy with something, trying to get the new curtains hemmed before bedtime, and his long fingers would come crawling, and she'd get irritated. But now she missed those fingers.

The night she finally slipped away with Lewis, three days after they got married, he led her around a field and over a stream, to an old barn with water running beneath it.

"You'll like the sounds in here," he told her. "It'll remind you of the river."

And Lil didn't tell him that she didn't miss the river. She didn't mention that she never intended to dig another worm as long as she lived.

He led her up to a loft in the springhouse, where he'd thrown an old sleeping bag over some hay.

"I got grape wine," he said. "And Dixie cups."

They toasted one another, and then he undressed her. It wasn't the first time she'd been undressed by a fellow, but it was the first time she liked it.

His fingers were rough, but not too rough. His kisses were firm, but not too firm. Then he moved on top of her, and she could tell that he'd been to war, that he had some of it left inside him. She held on while he met his needs, and somewhere outside, an old owl whoo-whooed, and beneath her, water passed softly over rocks and clay. And when he rested his face against her breasts, she ran her hands over his back and felt the soft hairs curling there.

He nuzzled against her breasts, his sweat dripping off and rolling between them, and he said, "My momma's gone."

She never knew for sure if he was crying.

LIL WOKE UP suddenly, in the dark, lost at first and wondering where all the bitterness came from. Her mouth was bitter, terribly bitter, and she needed to spit, or to swallow, to do something to get rid of the taste. It wasn't until she was on her feet that she figured out she had aloe resins in her mouth. It wasn't until she was by the sink, rinsing, that she realized the bed had been empty when she left it.

Tessa Lee was gone again. Lil pulled on her clothes as quickly as she could. The clock said 2:13. She was still tugging her top down over her head as she passed through the front door of the cabin, holding her breath.

But Tessa Lee was sitting on the porch in a plastic chair, wearing Sheila's old bedraggled housecoat, her legs stretched out, her heels resting on the railing. "You were snoring like an old pig," she said.

"Sorry, baby," Lil answered and took the chair beside her.

"I don't sleep good anymore," Tessa Lee admitted. "I used to sleep a lot better."

"Me, too," Lil said.

Everything was silent at Deep and Wide, except for a bullfrog off in the distance and some crickets. Lil and Tessa Lee sat in their plastic chairs and studied the darkness and watched the lightning bugs.

After a while, Tessa Lee asked, "How do you feel about stars?"

"Stars?" Lil replied. "You mean stars like the ones up there in the sky?"

But there weren't any stars in the sky that night. It was cloudy, and the stars were all hidden. There were only lightning bugs blinking, pretending to be stars.

"Well, yeah," Tessa Lee replied. "Do you like them?"

Lil considered for a minute, tried to remember the constellations. When Sheila was in elementary school, she'd helped her with a science project—they'd stuck white Christmas lights into black poster board to form the constellations. Now she couldn't remember any of their names—except the dippers. If she could just see them, she might remember some of their names.

"Sure I like them," Lil said. "What's not to like?"

Early the next morning, right after the sun came up, Tessa Lee followed her granny down the dirt path to the river, a box of garbage bags tucked under her arm.

"*Why* are we doing this again?" she complained. The night had been dewy, and now her ankles and feet were soaked.

"To look for treasures," her granny said. "It'd be foolish not to take advantage of local vegetation."

Tessa Lee was sore from her sunburn and stiff from sleeping in unnatural positions, and all she wanted was to go home. "What are we looking for?"

"Whatever we find," her granny replied.

Tessa Lee stomped along. It made her crazy how they always had to collect things. One time when they went to Williamsburg, they'd filled the trunk of Pop-Pop's car with magnolia petals that all dried up and turned ugly before they got back home. When they'd gone to a family reunion in South Carolina, they'd stopped beside the road to get cotton bolls, which weren't soft at all. They were prickly, and Tessa Lee was nervous the whole time they raided the field that somebody was gonna come with a gun and shoot them.

She knew what her granny was doing. She'd go home and brag to Rosie Jo about all the river stuff she'd picked up, and then she wouldn't have to feel so bad that Tessa Lee had run away from home in the first place.

"What kind of arrangements can you make out of mushrooms?" Tessa Lee grumbled and kicked over a mushroom that puffed up around her shoe.

Her granny tossed a handful of mushrooms into a bag. "I'll figure that out later," she said. "Or better yet, you figure it out, and I'll pay you for the idea."

When she was little, Tessa Lee'd come up with all kinds of craft ideas: Christmas tree ornaments made from dried beans, American flags made from bottle caps. She'd even assisted in the craft classes when she was younger, distributing ribbon and scissors, passing out paper towels or just unloading boxes from the van. Now she didn't care about crafts.

The river was narrow, more like a creek than the rivers Tessa Lee had seen before. A man in a little johnboat waved to them as they made their way to the bank. Her granny waved back, but Tessa Lee just toed the edge of the water and watched the tadpoles jerk.

"See there, over yonder? Let's head thataway," her granny said and pointed toward a place thick with reeds, so Tessa Lee followed.

Whenever they went to the beach, her granny collected sharks' teeth and angel wings. When they went to the farmers' market, she picked up all the corn husks that got dropped on the ground. She raided Christmas tree lots and took away the extra limbs to make wreaths.

Her crafts shed out behind the trailer was lined with shelves full of things she might need one day—and there was no rhyme or reason to what she collected, no organization. A box full of pinecones sat right next to a tin of old photos of people nobody knew. Tessa Lee asked her once about the people in the pictures, and they weren't even family. Her granny'd bought them at a flea market in case she ever decided to do a decoupage class.

When Tessa Lee was little, she'd organized her granny's supplies. Sometimes she still went out there to separate the ribbons from the stalks of eucalyptus. If it weren't for her, the fabric would be mixed right in with the seashells.

Tessa Lee stopped when she saw where they were heading. "Gross," she said. "It's all muddy down there. I don't wanna get all muddy."

"Fine," her granny said. "I'll do it myself, if you're too scared to help."

"I'm not scared," Tessa Lee said.

"Suit yourself," her granny replied.

So Tessa Lee found a log and peeked into each end to be sure nothing dangerous lived inside. And then she sat down on the flaky bark and watched her granny wade out into the shallow edges of the water.

"Look out for snakes," Tessa Lee warned. Then she checked the trees over her granny's head—to be sure no snakes were dangling down.

Because what if something happened to her granny? Now that she knew her momma was on drugs, crazy and never coming back, her granny was all she had left.

She saw something that might be a snake in the river, but then she figured out it was a turtle. There were lots of turtles warming themselves on roots and branches sticking out of the river. But some kinds of turtles were dangerous, too. Snapping turtles could nip off your fingers.

Her granny didn't seem worried. She cut the grasses and the cattails with scissors, loaded up her arms and then waded to the bank. Then she threw them down and tromped back into the bog.

"What are you cutting down cattails for?" Tessa Lee called. "We have those at home."

"These are different," her granny insisted. But they weren't different. They weren't different a bit.

Tessa Lee imagined her granny finding something in the reeds, something unexpected, like baby Moses in his floating cradle. Or what if her mermaid-momma was hiding behind the grasses, like Miriam from the Bible, except creepier? And what if she peeked out with her too-big teeth and her smeared-up face? Tessa Lee couldn't stand to think about that. It'd scare her granny to death, and what if she had a heart attack?

Then she pictured something impossible—crabs climbing out of the log she sat on. She hopped up, but there were no crabs there. What if her shrunken up mermaid-momma hid inside a hollow log? Like a wood nymph or a witch.

Tessa Lee called out, "Granny, you okay?"

"Yeah. I'm fine."

"I'm coming to help," Tessa Lee offered and made her way through the muck that sucked against her sandals.

So her granny cut the grasses and cattails, and Tessa Lee retrieved them, carried them to the bank and tucked them into the garbage bags, trying hard to arrange them so the sharp ends didn't poke too many holes. When they had as much as they could carry, they lugged the bags back to the van. Tessa Lee led the way.

For breakfast, her granny had doughnuts and a Pepsi from the vending machines, but Tessa Lee didn't eat. She was sick of all the junk food. She needed some fruit, but there was nowhere to get fruit at Deep and Wide Cabin Rentals.

Their clothes were all muddy and soppy wet, and her granny didn't have anything else to wear. So Tessa Lee put on her pajamas, which were just exercise shorts and a T-shirt, and while her granny showered, she took their muddy clothes to the laundry room across the gravel drive.

• • •

IT TOOK ALMOST two hours to do the laundry. Tessa Lee sat there while the clothes washed and waited, but it didn't seem that long.

Two hours was as far as her momma had been, all those years.

The whole tenth grade, Tessa Lee'd spent two hours in geometry on Monday, Wednesday, and Friday. Two hours in PE on Tuesday and Thursday, and all before 10 A.M. Two hours in school, and you still had two more to go before lunch.

Two hours was nothing.

Most times when she went to the movies with Amber, it took at least three hours. If you counted the time to get there and stand in line for popcorn, to watch the movie and go to the bathroom, and then out to the parking lot where her granny waited, it might even be four. Enough time for her momma to come to see her and drive back home.

Tessa Lee moved the clothes to the dryer and sat there with a handful of quarters, watching the clothes flop around.

Two hours was the length of Sunday school and preaching put together.

Two hours was how long it took her and Travis to wash the van and polish the hubcaps and vacuum out the interior and wipe down the vinyl with Armour-All. Lil paid them each ten dollars to clean her van like professionals. She thought they were saving up for college. Really, they were saving up for their bus fare to Massachusetts.

What if she'd taken Travis all the way to Massachusetts—when their momma was just two hours away?

Her friend Amber went nine hours away every summer, to West Virginia, to stay with her real dad. They drove all that way in a single day. To Amber, it didn't even seem like a big deal.

The night before Amber left for West Virginia, Tessa Lee slept over at her house. She got up that morning and had breakfast with Amber and helped load her suitcases into the trunk of her dad's car. She waved good-bye and walked home lonely, and when Travis asked her if she wanted to go fishing, she just sneered at him and went to her room to study for her driver's test.

That same day, Travis got killed.

By twilight, there were neighbors whispering in clusters all around their house, in the den and kitchen, outside on the deck. Tessa Lee was still in shock and didn't want to talk to anybody, least of all Amber's mom, who came over with a spiral-sliced ham.

"I just talked to Amber," her momma said. "And she's so sorry, sweetheart. None of us can believe it."

"She's already there?" Tessa Lee had asked. "In West Virginia?" It seemed impossible.

"Yeah, she's getting settled in. You wanna call and talk to her? I'll give you the number. You can run down to our house and use the phone, so it won't be on your granny's long distance."

But Tessa Lee couldn't.

The night before she lost her brother, she spent the night at Amber's house and didn't think about Travis at all. She told Amber she was going to Massachusetts to find her momma. Amber begged her not to, said hitchhiking was dangerous and buses broke down and Boston had a mafia bigger than the one in New York City. But it turned out her momma was just two hours away, and she didn't come when Travis died. She didn't even call.

Amber was nine hours away, and she still called. She called twice, but both times Tessa Lee said she couldn't talk, claiming they had company when they didn't, claiming they had to go to the graveyard when they'd just come back. Tessa Lee couldn't make the right sounds come out of her throat. After Travis died, her voice just sounded so funny, a low whistle, her words all hollowed out. She didn't want Amber to hear her like that.

After Travis died, Tessa Lee woke up in the night, startled, remembering that something was wrong, but not always remembering *what*. She woke up like someone had shined a light in her eyes, but there was never a light. Sometimes she wondered if maybe her momma had driven to see her and turned her car around, a three-point turn that shined into her window and woke her up so suddenly. It'd be just like a crazy drug addict to do something stupid like that, drive all the way to see her and then not even knock.

The sheet hurt Sheila when it touched her. It was a thin sheet, pink and worn, too loose and fine to make her skin ache the way it did.

She stretched out on her left side, sore side up. The soreness curved beneath her breast and around her back.

She tried to remember if she'd worn a bra with an underwire—because maybe the wire had broken and she hadn't known. She couldn't remember wearing a bra, except for the one she wore with the mermaid costume. That bra was made of scallop shells sewn onto elastic, but maybe there was a wire beneath it all, supporting the band.

Or maybe there was a wire beneath her bikini top. The day before her girl showed up, she'd worn it to the beach, then washed it out and left it to dry on a hook behind the clothes dryer. When she pictured it, it dangled limp, twisting too freely to have a wire. And anyway, her breasts were too small to need that much support.

She wondered if her bathing suit had been stolen yet. It was a nice one—a red crochet bikini. One of the girls from the jewelry stand would take it when they realized she was gone for good. One of them might be wearing it already, parading down the beach in Sheila's finest.

They all shared the laundry room, but they had separate living quarters. Reggie provided housing for his staff. Years back he'd bought an old cinder-block motel and converted it to apartments. Sheila's had been one of the nicest because she'd been there a long time. In addition to the bedroom, she had a living area with a kitchenette. The newer girls had to share rooms their first season, and they didn't have kitchens at all. Just hot plates.

Now that she was gone, someone else would get her apartment. Some other girl wearing her red bikini was probably already in her bed.

Sheila tried to stop thinking, and let the darkness come. But there was the pain in her side and the sensation of something crawling just beneath her scalp.

She kept picturing her daughter in her firefly cloak, standing before the window outside Fantasies of the Boardwalk. She heard her saying, "Momma, it's me. Tessa Lee," then watched her take off the cloak. Underneath, she wore the red crochet bikini.

She pictured Reggie yanking down the bottoms, her daughter beneath him, fucked in her own bed. But there was nothing she could do about it. Being fucked was inevitable, for everybody.

Sheila dozed off, but as soon as she turned over, she awoke to a deep throbbing burn. Had somebody burned her?

If so, there'd have to be a mark. In her half-sleep, Sheila imagined her pink sheet as an electric device. The old man had rigged it up to shock the CIA. She was under the pink electric sheet. She was in the CIA and no one had told her.

When she was younger, she'd burned herself. She'd done it as a distraction, to give herself something to focus on. Her momma never noticed, or if she did, she thought Sheila'd been clumsy with the iron, pressing the hems of Lewis's pants, the cuffs of his shirts. Sheila loved to iron. Dresses, curtains, sheets. It was her chore and her pastime. She loved the clean smell of a scald, and the edge of an iron left nice even lines. When she was stuck at home while other girls went to school dances or ball games or parties by the river, she marked those days in even lines along the inside of her arm.

After she left home, there were times when she didn't have an iron—when she lived in a motel, when she lived in a shelter. But she always had a lighter. With a lighter, she could heat the blade of a knife or the end of a screwdriver, make it hot and press it down. That sudden hot whiteness took everything away—the man who said he loved her but wouldn't leave his wife, the friend who took advantage, the job she didn't get—they all disappeared into the sudden blinding scorch.

Sheila finally got up, turned on the light, and stood before an old speckled mirror, examining to see if she'd burned herself by accident.

Her body was thin and tan. The sore spot beneath her arm sat directly in the white strip where she had no sun. She studied it closely.

At first, she thought the bumps were spots on the mirror. But then she felt them with her fingers. Three little red bumps. So she wasn't out of her mind. She had poison ivy. She probably got it out in the woods. Maybe she'd leaned against a tree, or slept on a sprig beneath the lean-to out back.

And once the bumps appeared, it seemed to itch more, like the poison oak she got as a kid, when she went to visit her great-aunt and -uncle, who lived way out by the river. It was fall, and she and her cousins went out to play and found the scarlet vine twining up a tree. It'd been Sheila's idea to pull it off and make crowns with the leaves. They wore them back up to the house, where the women exclaimed and scolded, then rushed them into tubs of hot water and washed them down with stinging lye soap.

She remembered the itching all over her face, her eyes swollen shut, the itching that climbed her arms and throat. The itching was awful. But there hadn't been pain. And the bumps had broken out quickly, in the first day.

What she had now was a different kind of itching, a different kind of poison. Poison with a kick.

Tessa Lee stayed in her room as much as she could and let her granny and Rosie Jo deal with well-wishers. Amber's momma came by, and Hully Sanders, and even her fourth-grade music teacher, who lived a few streets over. Tessa Lee spoke politely to them all and apologized for causing such a stir.

She expected to be scolded by all the adults, but they didn't fuss. They looked at her a little too long and made her worry that something was wrong with her face. As soon as she could, she hightailed it back to her room to look in her mirror.

She looked funny, but maybe that was just because her face was peeling from sunburn, and the skin beneath looked tender and pale. She looked shiny, like somebody else, not like herself.

Her room looked like somebody else's room, too. Everything was familiar, but somehow she wasn't attached to it. She looked at the medals she'd won from the science fair. In ninth grade she'd done her project on bioluminescence; in tenth grade, aggressive mimicry. For both projects, she'd studied fireflies. She even had models of fireflies on her desk.

There was such a huge space between her knowledge and her feelings. The awards were for her mastery of facts: fireflies light up to ward off prey, to indicate that they have defensive chemicals and taste bad. They also light up to attract mates. Different kinds of fireflies behave differently; some flash their lights rapidly, some more sporadically.

Then there was aggressive mimicry—and the habit of some

female fireflies who'd already mated to signal males of a different species. They were good warriors and would do anything to protect and nurture their eggs. When the male came to mate, the female attacked him, killed him and ate him.

It gave her chills just to think about—and it surprised her that nobody'd made a horror movie about female fireflies yet.

Tessa Lee'd checked out books at the library and studied articles on college websites. And she'd won the science fair two years straight. But the knowledge all came from outside her.

There was something else that came from inside, something more important running parallel to facts: the first sighting of a firefly's light, then the anticipation, waiting for it to blink back on, the surprise, even glee, when it streaked past.

Tessa Lee felt as far from herself as the feeling from the fact.

She felt like the tiny glowworm living under a rock, surviving on earthworms and just waiting for the right time to grow up. How did a glowworm know when to become a firefly?

She picked up one of her firefly models. She'd made it herself out of clay—not kid's modeling clay but real clay from the art store. She'd made one glowing and one just ordinary, to show how different they looked.

Glowing, a firefly had a lantern on its tail. But it was only pretty when it flashed. The other model, the plain one, didn't look the least bit interesting.

Fireflies were so complicated, not even *flies*, really, just skinny black beetles with wings trimmed in yellow, hanging out on the ground, sleeping under fallen leaves until nighttime.

But then, whoosh, they flew away, out into the night,

transformed themselves into something remarkable, blinking and glowing.

She and Travis had caught them, plenty of times, kept them in pickle jars with holes poked in the lids. But from inside glass, their flashes seemed desperate, and they couldn't survive that way long.

Where was that space between ordinary and magical? Between everyday and magnificent? Between the captured specimen and the creature in the wild?

Her momma had disappeared into that space.

Maybe when people died, they disappeared there, too.

Tessa Lee pulled out her firefly cloak and draped it around her. The tiny little fireflies were so faded that they hardly glowed anymore.

She stood before the mirror, examining herself in her old cloak, in her new skin, open and peeling away. She wasn't sure yet what she was becoming.

"I hope you're feeling some better today," the old man said to Sheila. "We got work to do."

He stood beside the bed and didn't seem to notice that she was naked.

She pulled the pink sheet higher around her neck and winced at the pain beneath her arm, gritting her teeth against the burning.

He had a caulking gun in his hand, and he pointed it at Sheila. "There's gonna be a war. We ain't got but about six hours to prepare, gotta make this place airtight. I done taped up the mail slot so they can't get in that way."

"I'm sick," Sheila muttered and covered her head with the sheet. "I was up most all night. Didn't fall asleep 'til after the sun was up."

"See here," he said. "I'm sorry, but you gotta get up." He prodded her with the caulking gun, and for a moment, before her head cleared, Sheila thought that was what had happened beneath her arm. The old man had shot her.

She peeled back the covers and pushed up on her elbows.

"I need your help," the old man explained. He had a mouthful of chewing tobacco and a brown line of drool had collected at the corner of his lips. "I'm gonna get all the windows and doors covered, but I need you to caulk around the baseboards." He spit over his shoulder, right onto the pink carpet. "Do you know how to caulk?"

"I think I've got the flu," Sheila told him.

The old man took a step back from the bed. "I hope you don't have the bird flu," he said. "The avian flu. You mighta got it from them birds."

"I'm pretty sure it's just the regular kind," Sheila replied. Her head hurt, and her legs ached, too. She'd feel so much better if she just had a cigarette. She wondered if she could smoke chewing tobacco, if she unpacked it, and rolled it in a coffee filter. Without thinking, she reached to scratch the poison on her side and flinched. "Hey, do you have any calamine lotion, or anything like that?"

"Why?" the old man answered, backing up another step. "You ain't itching, too, are you?"

"Yeah," she said. "I think I got poison."

"Let me see," he said.

Sheila pulled the sheet away just enough for him to catch a glimpse of her rash. By then, her bumps had multiplied into an irregular quarter-sized cluster, a raging, itching pod.

"Oh, no," the old man said. "Oh, Lord, no!" And he rushed out of the room, slamming the door behind him.

"Wait," Sheila shouted. "What's the matter?" She got up carefully, holding her side, and stood before the speckled mirror, where she flattened her breast with her palm and studied the growing rash beneath her arm. When she touched it, it almost took her breath.

Outside the bedroom, she heard shoving and a thud as the old man pushed something heavy against her door. Maybe the old wardrobe from out in the hall.

"I won't rub it on you!" she called. "What're you doing?"

Something else bumped against the door.

"Barricading you in," the old man shouted. He was panting by then, his voice high-pitched. "They've poisoned you," he said. "I hate to do it, but it's just like with them baby birds."

"No," Sheila said. She tried to soothe him, "No, honey, the CIA didn't do this." It was like he was tripping. She'd helped lots of people come down off bad trips before.

"They're trying to get to me through you. You're contaminated. You're done for." He started hammering, and the banging made her head throb.

"Come on, now. I'm here to help. Remember?"

"That ain't just regular poison," the old man insisted.

She tried to open the door, but it wouldn't budge, and the doorknob was loose in her hand, half unscrewed. "Come on, now. Let me out," Sheila said, shaking the knob, trying to get it to catch. "I've just got poison ivy. You can't get it unless you touch it."

"You gonna die," the old man said. "No need to fight it. You're done for, like my wife. They got you good."

"It's not serious," she tried to reason. "Please open the door. I need to use the bathroom!"

"Oh no," the old man said. "What you got is real, real bad!"

Then he started hammering again, and although Sheila hollered out to him, he wouldn't answer back.

She started to panic a little. "You can't just leave me in here," she said. "What if I die in here and decompose? Then you'll get sick for sure. If you don't have it already, it'll get you then."

No response, but she kept on talking. "The virus probably won't even activate until I'm dead, and then it'll be airborne. If I die in here, you're gonna die, too. You'll die with me."

The old man never acknowledged her threats at all, and after a while, she peed in the corner. Served him right. Asshole. She was so tired, and her arms were so sore, like she'd been rowing boats all her life, so she lay back down, pulled up the pink sheet, and went to sleep.

Some hours later, she heard a knocking against the side of the house. She went to the window and saw an extension ladder adjusted to reach the window's ledge. The old man stood below wearing a gas mask.

Sheila pounded at the window until it finally opened. She pushed it up as far as it would go. The old man ran back across the yard, looking in every direction for what might jump out from behind a tree. He pulled his gas mask back just enough to say, "Wait!"

So Sheila waited.

"Don't come out 'til I'm back in the house," he said. "When you go, take that ladder with you. Don't leave it here." Then he pulled down his mask and bolted for the door.

THERE WAS NO way Sheila could step onto that ladder with nobody to hold it. What if it tipped over? Her hands were too shaky, her bones too loose inside her skin. What if she fell?

Nobody would come if she fell.

She didn't like heights. She didn't even ride Ferris wheels.

When she'd first left home and gone to be with Lorenzo, the boy she thought she loved, the one her momma refused to let her date, they ran away together. They had to since Lorenzo worked for Lewis.

Lorenzo had family about an hour away, and so they went there. When they walked into his older sister's house, she shook her head and said, "I know you ain't brought home no white girl," but Lorenzo just grinned and hugged her, and the sister let them sleep on the screened-in porch, on an old piece of foam.

Sheila had cried those first days and especially those first nights, and Lorenzo tried to console her. He held her close in his big arms and told her not to let his sister boss her around, not to take it personally when she sucked her teeth and turned her head.

He tried to make her laugh. "Your momma don't like my pe-can tan, and my sister don't like your pale white tail," he joked. "But, baby, none of it don't matter, cause we got each other."

When Lorenzo was with her all that seemed true enough. But when he was at work, when the sister sneered or ignored her altogether, Sheila couldn't help thinking: I gave up my momma and daddy for *this*?

Lorenzo was learning to lay bricks, and he promised her they'd get a place of their own, as soon as they saved up enough.

There was a traveling carnival one town over. She'd read about it in the paper, and when the weekend came, Lorenzo took her there to ride the Ferris wheel. "It'll give you a whole new perspective," he said. "From way up there, you can see everything so clear."

But the world was more manageable to Sheila down low, with her feet on the ground. Up there in the Ferris wheel, dangling in that flimsy metal seat, she couldn't catch her breath at all.

Some people liked the feeling of being on top of the world, but up in that Ferris wheel, she could feel the contraption groaning and shifting beneath her. Not steady at all. One big gust of wind and the whole thing could topple.

Now Sheila sat in the windowsill, her legs dangling out, clutching the half-rotten window frame, soft and black from years of rain and mildew. She'd never make it down that ladder.

The first rung was only a few inches beneath the sill, but with nobody steadying it, she didn't have the nerve to take the first step.

At least this way she could see it. She knew that before she actually dropped down onto the ladder, she'd have to flip around and face the house. Her stomach fluttered at the thought. How could she drop out of the window without looking? Just trusting that the ladder would be where her toes landed? And she was barefoot. No treads at all. Just her toes to curl around each rung. She wasn't sure if she could trust them. She didn't know if she could trust her hands to stop shaking enough to hold on.

When she was little, her daddy'd built her a treehouse in the backyard. He'd hammered rungs into the tree for her to step on. She'd climbed up there beside him and pulled herself onto a higher limb and kept him company as he nailed down the platform where she spent her summers reading Nancy Drew mysteries and dreaming. She never fell out of that treehouse. She slipped once, when one of the rungs broke off, but her foot landed on the next one down and the only thing she suffered was a pulled muscle from trying too hard to hold on.

She closed her eyes and turned around in the window, clasping the soft wooden frame, her pelvis balanced against the mildewed sill. She took a deep breath and let her legs extend, let her body take that first tentative step into nothing. She found the ladder with her feet, tested it, felt the width of the rung, spaced her feet to get her balance.

Still, she wasn't ready to let go. She held onto the windowsill and felt the wood wiggle beneath her grip. Completely rotten. Time to leave. For all she knew, the ladder might push right through the house when she added her full weight.

She thought again of the swaybacked house, of how she'd

clung to it, too, how her fingers pressed into the soft walls. She hadn't wanted to leave there, either, hadn't wanted to leave the safety of being inside her momma. She never wanted to let go, ever.

The pain in her side spread around her rib cage. It felt like a broken rib coming right through her. It burned and tingled, pressed there against the rotten sill.

The pain in her side made her feel soft and mildewed and black. If she wasn't holding onto the windowsill so tightly, she could poke a finger right through her skin.

She had termites. She pictured them doing to her insides what they did to wood—gnashing something solid into pure powder. They were doing to her what they'd done to the old man's house.

She heard someone humming, and it sounded like her momma, like when she was still a baby and her momma rocked her to sleep each night, humming, maybe before she was born.

Her momma would know what to do about the poison ivy and the broken rib. Her momma would have calamine lotion. Quarts of it. She'd take the ladder along and give it to her daddy. He could lean it against a tree and build a tree-house for Tessa Lee and Travis. They could climb high and hide in the leaves, be held by the branches of a strong tree. They'd never fall again. Never.

The ladder jerked beneath her weight. She pressed her body close to it, let go, grabbed on, let go, grabbed on, and she hummed to herself, a song from another time. She hummed and the heat from the metal ladder warmed her hands. She kept her knees close to the ladder, let her knee bones kneel against the rungs, her toes dropping and grabbing, dropping and grabbing, the ladder warm against her hands, her hands sweaty but not slipping, her feet uncertain but warm, and always landing in place.

While Tessa Lee waited for her granny to finish her craft class, she wandered around the recreation center and looked at the pictures and collages hung on the walls. Each one told a piece of the story—how Hully Sanders overcame poverty and other obstacles to build the greatest mobile city on the East Coast.

When Hully first bought the land, nobody thought it was worth a plug nickel. It said that on a little white card beside the first picture, and there was a plug nickel displayed beneath the caption. There'd been nothing around except pine trees and chiggers. Hully'd used it as a campground at first, mostly for people with pop-ups or tents. Then as the surrounding area was developed, Hully started clearing his acres. One of his sons worked for an excavating service, and he borrowed a backhoe and dug some lakes on weekends.

Travis had always loved the pictures of the lakes being dug, especially the one titled "Man with a Vision," with Hully standing in a big hole next to the backhoe, his arms spread out wide. When Travis was really little, Tessa Lee'd had to hold him up so he could see. Sometimes when her arms got tired, she'd drag over a chair for Travis to stand on, and he'd study Hully and his lake-digging enterprises while Tessa Lee made bead necklaces or read a book. Then later, when they were far from the recreation center, when they were at the grocery store or in church, Travis would suddenly spread his arms wide like Hully and declare, "I'm a man with a vision" and make all the grown-ups laugh. Once he knew it made them laugh, he did it a lot. That was back before Pop-Pop died, before Travis got sad.

The next set of pictures showed the permanent sites being developed around the lake. That's when Pop-Pop and Granny had bought their lot. According to Pop-Pop, they got in just in time, before Hully hiked up the prices.

Some of the pictures had captions that read, "Prime Waterfront Acreage," but it looked more like swamp-front acreage to Tessa Lee.

Hully Sanders's Mobile City was nine blocks wide and thirteen blocks deep. The overhead shot, taken from an airplane, made it look like they lived right at the ocean, but they didn't. The entrance to the mobile city was just four blocks from the ocean, but it was a private beach for rich people who owned houses as big as malls. When they wanted to go to the ocean, her granny had to drive them down to the state park. They didn't go there much.

Tessa Lee still liked the overhead shot best. That was the one she studied the longest.

There was even a picture of their trailer on the wall, and beneath it, a picture of her granny, who was the crafts coordinator, and Pop-Pop, who'd been chief of security until he died. Their trailer was the very last trailer on a street that dead-ended at a lake. Sometimes the lake was pretty, but it hadn't rained much that summer, and the lake had pulled into its own middle, leaving a swampy muck around the edges. They were haunted almost always by mud-loving mosquitoes.

Whenever Tessa Lee complained about the mosquitoes or the smell, her granny just said they should be thankful for the view. It was true that in the mornings, from her bed, Tessa Lee could look out the window and see birds roosting in the branches of a tree that grew beside the lake. Sometimes there were herons, so compact, all pulled into themselves while they stood at the edges and fished, but then they opened up wide and flew away, their legs skinny and long and stiff as a rudder.

Sometimes the ducks came right up into their yard.

It was really a pretty good place to live.

Before Tessa Lee moved to Hully Sanders's Mobile City, the development already had the recreation center, the basketball courts, a grocery store, a church, and a playground. The pool was built the year after she and Travis arrived. That's where they'd both learned to swim. The year she was eleven, paddle-boats were added on one of the lakes. When she was twelve, Hully built a buffet restaurant. Now he'd opened a gazebo bar on the nicest lake, where people on vacation went to drink and dance.

And this year, they'd gotten the rickshaws.

Tessa Lee looked at the newest picture—five rickshaws parked in a line out in front of the recreation center, a boy named Leo who rode her bus sitting on the first one, waving at the camera.

The rickshaws looked like huge high-tech tricycles. The driver had the seat up front, the only seat with pedals. Then the riders sat behind, on an upholstered bench, beneath a little canopy.

The rickshaws were Hully's latest idea, a kind of cab service just for his mobile city. The drivers all had walkie-talkies. They got dispatched to pick up people from the transient section and pedal them over to the restaurant. Or to take people home from bingo or the pool.

It was the perfect job for Tessa Lee because she'd get to exercise the whole time she worked. She'd get paid to stay in shape. Leo told her that one Saturday night, he made thirty dollars just in tips.

But Hully was only hiring licensed drivers for rickshaw rides. He wouldn't budge when Tessa Lee asked him to make an exception. Not even when she repeated back the history of his mobile city and argued that nobody'd be a better tour guide, licensed driver or not.

So Tessa Lee'd planned to get her license right at the beginning of the summer and drive rickshaws the whole season long. But then Travis got killed, on the same day Tessa Lee was supposed to take her test, and now when she thought of rickshaws, she thought of Travis, too, even though Travis had never ridden a rickshaw in his life.

Sheila carried the ladder on her left side because her right side was too sore.

The sun was hot on her head and made the ladder hot to carry. Her feet were bare, and the sand on the dirt road was hot against her soles. She hoped she would come to water soon. She could cool her feet and her face in the water, then make a bridge with her ladder and cross over.

There was shade ahead, so Sheila walked toward it. She was in the shadows of trees and then out again and on a bigger road where a woman in too-short overalls was sure to be found if she dropped dead. Someone would stop for the ladder and see her there beneath it.

The first car that passed had a woman and children inside. The children turned back to stare at her and pointed all the way around a curve.

Then a work truck came by, full of Mexicans, who waved and honked their horn. Their big tires kicked up the dirt, and it settled on Sheila's sweaty skin.

She rounded a corner and saw a strange vehicle coming her way, maybe an army tank. Her vision was blurry, so it was hard to say. It was some sort of military vehicle, maybe like the one her daddy had ridden in when he was in the war.

It turned out to be a combine, a gigantic farm machine with wheels as tall as she was. Her daddy had driven those, too, so maybe it was her daddy, come to get her. It had metal arms with sprayers on both sides that were pulled in like an insect. The driver stopped right there in the road. He was way too young to be her daddy. He leaned out and stared at her so hard that she worried he may be up to no good.

"You heading anywhere in particular?" he asked.

Sheila shrugged. She didn't have the energy to do anything else.

"How 'bout I call my preacher, see if he can come give you a lift? Will that be all right with you?"

Before Sheila even agreed, the man in the combine pulled out his cell phone and started punching in numbers.

SHE WAS SITTING next to the ditch on top of her ladder when the preacher came. He was a wiry preacher with slicked-back hair and sideburns. He wore cowboy boots and a "Praise the Lord" belt buckle.

He had some twine that he used to tie Sheila's ladder to the top of his station wagon. The car was so old that it had lap belts for seat belts, and Sheila's didn't work anyway. The metal wouldn't click into place, but the preacher gave her a bible to hold and told her she was safe as long as she didn't put it down. The ceiling in his car was sagging, but he'd pushed it back up with smiley-face tacks.

He asked her what she needed, and when she told him calamine lotion, he took her to a drugstore in a tiny little town.

Bells tinkled when they walked in, Sheila first, the preacher right behind, holding the door. Everybody turned and nodded, then went back to reading the paper or taking inventory of the stock. The preacher called out to the pharmacist, who was behind the lunch counter filling up the ice machine.

"My friend here needs some calamine lotion. Where would that be?"

"Oh," the pharmacist said. "How bad's your poison?" He came right over and didn't seem to mind that Sheila wasn't wearing any shoes.

"Pretty bad," she told him.

"Let's take a look," the pharmacist said and led her to a storeroom, the preacher in tow.

Here we go, Sheila thought. She unhooked the right side of her overalls and delicately lifted the white T-shirt she was wearing beneath, careful to keep her breast covered. The preacher looked away.

"I hate to tell you this," the pharmacist said. "But that's not poison. Looks like shingles to me."

And Sheila thought of the old man's house, how the shingles had fallen off, how the guinea bricks along the side flaked and dropped to the ground as she scraped the wall climbing down the ladder.

"See how your rash is running around? See here? It's spreading out right along the nerve," the pharmacist said. "You need some medicine for that. You got a doctor you can call?"

Sheila shook her head. The pharmacist looked at the preacher, and the preacher just sighed.

The pharmacist leaned his head out of the storeroom door and yelled, "Hey, Doc? Hey, Doc, can you come here?"

"I'm retired," a man called back.

"Oh, put down your cheeseburger and get in here," the pharmacist demanded.

And soon another man was in the consultation room with them, studying Sheila's rash.

"Does it hurt bad?" Doc asked. He had little flecks of french fries in his gray beard.

Sheila told him that it did.

"Never had 'em myself, but I hear they're painful."

"Do they look like shingles to you, Doc?" Preacher asked.

"Might be," he said. "You got a thermometer? Let's take her temperature."

Sheila kept waiting for one of them to say they needed to do a breast exam. She figured that sooner or later, they'd say her uterus was involved and ask her to take off her pants so they could check that, too. But they never did. The man called Doc stuck the thermometer under her tongue, and said, "See here, Preach, one thing's for sure. She's undernourished. Needs some Angus beef if you ask me," and Sheila sighed, because there it was. She was no fool. She knew what the Angus beef stood for.

But they made her a big hamburger instead. Gave her ibuprofen to help with the fever. Nobody asked for a blow job. Nobody asked for a thing.

It turned out not to matter that Doc was a shrink and didn't know how long shingles took to heal. The pharmacist knew plenty and told him what to write on his prescription pad, and Doc obliged. Then while she and the preacher ate, the pharmacist filled it.

"You must've been under a lot of stress," Doc said. "You been under stress lately?"

"Sort of, I guess."

"Stress or chemotherapy. That's what causes shingles," Doc said.

The pharmacist folded over a little white bag and passed it to her. "Shingles is the same virus as the chicken pox," he said. "For most people, it stays dormant, but if it ever wakes back up, you get shingles."

"Is it serious?" Sheila asked.

"No, but it'll make you miserable. I put a little pamphlet about it in with the pills."

"Oh."

"You got a weak immune system," he told her. "Try to take care of yourself, okay?" And Sheila said she would.

She got her antivirals, lunch, calamine lotion, and a pair of flip-flops all courtesy of the preacher, the pharmacist, and the shrink.

When the preacher asked Sheila where she wanted to go next, she didn't give him her momma's address. She knew the address. She'd memorized it years before. But she didn't say that to the preacher. She just asked if he knew of a shelter in her momma's town. He called another preacher, who got directions to The House of Possibility. It was a women's shelter, and they just assumed Sheila'd been battered. She didn't tell them any different.

When they passed the entrance to Hully Sanders's Mobile City, Sheila's heart gave a kick. She memorized every landmark they passed after.

The House of Possibility was in a run-down neighborhood only a few miles away. A shabby Victorian, it had a big front porch and columns with NO TRESPASSING signs taped onto them. There was no sign advertising The House of Possibility. Just 206 Jefferson Avenue on a plaque beside the door. It looked like all the other old houses. The preacher parked on the street, opened Sheila's door, and helped her out.

"Can you use the ladder?" she asked the preacher. "It's all I've got to pay you with."

"Why, thank you," the preacher accepted. "I'll give you fifty dollars for it," and he opened his wallet. "I've been needing a ladder."

"But what about the medicine and lunch?" she asked.

"Courtesy of First Methodist of Haleyville," he told her. "One day you'll pay it back to someone else."

She walked into The House of Possibility amazed. Contrary to everything she'd suspected, all Christians weren't assholes after all.

EVERY FEW HOURS, Sheila checked her shingles to see how far they'd spread. They spread in either direction from the central cluster, a raging red band, multiplying, sometimes skipping ahead and leaving skin unblistered, and sometimes trailing along only to bloom into another clump of prickling, firey pimples.

They consumed her. Like algae taking over a pond. And they consumed her mind. She could think of nothing else—just the itch and throb, electric, numbing and shocking at once. And there were ghost pains. Pains in her knee, pains beside her navel, numb spots at the corners of her mouth.

The woman who worked at The House of Possibility went over the rules. No alcohol or drugs. No men. No going or coming after 10 P.M. Sheila tried to listen, but it took all her strength to try not to scratch. She wanted to tear off her skin in strips and shed it, like a tree or a snake.

The woman talked nonstop. She worked four days a week, afternoons and evenings. There was always someone there. They had twelve beds total, five were empty—now just four. She offered her soup and crackers, but Sheila just wanted to rest.

The woman led Sheila up to an attic where a rope was stretched from beam to beam, knotted to eyebolts, a makeshift closet. Along the rope, there were women's and children's clothes, all sizes mingled together, mostly out of style. Sheila and the woman sorted through and found a skirt, two blouses, some shorts and T-shirts, and a pair of old canvas topsiders. The woman heaped the clothes over her arm and took them down to wash while Sheila bathed and rested.

She couldn't stand for water to hit her shingles at all. She barely splashed them, didn't bother with soap or a rag.

They radiated around her, a wavy pattern weaving over her ribs. They might be pretty if they didn't hurt so much. Maybe she'd gotten shingles to help her go off drugs. Now she had a chance. Not like when she was the mermaid in the conch shell. She didn't have a chance then.

Her daddy would say the shingles were a gift from God. Maybe all painful things were gifts from God. Maybe God was the greatest sadist ever. Look what he put his only begotten son through.

When she worked in the conch shell, the Christians would come sometimes with their signs that said REPENT or THE WAGES OF SIN IS DEATH, and they'd march up and down in front of Fantasies and shout out their Bible verses and tell Sheila she was going to hell until Reggie came outside to run them off.

They tried to preach to Reggie, too, but he just said, "I'd rather be in hell than in heaven with you," and Sheila felt the same way. So often, God's followers were mean people, people who hated more than they loved. And what else could you expect—the one they worshipped kept beating them down. No wonder they had so much hate.

She'd already taken her pill at lunch and was supposed to

wait until bedtime for another, but what could it hurt, to double up?

Her bed was just a twin size, covered in a yellow chenille spread. Tessa Lee'd had a bedspread like that when she was a baby, and she'd sucked the knobs on it like they were nipples, always looking for comfort, never getting enough.

Sheila covered up in the yellow spread. She just needed to sleep awhile. When her legs and arms were stronger, when the termites stopped eating her up, then she'd go somewhere and buy a bottle. She'd get a pack of cigarettes. No need to give up everything at once. She had to be reasonable about it. Cigarettes were a gift from God, just ask the tobacco farmers.

There was a fan on the floor, off to the side of the dresser, and if Sheila just had the energy, she'd turn it on low. She'd close her eyes and sleep in the wind, let the wind blow her guilt away.

But the guilt was a gift from God, and so she kept it.

She hoped that God understood she'd had to leave. If she'd stayed behind, those children would've sucked her dry.

Maybe Lil had pushed too hard, forced her to take the test when she wasn't ready. Before Travis died, Tessa Lee'd talked nonstop about all the places she'd go once she got her license. She'd drive Travis to basketball camp.

She'd pick up Lil's prescriptions from the drugstore. It hadn't really occurred to her that Tessa Lee might fail.

Lil was proud of her, anyway. She didn't get upset in front of the people at the highway department. She was polite and nodded to the policeman, who told her she could try again in two weeks.

But once they got back in the van and headed home, Tessa Lee turned her face to the passenger window and rested her forehead against the glass.

Lil didn't ask questions or try to console her. There was nothing she could say.

When they'd first gotten the children, they'd been caught off-guard, so completely frazzled that it took them awhile to remember that their own trauma was nothing compared to what Tessa Lee and Travis were going through. Those first months had been filled with details—legal guardianship paperwork and court dates. Taking the children to a doctor, getting them beds and a dresser, getting their clothes in order, buying them books and toys, enrolling Tessa Lee in school, potty-training Travis.

Neither Lil nor Lewis had expected to work again. With the money they'd made from selling the farm and Lewis's pension, they had enough to enjoy their retirement. But once they had the children, Lewis went back to work as a security officer for Hully. Lil took in some sewing for a while, alterations mostly, and she made the bridesmaids' dresses for Rosie Jo's daughter's wedding.

It wasn't until six or eight months had gone by, when they were in bed one night, that Lewis pointed out that the children needed to have an experience.

She hadn't known at first what he meant. An experience

didn't seem like something you *decided* on. An experience happened *to* you.

She told Lewis she was too tired for any more experiences.

He put down the rifle magazine he was reading and took her hand.

She'd just painted her nails. They were still damp, and she didn't want to ruin them, so she pulled her hand away.

"I know you're tired," he said. "I'm tired, too. But those children haven't had anything to look forward to since they got left in the state park last year," he said. "They need some new memories, some good ones that include us—and not *her*."

Lewis was good that way, and he was right. He'd taken them on vacation, the four of them. Rosie Jo looked after the dog. They went all the way up to Williamsburg, Virginia, where they got Patriot Passes and explored colonial history. They spent three nights in a motel and had a holiday.

Now Lil could see that Tessa Lee once again needed an experience, something to reframe her summer, take her mind off everything that was wrong. So she asked her, "Do you want to go to Williamsburg?" It made her ache for Lewis just to say it.

But it was the wrong suggestion. Tessa Lee scowled, choked out, "No. Why would I wanna do that?"

Lil shrugged and remembered how cute Tessa Lee had looked in her black pilgrim hat. "Just wondered."

And then Tessa Lee broke down. Lil knew that she would. The sound of those great hiccupping sobs sounded so much like Sheila, so familiar.

FOR MONTHS, Tessa Lee'd pestered Lil about nonsense, like not signaling for a full one hundred feet before turning. She'd chastised Lil for passing a tractor trailer before they got to a stoplight, because it takes big trucks three times as long as cars to come to a complete stop. She'd fussed because Lil didn't use her emergency brake, even though they were parking on a flat surface. She'd reminded Lil about her blind spot. And on the day of Travis's funeral, when they were riding in the hearse from the church to the graveyard, Tessa Lee pointed out that cars were pulling over.

"They're showing their respect," Lil had said. "That's what they're supposed to do."

But Tessa Lee knew better. "No," she said. "When a funeral procession goes by, you're supposed to proceed slowly along your route unless a police officer tells you to stop."

So Lil knew it had to be nerves that would make Tessa Lee stop at a green light and go when it turned red. There was no other explanation. Even a monkey could pass that part of the test.

"It don't make good sense," Rosie Jo said. "Running a red light!"

They were at bingo, with a room full of summer friends and some strangers who would only be around long enough to play one night, maybe two. On bingo nights, they arranged the tables in the recreation center in long lines, so folks could sit behind them in rows and have plenty of space for all their cards.

"She must've been scared to death," Rosie Jo added. "No other way to explain it."

"She was," Lil said. "Anxious as she could be. And she's

been moping around the house for days. I tried to get her to drive us here tonight, but she wouldn't do it."

"No offense," Rosie Jo said, "but I don't believe I could have rode with her, knowing that she run a red light with a policeman in the car."

"He was a big black man," Lil said. "That's probably what made her so anxious."

TESSA LEE had always been anxious. On the day they'd picked her up from the state park campground, she'd been chewing her hair. Over the next weeks, she nibbled it off on both sides. It was a nasty habit, and after the first weeks, Lil told her that if she didn't stop chewing it, she was going to cut it short as a boy's. Tessa Lee kept chewing, and Lil got out the scissors and went to work. But when Tessa Lee didn't have any hair left to chew, she started chewing her lip, making little bloody ulcers all over her mouth.

"B-14," the caller said from up on stage. "B-14."

Lil checked her cards—she was playing six, and that was as many as she could keep up with. Rosie Jo played ten, but she was more of a competitor, and Lil just did it for fun. She used to share her cards with Travis, who loved bingo as much as she did and sat right beside her. Tessa Lee was never much for bingo, but she helped the rec center girls give out the prizes.

The bingo machine blew out another ball. "N-60," the caller said. "N-60."

The year Tessa Lee came to live with Lil and Lewis, she went into third grade at Pine Road Elementary. That fall, the teacher invited them in for a conference. Tessa Lee was making bad grades. According to the teacher, the problem wasn't her brain; the problem was her concentration. She was smart enough, but her mind wandered. The teacher called her spacey.

"G-9," the caller announced, and before she could repeat it, somebody across the room hollered, "Bingo!"

It took Tessa Lee a year to get her grades up, but she'd been making good grades ever since. She cried when she made a B in algebra. She was still spacey about some things, but she overcame it with her grades. She was a smart girl who scored in the highest percentile on all the state tests.

Being spacey hadn't caused Tessa Lee to fail her driver's test, though. Lil was sure of that. It was that black policeman. He was the reason she couldn't concentrate. They shouldn't let black policemen give the test to white girls. They should have a white woman to give the test to white girls.

She didn't believe in burning crosses or any of that foolishness. She just thought people ought to stick with their own kind. Bluebirds don't share nests with cardinals. Black ants and red ants work and sleep in different hills. What could be clearer than that?

After Sheila ran off to be with that black boy, who was nothing but a farmhand and would never own an acre of his own property, Lil dropped into the darkest space of her life. She quit going to church. She quit working with Lewis. She kept making her toilet-paper dolls but didn't go to craft fairs to sell them. She just boxed them up and left them in the basement. The basement was her favorite room, all damp and dark. She spent months in a kind of solitude she hadn't known since. Even though Lewis was right there with her, she was still alone. She talked to him and fixed his supper, but she felt no more connected to him than to the steak and gravy she spooned onto his plate. She most certainly didn't tell him that Sheila had run off with a black boy, but Lewis was no fool. He must have noticed that Sheila and Lorenzo disappeared at the same time.

They never spoke about it.

One night many months after Sheila ran away, Lewis talked her into going out to supper. They went to a seafood place about forty miles south, a place not far from where Lil had grown up. They'd just finished their main course and were waiting for the dessert when a cousin she hadn't seen in years approached the table. He hugged Lil's neck and shook Lewis's hand, and they talked a long while before he told her that a whole bunch of her relatives spent Saturday nights at the Cock-a-doodle-doo, a bar not far from there.

Lil'd forgotten all about the Cock-a-doodle-doo. She'd gone once or twice before she married Lewis. It was a place where people played cards and pool, drank beer, and danced. Since Lewis was a churchgoer, she didn't frequent bars. She didn't even know the Cock-a-doodle-doo was still open.

The cousin invited Lil and Lewis to join him there, and Lewis agreed, maybe because it'd been so long since Lil had laughed, even longer since she'd danced. So she and Lewis followed her cousin to the Cock-a-doodle-doo, and they went inside and had a reunion. Lil had a beer, though Lewis stuck to sweet tea. Her cousins showed them pictures of their children and grandchildren. They recalled old times and joked about when Lil was known everywhere as the worm woman.

"You wouldn't believe how far she could stretch an old

worm," her cousin said to Lewis and slapped his knee. "She could pull 'em a foot without breaking 'em!"

"I believe it," Lewis said, and everybody laughed.

When they asked about Sheila, Lil told them she'd gone off to college in Florida. She didn't miss a beat, and though Lewis looked surprised, he didn't dispute it.

"College?" one of them said. "Well, my, my!"

She and Lewis were out on the dance floor when three black men came into the bar. The whole placed shushed, no sound at all except for Merle Haggard on the stereo and somebody hitting the cue ball hard, popping another ball into the pocket.

The Cock-a-doodle-doo catered to locals, white ones. Everybody knew that.

"They ought not be in here," Lil said. It made her seethe to see the black men go up to the bar and speak to the bartender like they had the right.

"Now, Lil," Lewis said. "It ain't none of your business."

"They got their own bars," Lil said. "No reason to come here." She had her eye on the biggest of the three. He was arrogant, she could tell. He probably went with white girls. Might be looking to pick one up.

"You oughta run 'em outta here, Lewis," she said into his collar.

Lewis didn't reply.

When the song changed to something more upbeat, Lewis took her hand and tried to lead her to the table, but one of her cousins cut in, and so Lil danced with him back out onto the floor.

"I wish somebody'd go knock their teeth out," Lil told her cousin.

He haw-hawed and said, "You always were feisty, Lil. You want me to go fight 'em?"

"Watch this," she said, and she danced over to the bar where the three men still waited to be served. She wiggled her hips like she hadn't done in years, held her arms up high over her head, and shimmied. Oh, she could still shimmy. She danced up close to the biggest one, who had noticed her by then and was smiling nervously.

Then Lil hauled off and slapped his face as hard as she could.

It rang through that room, that slap. It rang up her arm, prickly, cold fire.

"Excuse me, sir," Lil said. "Sometimes when I'm dancing, my arms just go all over the place," and she danced away, her cousins cheering all around.

"YOU GOT IT, Lil," Rosie Jo said, "Bingo, BINGO!" she shouted.

If Travis had been there, he'd have been jumping up and down in his seat. He wouldn't even care that she'd won kitchen goods instead of the free passes to the state zoo or the badminton set that had been given away earlier. Travis was excitable, nine years old but still apt to flap his hands about when he got happy, still a little boy, beautiful to look at with that black hair and those bright green eyes. He was a strong boy, not exactly fat, but sturdy. He was sweet and soft on the inside, though, and Lil missed him terribly, especially at bingo, where he should have been sitting beside her. And she missed Tessa Lee, off sulking in her room. She should've been there, too.

The darkest moments could come at the strangest times, even in the middle of bingo. She could be sitting in the rec center, with bright lights all around, and in her heart, she was back in the basement of that old farmhouse. If Lewis was there, he'd know what to do. He'd come down to her basement, take her hand, lead her back up the stairs.

"I can't stay," Lil whispered to Rosie Jo. "Can you get a ride?"

"Yeah," Rosie Jo said. "What's the matter?"

"First time I won since that boy died," she admitted.

"Oh, honey, you want me to come?"

"No," Lil said. "It's okay. But play my cards. They might be lucky."

Tessa Lee had cramps. She crouched on her bed in the position that supposedly helped with cramps—she'd read about it in a magazine—and tried to write a letter.

"Dear Amber," she wrote. "I wish summer was over and you were back home."

Too misty. She balled it up and flicked it toward the wastebasket. Writing that letter would make her all soggy, and she didn't have time for that.

"Hi, Amber. What's up?" she tried. "Have you met any cute guys over there in West Virginia? Don't you come back with a funny accent, now!"

She balled that one up, too, grimaced, adjusted her pad. She must have a clot that needed to drop. That was why it hurt so much.

"Hola, Amber," she wrote on the next sheet. "Que tal?"

That was better.

"I met some guys who were going to a wedding. They couldn't speak English, and all I could think of to say was 'Te gusta la sandia?' Can you believe that? I sounded so dumb, asking them if they liked watermelon. (Señora Ortega would laugh at me for sure!) But they didn't care. They said, 'Si, si!' and gave me a drink—maybe sangria. It was good.

"Granny's been real sad since Travis died. Me, too. He was a pain, but he was still Travis. The weird thing is that I forget sometimes. Yesterday I was sitting on the couch, and I thought I saw him over in the chair playing his Game Boy."

She balled up that sheet, too. There was no way she could write to Amber. What she felt was unspeakable, unwritable. Everything she felt was wrong.

She stood up and did some deep-knee bends, trying to get the blood out. The pain made a black edge around her vision, made it seem like everything was outlined or framed. Not a real thing. Just a picture of a thing.

"Dear Amber," she began again. "I didn't pass my driver's test. I think I was PMSing. Besides that, the policeman who gave it to me was really hot. He had these dimples like you wouldn't believe. He looked sort of like Rich Eberly, but with a broader chest. Real cute. Anyway, I almost passed, but I didn't. I think it'd be easier if the policemen were all fat and ugly. They say it takes most people two times, so I wasn't upset. But let me give you some advice: be sure to practice on your three-point turns. If you bump the curb, they'll fail you."

Tessa Lee stopped. Was that a lie? Not really. She knew it sounded like she bumped the curb, even though that wasn't what happened. But she didn't actually *say* that. And they *would* fail you if you bumped the curb. She'd just neglected to mention the red light.

So Tessa Lee went on: "I found out my mom's not in Massachusetts after all. She's on drugs."

She drew a little monster face after the word *drugs* because she'd ruined that letter, too. She couldn't send it. She twisted that page into a tight little log, then picked up all the other letters and tossed them into the wastebasket.

She didn't need Amber. Amber wasn't strong, and she was spoiled. She was a baby. She didn't even start her period until the end of eighth grade. Tessa Lee got hers in sixth.

On the day that Amber started her period, Tessa Lee went over to her house, and Amber was in her room, playing a game on her computer. There were towels all over the floor. Tessa Lee didn't know why they were there at first, until Amber picked one up, reached between her legs, and wiped the thin swipe of blood.

"I can't stand it!" she said. "It's gross."

"Don't you have a pad or something?" Tessa Lee'd asked her.

"Yeah," she said, and she pulled back her panties to show a panty liner, vaguely stained.

"That won't last long enough," Tessa Lee said. "You need a real pad, a bigger one."

"I can't stand those," Amber said. "Feels like I've got a boat between my legs."

Tessa Lee should have known then that Amber was a

baby. If she couldn't handle her own period, how could she handle the rest of life?

Amber's mom had come into the room later that night and collected all the towels. They were only slightly bloody, but Amber would use them each just once. Every time she felt the blood, she wiped it away.

If Tessa Lee'd wiped menstrual blood on her granny's clean towels on purpose—well, she didn't even know what would have happened.

She didn't need Amber. She didn't need anybody.

She took the firefly cloak out of her pillowcase, put it on, and spun around and around and around until she was dizzy. She let the blood run down her leg and dabbed it up with the cloak.

The antivirals should have taken ten days, but Sheila finished hers in eight. Most of those days she slept, and in her sleep, she'd think someone had shot an arrow in her back, below her shoulder blade, where the shingles wrapped to the middle. She dreamed she had an arrow there, and no one would pull it out.

Or she dreamed of being underwater, the mermaid swimming on the ocean floor, until the shadow of a pirate ship crossed above her, darkened her sea. The spear pierced her from behind, and when she turned around to see, there was Reggie in his eye patch, grinning gloriously.

He stabbed her through the gills. He left her panting, left her gulping and desperate.

The shelter director took her to the doctor in her second week, when her drugs had run out but her rash was still prominent. The doctor said it was normal for her to be so tired. The shingles were running their course; the blisters were scabbing. It'd take a month to six weeks for her to heal up completely.

They looked like scales on her body, like she was turning into a fish.

"Try not to scratch," the doctor said.

When she was a little girl, she'd gone fishing with Lil and Lewis lots of times. Whatever they caught, she was responsible for scaling. She took a big spoon and scraped against the scales, flecking them everywhere, all over her hands, all over the table, in her hair. She wished she had a big cold spoon to scrape the shingles off her side, to scrape them from beneath her breast. If the handle of the spoon was long enough, she might be able to fleck them from her back.

But then she wouldn't be waterproof.

The doctor ran blood tests and gave her some ointment for the itching and told her to rest.

So she ate a little and slept a lot, sometimes waking when the baby in the next room cried.

Sheila'd been in a shelter before, with Tessa Lee, before Travis was born. She'd spent eleven weeks there—and then a year in a halfway house when Tessa Lee was little, after they'd left the road, when she was cleaned up and working toward her cosmetology license.

Before the shelter, she traveled with a carnival every season until Tessa Lee was three, dancing in a girl show. Then one night she went back to the motel where they were staying, and her friend who'd been babysitting, a dancer too pregnant to be onstage, had overdosed. She was already dead, blood and foam trickling from her mouth and nose, and six little children, newborn to four, crawling all over her, crying in the corners.

Sheila knew she had to go then, get out of that place, get Tessa Lee away from that life.

SHE'D STARTED working in the girl show right after she left Lorenzo, because one day when they were still together, he'd taken her to ride the Ferris wheel and she'd met a man at the carnival.

Lorenzo had gone to get corn dogs. He stood in line a long time, and while he was away, the barker approached her. Sheila'd seen him before, with a couple of girls all dressed up in shimmery costumes, sequins and veils and high heels.

"You need a job?" he asked. "I got a job for you. Can you dance?"

Sheila told him she already had a job. Maybe he knew she was lying.

"You making good money?" he asked. "'Cause I can earn you a hundred a night. Minimum. You'll be making two hundred in no time."

"I don't think so," Sheila said. She looked to the concession stand where Lorenzo was paying.

"Some girls make fifty grand a year," he told her, lifting one eyebrow for emphasis. "Pure profit. All expenses paid.

You think about it," he said. "Come back tomorrow. No later. We leave the day after."

That night it rained, a blowing rain. Sheila was sleeping next to Lorenzo on his sister's porch when the wind blew the storm right onto them. It was like trying to sleep in the shower. Lorenzo kept on snoring, oblivious to it all.

Sheila knew if she stayed there, she'd spend the next night on a piece of foam just beginning to mildew.

On top of that, his sister had picked out a different girl for Lorenzo, a black girl with a pretty broad face, a gap between her teeth. She was sleeping in the guest room, just waiting for Lorenzo to come to his senses. His sister'd be happy if the rain washed Sheila off that porch.

She pictured herself in shimmery costumes and feather boas. She pictured herself in Vegas. She'd never been.

Lorenzo kept saying they'd get a place, but he didn't have any money. What he had, he spent on carnivals and record albums and football games. Sheila didn't want to be like her own momma, who depended on her daddy for everything, even grocery money. She wanted to make a salary of her own. Maybe she'd become a nurse.

If she could make fifty thousand in one year, she could go to college. That'd pay for college. Two years of dancing, and she could show up on her momma's porch one day with a degree in hand. Then her momma'd be sorry.

So the next day, Sheila asked Lorenzo's sister for a ride back to the fairgrounds one town over.

The sister looked her up and down, considering. "I'll take you if you promise not to never show your face here again," she said.

. . .

THE SHOW MOVED from town to town—not big towns or state capitals—little places where the police could be bribed with special shows, where girls could strip down to nothing and they could all make more money.

Sheila saw the country, one run-down town after the next, dancing outside a paper mill where the stink made everybody queasy. Dancing in the parking lot of an abandoned Kmart, outside a Feed and Grain, on fairgrounds, in county airports. They moved from place to place, following the weather, a week here, a week there.

Only men were allowed inside the tent to see the shows. Sometimes the same ones came back night after night. Sheila was loaded most of the time. At first it took a lot of wine for her to go out there and dance. Then being drunk was just a habit. She could drink it by the jugs. She could drink it until she threw up behind the tires of the trailer that formed their stage, and then she could go right back on and dance some more.

When she started, she said she wouldn't stick it in their faces. Other dancers could do that, go push it to the edges, let men too drunk to stand up straight nudge it, eat it. Sheila never meant to do that. Those first weeks, she teased, backing away from all the mouths.

At first, it seemed like the room was full of mouths—open, wet, ringed with hair, or baby-faced bare, surrounded by acne, or old wrinkled mouths pulled asshole tight. Mouths with chewing tobacco oozing out the edges, with cigarettes loose in the corners, mouths smacking gum.

At first, it seemed like the room was full of tongues, thick, flicking at her, circling, beckoning, lolling around.

Then she stopped looking at the mouths and just danced. And what was the difference anyway between a tongue on her thigh and a tongue between her legs? Those couple of inches meant a lot more money. The longer she could stand it, the more she could make.

It was hard at first, but the wine dulled her, and after a while, nothing mattered but the cash. They could ram their tongues wherever they wanted, as long as they paid hard cash to do it.

The first year she kept imagining she might go home one day, back to her momma and daddy. She might finish school. But what would they think, when they found out where she'd been? Her daddy was a deacon in the church. Her momma directed Vacation Bible School.

SHE GOT PREGNANT with Tessa Lee on the road. Second season. She was turning tricks by then.

She'd never thought she'd turn a trick, and the first time it was just as a favor, to help out a friend. It didn't seem real that first time. But after she'd done it, it seemed crazy to pass up good opportunities when they came. She only did it sometimes, never with weirdos, never with anybody who just assumed she'd say yes.

Every few weeks she might turn a trick for a hundred and fifty, two hundred, plus dinner. She wasn't a whore. She was a dancer, a stripper, and only temporarily. She was saving up to get her own place.

None of the tricks got her pregnant, either. She was

careful. She knew whose baby it was. She had a boyfriend, but he was married. His wife and little boys stayed home when the carnival went on the road.

When Sheila was pregnant, they fought because he wouldn't leave his wife and be with her. He'd disappear for days at a time, go home to Marsha even though she was frigid.

"I won't never divorce her. Never!" he said. "So shut up about it. She's the mother of my children."

And Sheila just stood there, hands on her belly, accusing him with her stare.

"I never lied to you," he said. "I told you all along what was what."

But Sheila'd hoped that things might change, that he might change his mind.

She'd have kicked him out of her bed, except it was really *his* bed, since he owned the show. He paid for all the motel rooms, so he could sleep wherever he pleased. And anyway, she didn't want to kick him out because he made her laugh and brought her ice cream and took her to watch the sunrise over the ocean on the day she turned twenty. He understood that who she was onstage wasn't who she *was*. A thousand men could lick her and prod her, but that didn't count. What counted was after the show.

When she was pregnant, he made sure they kept Sheila on. Sometimes she worked concession, serving up chili in cold states and Icees in warm ones. Sometimes she stayed back at the motel and watched the other dancers' children. In one town, she even parked cars. Two weeks after she gave birth to Tessa Lee, she was back onstage dancing. It didn't matter that her stomach was still squishy and loose. What mattered was how she moved, so she moved.

The blood would have mattered, but she used a sponge to keep it inside her while she danced.

She didn't do any drugs at all once she found out she was pregnant. Other girls could take their chances, but she didn't want any waterheads or freaks.

She drank a lot, but no drugs. The night she went back onstage, she was so sad and depressed that she shot up. After that, she didn't feel it. For two or three days after, she didn't even remember she'd had a baby.

There was something appealing about that kind of oblivion. A single dose and you could forget your past, forget the whole world. No pain at all. No itching. A single dose and the arrow in her back would become wings. Fuck mermaids. Fuck fish. She was growing wings right out her back. She could fly beyond and beyond.

Friday nights were movie nights at the recreation center. They showed three movies each night, a rated G at 5:00, a PG at 7:00, and an R at 10:00.

Before Travis died, they always went to the Gs. Tessa Lee and Amber could stay for the PGs, but Travis had to go home when the kid flick ended. Since Travis died she hadn't been to the movies at all, and now suddenly her granny was giving her permission to stay for the R.

"You need to spend some time with your friends," her granny said. "People your own age."

"I don't have any friends," Tessa Lee replied.

"Sure you do," her granny said. "What about that little Beverly girl?"

"I don't wanna go to the movies," Tessa Lee told her.

But she could see that her granny was worried, and she didn't want to upset her any worse. She'd already upset her enough. And maybe her granny was tired of her. Maybe she needed some space.

All that afternoon, her granny kept checking her watch to make sure Tessa Lee didn't miss the show.

"I'm not leaving 'til 7:00. I'm not going to the G," she explained.

"Why not?" her granny asked.

"I don't wanna sit through three movies in a row!"

So Tessa Lee had supper, then changed and left on foot. She didn't even know what movies were playing.

But she bought her ticket and went inside and talked with some kids she knew from school. They were polite to her, let her into their circles. Leo was there, and he said, "Hey, look who's here!" and he invited her to sit with him and his friends, but Tessa Lee could tell that they didn't know what to say.

She was like a stranger. She had a reputation now, since Travis had died, and since she'd run away from home. The other kids whispered when they didn't think she was looking.

When the lights went out and the movie started, it just got worse. Tessa Lee couldn't concentrate. The sounds were too loud, the faces on the screen too big. There were too many smells that didn't go together. Leo was wearing aftershave and it clashed with the butter from his popcorn. The room was too hot. The chairs were too close together, and she was touching legs with Leo on one side and a girl named Katie on the other. She tried to watch the movie, but in a while she got up, like she was going to the bathroom, and she left.

She couldn't go home yet, though. Her granny was playing cards with Rosie Jo at their house, and she didn't want them to know she was too jittery to sit through the movie. She'd look totally pathetic if she went home too soon. So she walked around a long time, up and down the streets, until she came to a yard where a trailer had burned down the winter before. Everything had burned away except for the foundation, and even after Hully's crews had cleaned up the debris, there were cinder blocks left behind, the underpinning outlining what had once been there.

Tessa Lee went over to the burned-out site and walked along the blocks, like she was on a tightrope. Tall weeds had grown up inside, green where everything used to be black. A cloud passed over the moon and gave it a beard, and Tessa Lee watched the beard blow away as she walked around the perimeter of what had once been somebody's home. She was circling the edges of another family's tragedy.

She hadn't known the people who'd lived there, but just the Halloween before, Travis had gone trick-or-treating at that trailer. Tessa Lee and Amber were with him. They were too old to ask for candy, but they still dressed up. Tessa Lee had trimmed out her witch's hat with a thin green boa, and she'd trimmed the neck and cuffs of her dress in the same way. Amber was a vampire, and Amber's cousins, who went to school with Travis, were both Ninja warriors. Then there was another boy dressed as the grim reaper.

But Travis was dressed like a dog. He had a furry hood with floppy ears their granny had made for him, and a brown fur suit to match. Tessa Lee'd tried to talk him into being a superhero, at least, or maybe a werewolf. A wolf was kind of like a dog.

But Travis wanted to be a circus dog. He didn't even seem to mind when the other children made fun of his costume.

Travis loved Halloween and ran ahead of all the others toward the porch lights. Tessa Lee and Amber could hardly keep up. The other boys would be demonstrating their Ninja kicks to the adults with the candy, or pretending to cut off their own heads with swords while Travis raced to the next door.

The burned-out trailer wasn't burned out then. It was all decorated with jack-o'-lanterns and spiderwebs, and Travis ran up to the front deck before any of the rest of them.

He must have thought the masked man sitting on the deck was a decoration, because when the man reached out to hand him candy, Travis jumped back and screamed, high-pitched, and ran backward to Tessa Lee and grabbed onto her with both arms. He cried like a baby. He cried hard and loud, not like a nine-year-old, and the other kids laughed just as hard as he sobbed.

He didn't want to go up to the deck again after that, even after the man took off his mask so Travis could see that he was just a regular guy, probably somebody's granddad.

"Get up there," Tessa Lee said to him, and she shoved him. "God, you're pathetic," she said to the floppy-eared dog.

The craft fair along the boardwalk was the biggest show of summer. Lil set the alarm for early so she'd have plenty of time to get there and arrange her wares before the crowds picked up.

She packed her hand-painted napkin holders—two boxes of those, because they were bulky. One box of the cross-stitched matchbox covers for fireplace matches, the long ones. Those were all Christmas-themed and a little bit iffy for early August. She packed two boxes of her wooden geese with clothespins for beaks. Those held mail and were popular everywhere she went. She lugged the boxes to the van, pushed them back as far as her arms would reach.

"You want these?" Tessa Lee called from the shed, and when Lil leaned out of the van, she could see Tessa Lee coming her way with a box of toilet-paper dolls.

"Well, good morning," Lil said. "I didn't mean to wake you."

Tessa Lee was already dressed. "You didn't. I set my alarm," she said. "Do you want these or not?"

Lil hadn't intended to market the toilet-paper dolls at this particular show, but since Tessa Lee had pulled them out, she said "Why not?" and loaded them into the van, the dolls and also a few toilet-paper animals.

Lil picked out fifteen of her best seashell wreaths and finished up with three sets of placemats woven from the cattail grasses. She'd see how they sold. She'd never tried those before.

The craft fair along the boardwalk was almost an hour's

drive to the north. There were hundreds of vendors and concession stands and musicians. Lil looked forward to it every year. This year she was looking forward to it less. Travis had loved the craft fairs. He was such a little talker, telling patrons about each item, taking their money. In her lifetime, Lil hadn't known very many people who stammered, and the ones she knew were ashamed of it and kept quiet for the most part. But Travis was a stuttering little motormouth, and while children his own age made terrible fun of him, adults were mesmerized. Seemed like they just loved to hear him talk.

Travis had been her right-hand man, running to get her a soda when it got too hot, making friends with the vendors at nearby booths. That was just good business. If he'd lived long enough, he'd have made a good businessman. Either that or an auctioneer.

Tessa Lee hadn't even gone to the boardwalk show for the past couple of years. The night before when Lil'd asked her about it, she'd said she'd rather stay home and read. Being a teenager had taken all the craftiness right out of Tessa Lee. As far as Lil could tell, she didn't do much of anything anymore except take Excedrin and brood.

But here she was.

"I thought you wanted to stay home," Lil said.

"Changed my mind," Tessa Lee replied. "Can I drive?"

Lil's heart did a flip-flop, then straightened itself out as she tossed Tessa Lee the keys.

Sheila was tempted, she had to admit. When the shelter director first put up the sign-up sheet for the boardwalk art show, she figured that her momma would be there. She'd done crafts as long as Sheila could remember. The tackiest shit in the world.

The sign-up sheet was on the bulletin board, next to the schedule for Bible study and AA and NA meetings. There were only seven spaces available, because that's how many could comfortably fit in the van. It was a first-come-first-serve sign-up, open to anybody who wanted to ride, tenant or worker.

But the craft show was north, midway between where she was and where she'd come from. She could just see herself bumping into one of the jewelry workers on the boardwalk. She didn't remember Reggie ever taking the spools of jewelry to art-walks, but you never knew.

Besides that, if her momma was at the craft fair, then it was a perfect time for Sheila to scope out Hully Sanders's Mobile City.

The only problem was her clothes.

When the shingles were at their worst, Sheila didn't even notice what she was wearing. But the better she felt, the worse those hand-me-downs looked. One of the blouses she'd been given was okay, but the skirt made her look Amish. She couldn't go out in public wearing those shorts, either. They were fine for sitting on the porch, even going to the doctor. But there was no way she could wear them out.

The sheets on her bed were more stylish than her clothes,

light blue with deeper blue flowers, kind of vintage-looking. People spent a lot of money for those old-fashioned patterns. She pulled the pillow out of the case, measured it against her hips.

When she went downstairs to ask for a needle and thread, the woman on duty tried to talk her into joining them at the craft fair. "We're leaving in about an hour," she said, "And there's still one seat open."

Sheila shook her head and fished through the sewing box looking for blue.

"It's so much fun," the woman told her. "If you want, you can just sit on the beach all afternoon. That's what I'm gonna do, get some vitamin D."

"It's too far," Sheila said. "The seat belt rubs against my shingles." It was true that the seat belt hurt, but she was getting better by then. She could have tolerated it if she'd wanted to.

She asked the woman if there was a park in walking distance, and the woman tried to discourage her, tried to act like the backyard was a tropical paradise. But Sheila persisted and the woman gave her directions. "I'm not sure it's safe after dark," the woman said, and Sheila assured her she'd be back long before the sun went down.

It only took ten minutes to make a pillowcase skirt. She used her shoelaces as a drawstring because she planned to wear her flip-flops anyway. Naturally, as Lil's daughter, she was handy with a needle and thread.

There was no parking allowed along the boardwalk, even for the vendors, so once they'd unloaded their boxes, Lil left Tessa Lee behind to arrange things while she moved the van to a city garage a block and a half away.

When she got back, her booth looked like a hippie hideout. Tessa Lee had draped colorful, fringed sarongs across the table. She even had a spray bottle to spritz the wrinkles out of the fabric.

Lil borrowed the bottle and spritzed her face, then dabbed it off with her shirttail. "Looks nice," she said.

She hoped Tessa Lee's display wouldn't keep Christians away. It looked like the kind of table where you'd buy mushroom candles and incense. Maybe big golden hoop earrings. If Sheila'd done the same thing years before, Lil would've flat refused. She'd have insisted on her off-white tablecloth, just like always. But she'd learned the hard way.

All she'd ever wanted was to give Sheila the life she hadn't had herself. Mostly she'd wanted to keep her safe, pass along strong values, not let her be mistreated or experience adult things too soon. So she'd put her foot down when Sheila brought home the permission slip for the overnight school field trip with the biology club. She didn't know the chaperones and couldn't take that chance. Sheila joined the swim team once, and Lil was fine with all the home meets. She hollered and clapped as loud as anybody. But she hadn't let her compete when the team went away. The coach was a muscular horsey-faced gal, and Lil was scared she might like women instead of men.

She hadn't allowed Sheila to attend the prom when she was invited by an older boy.

Year after year, she'd taken Sheila to a nice dress shop on her birthday, and she'd bought her pretty dresses for church and special occasions. But they weren't the kinds of clothes Sheila wanted to wear. One morning she even caught her changing clothes in the barn, whoring up between the time she walked out the door for school and the time the bus came to get her.

Lil just wanted to protect and guide her, and look what happened. It couldn't have backfired any worse.

While Lil recounted the change in her cash box and waited for customers, Tessa Lee hung the sun tarp over their heads. Then she sat down on one of the stools and read a paperback from her summer reading list. She wasn't as much of a salesperson as Travis had been, but she stayed close by, like when she was a little girl and wouldn't let Lil out of her sight.

It'd been such an adjustment back then, to go from having nobody but Lewis to having two little ones trailing her every step. Lil'd go to the kitchen to fix a glass of tea, and there they'd be, just looking at her. She'd go out to the backyard to water her flowers, and one of them would turn on the hose while the other shook out the kinks. She got used to their shadowing pretty quickly, stopped letting the door slam in their little faces.

Sheila had never been so clingy, or if she was, Lil didn't recall it.

She'd run herself a tub of water, peel off her clothes, and settle in the tub, only to open her eyes and find Travis driving his racecar around the rim of the toilet while Tessa

Lee sat on the counter next to the sink and counted her eyelashes.

Now she just had Tessa Lee, sitting to the side, acting aloof, but paying attention nonetheless. Whenever somebody would buy something, Tessa Lee would jump right up and rearrange the items on the table, making everything neat and orderly, putting everything in its place.

There were vendors on either side of the street, for blocks in either direction. Their booth was wedged between a portrait artist and a welder who made yard ornaments out of discarded springs and shovel heads. Across the way, there were people selling sachets that smelled like cedar and lavender, and a jeweler who worked with glass.

And way on down the block, almost at the end, there was Rash, the sandspur boy, selling hemp bracelets and handmade hats and dried arrangements of sandspurs in glass bottles.

"Hey, Firefly!" he said. "How you doing?"

"Good," Tessa Lee replied. "I didn't recognize you at first."

"It's the hair," he said. "I needed a change."

His hair was hot pink. It stood straight up and made him look like a rooster. "How'd you get it to do that?" she asked.

"You mean stand up?" he said. "Gelatin."

"Must be cherry-flavored," she joked. She fingered his sandspur arrangements, spacing them even. "You got your own booth?" She didn't know that teenagers were allowed to rent spaces and wondered if he'd needed an ID.

"Sharing one," he said. "My friend Tabitha makes the bracelets, and her girlfriend Frieda does the hats. They're off getting their belly buttons pierced. You wanna sit?" He offered her a chair behind his station.

While he was talking to a customer and folding a hat and putting it into a bag, she pretended she was there with him, not with her granny at all. If something happened to her granny, she might be okay. She might be able to support herself making hats and bracelets. Once she got her driver's license, she could take herself to craft shows, maybe share a booth with Rash. She could drive herself to school and to the dentist when it came time for her cleaning.

She wondered what she'd look like with pink hair. Or with short hair, spiked up on purpose.

When he was done with his customer, Tessa Lee said, "I can only stay a minute. I'm helping my granny."

"Your granny!" he said. "I remember."

"She makes these totally dopey crafts," Tessa Lee said. She felt bad for talking about her granny's crafts that way.

"Like what?" Rash asked. "Does she paint on saw blades? I love those painted saw blades."

"Toilet-paper dolls," she said.

"Even better!" Rash replied, and he promised to come see them when Tabitha and Frieda returned from the Body-Art Saloon across the street.

All the way back to the craft stand, Tessa Lee fantasized about what she'd do if something happened to her granny. Maybe Hully'd give her a job in the office, let her answer the phones or something. Maybe she'd teach her granny's craft classes. She knew how to make a seashell wreath. She'd had plenty of practice with glue guns.

Her granny's birthday was coming up, and she'd brought along her money, in case she found the right gift. There was no need to hang onto all the money she'd saved—now that she knew her momma wasn't in Massachusetts, anyway.

She stopped by a stand where there were pictures of lighthouses and seascapes. Maybe she'd become a painter. How hard could it be to paint a lighthouse?

A few summers back, there'd been a man who'd come to the recreation center twice a week to teach oil-painting classes. At the time, Tessa Lee was in one of her Massachusetts phases, doing odd jobs for money. She'd just washed and waxed Hully Sanders's red truck, and as he was paying her, the oil painter drove up in his dented old Buick and tripped on the sidewalk and spilled all his brushes. So Hully offered her ten dollars a class to be the oil painter's assistant. It was a lot of money to pay somebody too young to even get a work permit, but Hully felt bad for them, because Pop-Pop had just died, and he wanted to put some joy into Tessa Lee's life. She could tell. She could see right through him.

From then on, she rode her bike to the rec center every Tuesday and Thursday morning and put butcher paper on the tables and passed out paper plates. On each plate, she dabbed out squirts of blue and green and white and black. She passed out canvases and brushes and paper towels and watched the oil painter work.

He taught just two pictures—one of a sunny day out on the beach and one of a sunset over the water. He wasn't that great a painter, and nobody ever came back more than twice. But he was a pro at those two seascapes, and week after week, Tessa Lee listened to his instructions. She was surprised to learn that you should never put the horizon at the center of the canvas. If the oil painter hadn't taught her differently, that would have been her first instinct, to center it. Up until then, it had always seemed like if there was a dune on the left, there ought to be a dune on the right, to balance it out. But according to the oil painter, balance wasn't realistic. It was a construct of the human mind, an attempt to control things, he said.

Tessa Lee listened and took it all in. That was the summer after Pop-Pop's heart blew out, and she was still so sad and missed him so much, missed standing in church beside him and sharing his hymnbook and singing along with his deep voice that could do the low part when they sang, "Now Let Us Have a Little Talk with Jesus." She missed him like crazy, and she wanted her life to be balanced again. She wanted a Granny and a Pop-Pop both.

But in real life, you didn't get equal shares of water and sky. Maybe you got a whole lot of sky and just a little bit of water. Then you had to learn to love the clouds more and forget about splashing around.

If you ran out of blue paint, you had to use more white, make a grayer sky, a grayer sea.

Before, she'd always thought that people had heart attacks in times of stress, or when they were shoveling snow, or straining too hard on the toilet like Elvis. But nothing was predictable, and Pop-Pop's heart exploded while he was sleeping, in his own bed.

And then everything was off-balance and nothing made sense. Granny spent all her days cross-stitching, making tiny little Xs spell out "Noel" and "Joy to the World." Even when they went to the pool, Granny sat beneath the sun umbrella and cross-stitched "Merry Christmas." All her holiday matchbox covers smelled like Coppertone.

When Pop-Pop was gone, Travis quit talking for a while. He just nodded and motioned for things. He was only in second grade at the time, so it didn't matter much that he made U's on his report card, for "Unsatisfactory," because he wouldn't read out loud or recite anything. Granny just kept on cross-stitching, and then it was summer.

Tessa Lee lived for Tuesdays and Thursdays. She could make cleaning the brushes take two hours. While she helped the oil painter, Travis stayed home with Granny and sat on the floor and made potholders, or read from his storybook, or drew pictures of boats. Then when he started second grade for the second time, when he took up language again, he'd picked up that stutter. His mouth kept repeating sounds, like popcorn in the microwave.

Tessa Lee tried to undo her ideas of symmetry, because in her heart, she knew that speaking clearly didn't get you what you wanted any faster than spitting it out in a thousand pieces.

SHE STOPPED at a craft stand where a woman made ornaments out of broken glass and tiny mirrors. They were all sizes and hanging up from fishing lines stretched between several poles. Tessa Lee walked beneath them and admired what they did to the light, and she decided to buy her granny a birthday present from Travis, who knew how a thousand pieces could come together and shine. She picked out an ornament the size of an orange, with blue and silver mirrors all over it, shiny as mylar. She bought it with Travis's money and had the woman pack it in bubble wrap before she paid her.

She felt bad for her granny, who might not have but one more birthday. It made her sad that her granny would die, but she cheered up some at the next craft stand where a man sold light-switch covers, painted with swirls and splatters in every imaginable color. Tessa Lee flipped through purples and reds, through golds and oranges. She couldn't remember if her granny's bedroom had a double plate or a single, so she bought one of each, in aqua and pink and white, and the man at that stand wrapped the plates in blue tissue and taped them up to protect them.

Tessa Lee walked along with her packages for a while and tried to look like a normal girl. She wondered if she looked normal, like a regular teenager just shopping for presents.

She wasn't sure if she wanted to blend in or not. She wanted to be *able* to blend in, but then she still wanted the option of standing out. Sometimes she wanted to do both things at once. It made her crazy, how her own desires fought against each other.

One day after the oil painter's class, she'd gone home and taken down the posters on her bedroom wall. Pop-Pop had helped her hang them the first time. They'd used his level and also his stud finder, and so her posters were all even and symmetrical before she took them down. When she put them up again, she didn't bother with tools. She hung some high and some low.

But they looked ridiculous that way. Even when she was trying to do something else, like talk on the phone to Amber, she kept arranging those posters in her mind, putting them back where they belonged.

Everything looked ridiculous then, even the oil painter, with his streaked up apron and his knobby fingers and his gray hair that sprouted out like moss. What did he know? And everything *sounded* ridiculous—words didn't mean what they said, and silence didn't mean what it said, either.

The oil painter taught her that when you make a mistake, you have to turn it into something deliberate. "You can't just wipe a blob of paint away without leaving a streak," he said. "If you try to wipe it off, you break the integrity of the brush-stroke."

But Tessa Lee learned that a blob of paint could be thinned out, spread wide, incorporated into something else.

One Thursday the oil painter didn't show up for his class. There were five women and a teenage boy seated at the table, ready to do their seascapes. Tessa Lee had already put the paper down, the canvases and brushes. She'd already set up the artist's easel, squirted out the paint. She'd taken their money and told them which painting they were doing. She had the model up on the wall so they could see it.

Finally, when it was clear that the painter wasn't coming, when the vacationing would-be artists started squirming and asking questions, Tessa Lee began the class without him.

"Start with the horizon," she said. She picked up her brush and dipped it in the paint and spread it across her canvas like she knew what she was doing. "You never, ever center it. You want your eye to be drawn away from the center because that creates dimension."

And they believed her. They did what she said.

She blended colors, added white to make the caps on the waves. She made a dune with sea grasses. She even added a seagull, just one, just a thin black M in the sky. The oil painter had never included seagulls before.

Tessa Lee could support herself if she had to, if her granny got cancer and couldn't work. She could teach oil painting. She could get her driver's license and drive her granny to chemotherapy. She was old enough to stay with her in the hospital. And if she died, well, Tessa Lee would handle it.

Maybe her granny would like a handmade tile for her birthday, something pretty to set her coffee cup down on so it wouldn't leave a ring on the table. She inspected the painted tiles, bright with their sunshines and flowers and Celtic designs. There was a tile with a dog in a sailboat—two of Travis's favorite things—and so she bought that, too, to give to her granny from Travis, and then all of Travis's money was gone.

When Travis's money was gone, he seemed deader than before, and Tessa Lee was lonely. She knew she needed to get back to her granny, but she was too lonely to see her granny just then.

So she stopped at a booth where a woman sold stepping-stones with words etched inside. Some said "Welcome." Some said, "You are here."

In her mind, she went to the graveyard where Pop-Pop waited for Granny, her name already there with his, on the other side of the huge praying hands. And next to Granny, there was Travis's place. He didn't have a stone yet, just a little temporary marker holding his place and a plant in an urn. They'd ordered a stone for him, a little fat one, shaped just like him, with his fourth-grade picture next to his name, but it took a while to get it custom-made and it wouldn't be delivered until September.

When she died, who would order a stone for her? Not her momma. Her momma wouldn't even know that she was dead.

When Travis died, they picked out his favorite clothes for him to be buried in. The coffin was closed anyway, so nobody knew he wasn't wearing a suit and tie. They picked out his favorite shirt—a button-up blue shirt with little sailboats all over it—and jeans and his new high-tops that Granny had just bought him because he was supposed to go to basketball camp in a couple of weeks.

If her granny died, she'd know what clothes to bury her in. Granny'd want to wear a dress, because Pop-Pop had been buried in a suit, and she wouldn't want to be underdressed lying next to him like that. She'd want to have on either the blue dress she wore to the Easter Cantata or the burgundy velvet skirt with matching jacket that she wore when Tessa Lee got inducted into the Spanish Honor Society. It depended on the season.

Nobody'd know what to bury her in, though. She'd have to leave a note for Amber, tell her where to find the firefly cloak. Or else she could just die in it, and maybe when they found her, they'd let her wear it to her grave, since nobody'd know what else to dress her in.

She wandered along, dreamy and slow. She watched the glassblower spin glass through his blue flame. She liked that blue flame, the way it flickered and surged, and she figured she could learn how to do that, bend glass, if she had to.

It reassured her to see the glass softening. If glass bends, anything can.

In a way, it'd be better if she died before her granny because she didn't want to go through all that again. Picking out clothes for the burial, picking out caskets and hymns. Dying was a lot less work than being left behind.

At her Pop-Pop's funeral, people lined up to walk by his casket and say good-bye. For some reason, Tessa Lee had a puzzle in her hand. It was a hard plastic square broken into littler squares, and you could twist and turn in every direction to try to make each side a solid color. She wasn't even sure where the puzzle had come from, but she'd been twisting it for two or three days, trying to separate the reds from the blues. When she got up to Pop-Pop's casket at the front of the church, for some reason she threw the puzzle. She threw it a long way—she didn't even know she could throw that far—and it broke a big glass window off the side of the sanctuary. She didn't remember doing it. Even though she saw the window break and heard the glass tinkling, it didn't seem like she had any connection to that noise and mess.

Later, it didn't even seem real. She'd thought the windows in churches were stronger than that.

It didn't seem real that Travis was dead, either. Nobody gave her a puzzle to play with when Travis died, and maybe it was a good thing.

If her granny died, then she'd have to ask Rosie Jo to take her to the highway department for her driver's test. She'd have to be sure to pass, though. It'd be too much to ask a neighbor to take her there twice.

It wasn't Lil's birthday. Her birthday wasn't until the end of September. So she didn't know what to make of Tessa Lee's strange grin and the bags she dumped in her lap.

"Go ahead. Open them," Tessa Lee said. She smiled like she was apologizing for something.

"What's all this?" Lil asked.

"Birthday presents," Tessa Lee said.

"For me?"

Tessa Lee nodded.

Lil put the bags aside. "Well, that's sweet of you," she said, "but it's not my birthday."

"I know when your birthday is," Tessa Lee sassed. There was something funny about her voice, something shaky underneath it. "But you might as well open them now, since they're here—and *you* are!"

Tessa Lee could be so odd. "I don't *want* to open them today," Lil told her.

Tessa Lee collapsed onto her stool and picked up her book and started reading. Lil couldn't tell whether or not she was crying. Having a teenager was exhausting. It was impossible to keep up with all the moods.

"I'd rather look forward to them," Lil explained. "If I open them now, I won't have anything for my birthday."

But Tessa Lee didn't reply.

Lil debated opening the presents but decided against it. She had to stay the course. "Maybe you could wrap 'em for me," she suggested. It seemed like a reasonable request, a little wrapping paper, a bow or two.

"They're sort of wrapped already," Tessa Lee whispered from behind her book.

Lil kissed her head and said, "Thank you, honey. I really do appreciate it. But I'm gonna wait to open them."

"Whatever," Tessa Lee said.

Tessa Lee was fingering the skirt of a toilet-paper doll, trying to make all the flounces sit even on the table, and feeling a little homesick even though her granny was right there when she saw Rash shuffling down the sidewalk.

"There he comes," she told her granny. "Don't say anything stupid."

"Well, I beg your pardon!" her granny replied.

She knew her granny wouldn't like it that he was smoking. She wished she'd thought to tell him.

"You don't smoke, do you?" her granny asked as Rash spotted them and waved.

"Me?" Tessa Lee asked. "No. Gross."

Rash put out his cigarette in the grass, toeing it hard. Then he picked up the butt and threw it in the trashcan. At least he didn't litter in public.

When she introduced him, her granny smiled too big,

for too long. "Your name is Radish?" she asked. "Radish?" and Tessa Lee wasn't sure at first if she was making fun.

"You can just call me Phillip," Rash said.

"That's better," her granny replied. "Do you have a last name?"

He told her it was Caldwell, but no, he wasn't related to the Caldwells who had the personal injury law firm.

Her granny thanked him for watching out for Tessa Lee when she took her "private vacation." She winked when she said that, and Tessa Lee finally exhaled.

"You're welcome," Rash said and laughed. "You didn't tell me your granny was cool."

And before Tessa Lee could get the two concepts together in her mind—her granny and being cool—Rash was back behind the craft stand, seated on a stool, while her granny examined his ears. Tessa Lee winced and hid her face as her granny studied the safety pins he'd stuck from top to bottom.

If she married Rash, her initials would be TLC. She didn't want to get married, but if something happened to her granny she couldn't pay all those bills by herself—the light bill and the cable and everything else. She knew she'd probably never marry Rash. She'd pick a boy with regular hair, just brown hair, like the violin player's.

Rash had twenty-five pins through his ears by then. Her granny was twinging them with her red fingernails, playing scales on his ear.

"Doesn't that hurt you, honey?" her granny asked.

"Not bad," Rash said.

"Do you use a piercing gun?"

"Just an apple," Rash said. "Or a potato. I just stab 'em right through and close 'em up."

Tessa Lee cringed. Her granny said, "How about that," and looked over at Tessa Lee and rolled her eyes.

"I put alcohol on 'em every night," he said. He picked up a toilet-paper pig and dallied with her pink yarn skirt and laughed out loud.

Tessa Lee thought at first he might be mocking her granny. If he mocked her granny, she'd have to make him leave, and it made her stomach hurt to think about it. She hadn't had to defend anybody since Travis died, and realizing that made her stomach hurt, too.

But Rash wasn't joking when he said, "She's so cute! What a great idea."

"Glad you like it," her granny replied.

"How much are they?" he asked. "My dad'll love this. No kidding."

"You say you're selling flower arrangements up the way?"

"Sandspur arrangements," Tessa Lee clarified. Her granny would hate them. She was sure of it.

"Yep," Rash said. "Our stand's maybe twenty or twenty-five down, on the left."

"I'll swap you," her granny said. "Go ahead and take your pig, and after a while I'll come down to where you are."

Rash hopped up and claimed his toilet-paper pig, clearly pleased. "I love the little hat," he said, and her granny showed him how she used a stickpin to keep the pig's hat on. The pin pushed through the yarn and through the pig's soft plastic head.

"Be sure to save me an arrangement, now," her granny told him, and she gave Tessa Lee the eye, like she knew nobody in their right mind would ever pay for sandspurs.

Tessa Lee wasn't sure what had come over her granny, or

why she was being so accommodating. Maybe she had lung disease and wanted to give her one last happy day before she broke the news.

"Do you wanna go walking and see the other booths?" Rash asked.

She'd just gotten back not a half hour earlier. She'd barely had time to restock the seashell wreaths—and now her granny might have lung disease.

"I should stay here and help Granny," she apologized.

"Oh, get outta here," her granny said. "Can't you see I'm fine?"

Sheila stopped at a store for a pack of smokes and a lighter. The plastic around the outside of the pack crinkled. She'd forgotten that sound, the anticipation that went with it, like the wrapper was laughing. Her fingers trembled as she packed the tobacco against the heel of her hand, then tore away the foil at one corner and admired the tight little bodies nesting inside.

Beautiful.

The first cigarette singed her throat and made her dizzy. It was delicious and nauseating at the same time. The second one burned smooth. She sat on a bench in the park and smoked four or five in a row and let the sun warm her head while the smoke coated her throat.

She'd only been there a little while when a fellow came up to bum a cigarette, a nice-enough man hard on his luck, living in his car. It was parked a few blocks down the street. He was going to his cousin's to take a shower and get high, and he invited her to come, if she wanted to.

She wanted to, all right.

But all the way there she tried to talk herself out of it. If she stayed clean, she could see her momma. She could find out what happened to Tessa Lee. If she stayed clean, she could go back to The House of Possibility until she figured out if she really wanted to know what bad thing had happened to her daughter.

And what if his cousin knew Reggie?

"What's your cousin's name?" she asked the guy.

"Carl," he said.

"I can't go," she told him.

"You got something against Carl?" the guy replied, and when Sheila smiled at him, he said, "Suit yourself," and pointed her toward a bar.

She could see the sign up ahead, but she walked and walked and didn't seem to get closer. Cigarettes didn't usually do that to her. It was nice to get high off cigarettes—a cheap high. But she kept her eyes open for a closer bar, somewhere to stop and sit down. She was sweating, and the perspiration irritated her shingles and made her itch.

By the time she got to the bar, she decided to have just one drink, then call a cab to take her back to The House of Possibility. She had a chance to make a new start. It'd be stupid to throw it away.

She settled on a barstool and ordered a beer, then another one to help her recuperate. The air conditioner felt good, and the bartender gave her some pretzels to snack on. A bearded fat boy ordered her a third beer and told her all about the fight he'd had with his girlfriend. Then his cell phone rang, and he left, and a different guy bought the next couple of rounds, plus the potato skins they shared while they watched a ball game.

"You ever been to a place called Hully Sanders's Mobile City?" she asked him.

"Every day," he said. "I work for Hully."

She hadn't thought of Hully as a real person before. She thought of Hully Sanders as a cartoon character, like Yosemite Sam. She pictured Hully swinging his guns, a long red beard down to his belt. "What do you do?" she asked.

"Ride the trash truck," he said.

"You gotta be kidding."

"No kidding," he swore. "Pays good, and I get a trailer to stay in as part of my contract. I been there almost a year."

"I never been," Sheila said. "I passed the sign on the road. Looks like a nice place."

"It is," the trashman said. "Some of it's real nice." He sucked hard on his beer. "One side's got permanent sites, where people live in full-sized mobile homes. Stay there year-round. Other side's wooded, more like a campground, with a lot of pull campers, Airstreams, you know, and Winnebagos. That side's nice, too, 'cause they got water and electric hookups and good-sized bathhouses."

"Huh," Sheila said.

"Now my place ain't in the nice part," the trashman told her. "It's at the back, near where we park the trash trucks and stuff. It's all the old trailers they can't rent out no more to people on vacation and stuff."

"I bet you smell good when you get home, don't you?" Sheila joked.

"Yeah," he said. "Even the dog runs away."

"What's your wife think about living with the trashman?"

"Ain't got no wife," he said.

"Come on, now," Sheila said. "I've heard that line before."

"I don't," he said. "You think I'd be sitting here buying you drinks if I had a wife?"

After they'd wandered past craft stands awhile, Tessa Lee and Rash walked down to the ocean, kicked around at the place where the sand turned to surf. Tessa Lee looked for angel wings, and Rash looked for mermaid purses. He found one and held it up for Tessa Lee to see. When she shook it, something rattled inside, maybe sand or maybe dried-up eggs.

"Speaking of mermaids," Rash said cautiously, "I guess you should know that Juana never came back to work. After that day that you showed up, I mean."

"Really?" Tessa Lee's cheeks flushed and her head went light. Why did her momma hate her so much?

"Yeah," Rash said. "I hoped maybe she was staying with you and your granny, but since you didn't mention it. . . ."

"No," Tessa Lee said. She dragged her toes through the

little bubbles, the crushed-up shells that crunched beneath her feet. "I wonder where she went," she said.

"It's weird," Rash replied. "Nobody's seen her for weeks. And she'd been working in that conch shell forever."

Tessa Lee leaned over to study a hermit crab, and as soon as she got close, it took off toward the water. She hadn't even touched it yet.

Part of her wanted to stomp that little hermit crab deep into the sand.

"Reggie came over to the arcade and asked a bunch of questions," Rash said. "He was pretty upset, you know? They were tight. He thought maybe she left with you."

"She didn't even recognize me."

"Sure she did."

"I told her who I was," Tessa Lee admitted. "And she said she didn't have any children."

"I guess you caught her off guard," Rash replied. "I told Reggie that your granny came to get you, and that Juana wasn't with you when you left."

"She hates me," Tessa Lee said.

"No, she doesn't."

"It's okay," Tessa Lee said. "I hate her back."

"No, you don't," Rash said.

But it was true. She did hate her. "It's like she left me twice," Tessa Lee told him, and she walked out into the water, not even caring that she didn't like the ocean. Not even caring that she didn't have dry clothes. She walked into the ocean to get away from herself, but of course it didn't work. The waves broke over her knees and splashed up onto her shorts.

Rash followed, grabbed her arm, and they waded out farther.

Tessa Lee kept her feet up as much as she could, jumping even the littlest waves. She didn't like not seeing where she was stepping. "In a way, I'm glad she didn't recognize me," Tessa Lee said.

"She recognized you," Rash assured her.

"I always thought if she saw me, she'd want to be with me again. But if she's on drugs like you say, then it's good she didn't."

"I guess," Rash said. He got a big mouthful of water and sprayed it out like a whale.

"I hope nothing happened to her," Tessa Lee said. She turned her back to a wave and let it slap across her shoulders.

"She probably just decided to start over somewhere else. Maybe she went somewhere better. Or to rehab or something."

"You think?"

"Don't know. Maybe." Rash dove under, but Tessa Lee didn't, and a big wave broke over her head, sent her tumbling.

She came up spitting and coughing, almost back to the shore.

Rash was laughing behind her. "You okay?"

"Yeah," she said. Water in her eyes, burning at her throat, sand everywhere. It felt perfect, really. She was insignificant, a blot of paint in somebody else's painting. She wished somebody would just smudge her out.

"Come on," he called. "We'll get out past them."

So they went deeper, beyond the waves.

Tessa Lee dove under and swam against the current.

The first time her momma left, she'd expected her to come back any minute. Every time a car pulled up outside the trailer, she thought her momma might be in it. Every time the phone rang, Tessa Lee leaped to answer it. She volunteered to walk to the mailbox at the end of the street and check the mail, searching every envelope for her momma's handwriting, a return address that might tell her where her momma had gone.

Once when she was eleven, a letter came addressed to her, with a return address that looked like it'd been written in her momma's slanted cursive. It took her two days to get up the nerve to open it, and then it was just a subscription renewal for a magazine she'd gotten the year before as a birthday gift from Amber. The slanted cursive was a hoax. When she looked up close, she could tell that it'd been printed from a computer, not written at all.

Tessa Lee put her foot down, and suddenly the ocean floor wasn't there. Rash was right beside her, but the water was over her head, and when she realized it, it made her almost too scared to swim. Rash was saying something, but she couldn't tell what because the ocean was too deep. She kept dipping down to touch bottom, but she had to go under to do it, way under, and there was seaweed down there and something else spongy, and she got some water in her throat and choked.

"It's too deep," Tessa Lee cried. She had salt in her eyes, and everything burned and went blurry. "We're out too far," she said.

"It's okay," Rash assured her. "Plenty of people are deeper than we are. Look."

"I'm gonna drown," she said.

"No, you're not," he replied. "You're not even close to drowning." But he grabbed her arm and pulled her back in some, and then she was able to swim again.

And then she could touch the bottom and didn't mind the idea of crabs as much.

"I used to close my eyes and concentrate so hard," she said. "I'd picture my momma in all kinds of ways, like with her legs broken. I figured if her legs were broken, then it made sense why she hadn't come to get me. 'Cause she couldn't walk. And then sometimes I pictured her with a big tumor in her throat, because if she hadn't called, it must be because she couldn't *speak,* you know?"

"Don't you hate it when you can't tell whether you're a psychic or not?" Rash asked.

"Yeah," Tessa Lee said.

They bodysurfed up to the beach, then settled there in the shallowest water, where the foam from the waves made a ruffle.

Tessa Lee didn't tell him how she'd prayed to Baby Jesus, night after night, begging for healing for her momma's tumor, so she could speak again and call home, tell Tessa Lee to pack her bags.

She didn't tell him how she'd prayed for her momma's broken legs to heal. Baby Jesus was 100 percent useless where her momma was concerned.

Rash dug his heels into the wet sand and let the waves push over his knees. He turned his face up to the sun, and Tessa Lee watched him. He looked pretty normal. If it weren't for all the pinkness and all the safety pins, he wouldn't look weird at all.

"I had a brother," she said. "But he got killed." She could say it because Rash had his eyes closed, but then he opened them.

"Really?" he asked. "When?"

"Couple of months ago."

"Oh my god," Rash said. "I'm sorry."

"Yeah," she told him. "If you see my momma, if she goes back to work as the mermaid when she gets out of rehab, tell her Travis is dead." She got up and Rash followed.

They dripped across the sand and up to the boardwalk.

"That's why I was looking for her," Tessa Lee said. "That's all I needed to tell her in the first place."

"What happened to your brother?" Rash asked.

"Got hit by a trash truck," Tessa Lee replied. "It was his own fault. He wasn't paying attention."

"So what?" Rash said. "That sucks."

"Survival of the fittest. Didn't you study that in school?"

Rash looked horrified, and she wasn't sure why she'd said it. It wasn't what she felt. Not at all.

Lil stood before the pink-headed boy's craft stand. Most of the spikes had washed out of his hair when he went swimming, and now it lay down like a respectable boy's hair. If you overlooked the fact that his hair was pink, he looked fine.

But his friends weren't doing a thing to help his reputation. The two girls were holding hands, and they weren't little girls, either. They were teenagers, nearing twenty. One of them wore a T-shirt that said RADICAL FEMINIST, like that was something to brag about. The other one had rings through her nose, and her hair hung in long clumps that looked like turds. Same color, same thickness.

"This is Tabitha and Frieda," Phillip said.

"Nice to meet you," Lil replied. She wasn't accustomed to shaking hands with girls, but these girls offered their hands just like a man would.

She asked the turd-headed girl who made the bracelets how she tied the knots, and the girl showed her. Her fingers were quick, and Lil admired her artistry. Nice tight lines. Very professional. Too bad she didn't take better care of her tresses and find herself a boyfriend to hold hands with.

Lil bought a bracelet for Tessa Lee, and also a hat. She didn't think much of the hats, really, with the stitching on the outside, in a color that bragged against the corduroy, but what did she know? She saw that same style in fashion magazines when she went to get her hair cut, so maybe it was a classy hat. Besides that, in the craft world, there was an unspoken expectation that the artists support one another, and the girls were Phillip's friends. And Phillip had been the one who sent Tessa Lee back home to her. If he'd wanted to, he could have talked her into staying at that seedy beach. But he didn't.

As for the sandspur arrangements—well, she had to keep up her end of the bargain. The arrangement he'd picked out for her was as big and unruly as a hooker's wig, a rumpled thorny spray in a blue glass bottle.

"I don't want to take your biggest one," Lil said. "Just give me a little one," and she tried to swap the arrangement for a smaller spray, one that wouldn't take up too much room in the trashcan.

"Oh, no," Phillip said. "You gave me a toilet-paper pig! So I want you to have my best work." He pushed the large arrangement toward her again. "I call this one Astria."

"Astria?" Lil asked.

"Like I told Firefly," Phillip said to Lil. "A sandspur's like a star, right here on earth where we can touch it."

"Huh," Lil said.

"And sandspur arrangements are like the antithesis of roses," he continued. "A way to say 'I love you' that acknowledges the pain in life, not just the beauty, you know?"

"I reckon so," Lil said. She took the arrangement from Phillip's hands. There must have been forty sprigs of sandspurs in it.

"Careful," he said.

A sandspur caught the sleeve of her shirt and when she pulled it away, another one snagged the fabric over her breast.

"These are dangerous!" Lil said.

"Everything beautiful is a little bit dangerous," Phillip explained.

One of the girls, the hatmaker, said, "He's full of it, Lil. He just likes sandspurs because nobody else does."

"That's not true," Phillip insisted. "I like sandspurs because I *am* a sandspur in a world that admires roses. And so are you!"

"Well, how about that," Lil said.

"Firefly's a sandspur, too," he said.

"Oh no, baby," Lil replied. "She's always been a rose."

One sarong at a time, Tessa Lee changed the display at the craft stand, putting Lil's white tablecloth beneath what was left of the wooden napkin holders and the toilet-paper dolls. The seashell wreaths were gone, and she'd just sold all three sets of the cattail-grass placemats to the same buyer, who left her card in case her granny had more in stock back home.

She took the cash box with her when she stole off to the port-a-potties, just for a second, and stripped out of the wet clothes. She tied the first sarong around her waist as a skirt. The second one she tied tightly around her breasts, like a strapless bikini top.

It felt naughty, not wearing underpants or a bra, and somehow it made her feel confident, too.

She wasn't sure what her granny would say when she got back, whether she'd care. It didn't really matter if she cared because soon she'd be dead, and Tessa Lee'd be on her own, anyway.

When Travis had been little, Tessa Lee'd tried to teach him to color inside the lines. Tessa Lee loved the lines, but Travis ignored them altogether. She'd tried to teach him to use the right crayons, to make the horses brown or black, the grass green. But Travis knew something she didn't, like the oil painter. It didn't matter if the grass was green. It didn't matter if the grass was *grass*. Sometimes it was more real to put the sky on the ground, the grass in the sky.

She hoped nothing had happened to her granny. She'd been gone awhile, too long. She wondered if her granny was carrying an ID, if she'd taken her fanny pack or at least put her driver's license in her pocket so that if she dropped dead along the boardwalk, somebody could identify her.

Would anybody know to come tell Tessa Lee if her granny dropped dead? What if everybody started taking down their stands and leaving before her granny got back? She wasn't allowed to drive without an adult in the car. She wasn't even sure she knew where to turn to get onto the road that took them home. She'd have to stop by the hospital, to see if her granny was there. If her granny wasn't at the hospital, who would she call? The police?

It made her mad that her momma wasn't there, that she didn't even have a phone number for her momma. When she thought about her momma now, all she could picture was a screaming mermaid doll, but she wasn't even a mermaid anymore. There was no way to picture her at all, no place.

She didn't have a backup relative.

She needed a boyfriend, one old enough to marry if worse came to worse. So she pushed out her chest and smiled at all the boys who looked her way.

When Lil got back to their booth, Tessa Lee was standing there with her hand on her hip, dressed up like a Hawaiian, her little belly pooching out for all the world to see. She was flirting with some boy, a fellow with a ponytail, maybe a Greek.

But that wasn't what worried Lil most. "You better not be no sandspur," she said in a tone that sent the boy on his way.

Lil sat the arrangement Phillip had given her down on the ground, beneath the table where nobody could see it and mistake it for one of her own creations.

"What?" Tessa Lee asked.

"You better not be no *sand*spur," Lil repeated. "And if I ever catch you holding hands with a girl, I'll whip your ass," she added in a whisper.

But Tessa Lee spoke at full volume when she asked, "Why would I hold hands with a girl?" and Lil said, "Shhh," because a customer was coming, and what if the customer was a Christian!

The customer had lots of questions about the kind of glue Lil used, whether hot-glue bonds were permanent, whether she'd ever heard of Gorilla glue, if she'd ever tried it. All the time Lil talked with her, she thought about what she'd said to Tessa Lee—and what she'd said to Sheila so many years back.

She thought about her grandchildren, and how little it mattered that they clearly had different daddies, Tessa Lee so freckled and lanky, Travis with those bright eyes and a sumo wrestler build. She didn't love them any different because of their DNA.

Deoxyribonucleic acid. She still remembered when Sheila had to spell it at a spelling bee. She lost on that word. Got her *i* and her *e* twisted around. Sixth grade, and she and Lewis were there. They thought she did great just to get to that level. Did they expect too little of Sheila? Or did they expect too much?

The customer looked over every cross-stitched matchbox cover, deciding at last on "O Holy Night." Tessa Lee was right there to wrap it up for her, carefully peeling the ten-dollar sticker off the bottom because it was a gift.

She was a sweet girl, a good girl. Would it have mattered one iota if she'd been half-black? Lil'd always assumed mixed-race children had a harder time in life. When she saw them in the store, she felt sorry for them, felt like they had to pay for their parents' transgressions.

But maybe she was wrong. A mixed-race child with two parents, four grandparents, maybe even eight great-grandparents would have a whole heap more support than one white Tessa Lee, with her one white granny to her name.

Tessa Lee counted out the customer's change. She was a smart girl, an honest girl. Lil'd never had any real trouble with her, except for the running away. She'd never taken money from Lil. Her brother Howard's youngest boy was in juvenile detention for stealing, and he had two white parents.

And then she thought about Sheila. Wouldn't it have been better for Sheila to settle down with Lorenzo than wander from place to place, man to man? If Lorenzo loved her, if Lorenzo was a good husband and father, then couldn't Lil have learned to love him, too?

It would've been better, Lil decided. For the children and for Sheila. Love trumped everything else, when it came right down to it. Lewis always knew that. "What business is it of yours?" he'd have asked her—if she'd given him the chance.

When the customers had gone, and it was quiet around the stand again, Lil looked at Tessa Lee and said, "If you ever decide to hold hands with a girl, you just need to understand one thing: I'm gonna raise hell about it. But I'll get used to it after a while."

"Okay," Tessa Lee said. "But why would I hold hands with a girl?"

Tessa Lee never intended to go listen to the wind ensemble that was scheduled to play at four at the north stage. And it wasn't true, either, that the violin player from her Sunday School class was performing there. The violin wasn't even a wind instrument, but maybe her granny didn't know that. She lied to her granny, right to her face. It wasn't that hard to do. She told her she'd be gone for an hour or two.

"You be back here by six thirty," her granny said. "The show ends at seven, and I need you to help load up."

"Okay."

"And go put on your clothes," her granny said. "You look like a tramp."

"They're wet," Tessa Lee replied. "I look fine." She left before her granny had a chance to complain. Served her right, for staying gone so long.

FRIEDA AND TABITHA were proud of their belly-button rings. The skin was red and irritated at the place the metal passed through, especially on Frieda's belly, but they looked impressive.

"They're pretty," Tessa Lee said. "Did it hurt?"

"Not bad," Frieda said. "It was quick."

"Yeah, it hurt," Tabitha admitted. "But it's worth it."

"I've been thinking of getting one," Tessa Lee said.

"No kidding?" Rash said. "I'll go with you."

THE BODY-ART SALOON was just across the street. The storefront had paper in the windows so nobody could peek in, and the sign itself was spray-painted in graffiti letters. It looked a little scary, and there was a sign on the door that said, ID REQUIRED. ABSOLUTELY NO ONE UNDER 18 WITHOUT PARENTAL CONSENT.

Tessa Lee was relieved. She thought she might go hear the wind ensemble after all.

She liked the way piercings looked, though. She'd even taken an earring—a little hoop—and pinched it under her belly button before. Amber'd done it, too, with the other earring, and when they'd shown Amber's mom, she'd choked on her coffee.

"Too bad," Tessa Lee said. "I'm not old enough."

"Baloney," Rash replied. "They have to say that. We'll tell

'em you're eighteen." And before Tessa Lee could protest, he'd pushed the door in and they were at the counter.

The girl who worked there said they really did have to prove their age or else have a parent sign. But Rash charmed her with all his safety pins, and it turned out she knew a guy around the corner who did tattoos and piercings out of his apartment, no questions asked, and she wrote down his address and sent them away.

WHEN THEY KNOCKED on his door, he answered it without his shirt. It looked like they'd woken him up, but he was friendly about it, said that he had time to do Tessa Lee's belly button, if she had fifty dollars. He was at least twenty-five. Maybe thirty. When he wiped his eyes, Tessa Lee was surprised at how much hair he had beneath his arms, long hair. He had tattoos up both arms, all over, and a shaved head, and a little mustache and goatee. "You'll have to wait outside," he said to Rash. "'Cause I can't work with an audience."

"I don't know," Rash said.

"Come on, man," the guy replied. "You think they'd give out my address at the Saloon if I was a killer?"

It all happened faster than Tessa Lee could think. She was looking around at the guy's apartment. The ashtray on the coffee table had spilled onto some tattoo magazines, and there was dirty laundry heaped into a corner.

"You sure you wanna do it?" Rash asked.

Tessa Lee nodded.

"I'll be right outside," Rash said, and he left.

The guy didn't have much of a selection of body jewelry.

Just silver rings in a few different sizes. They were in little plastic packets on his table, right next to the honey and the salt and the Splenda. He didn't have the littlest size, though. When she'd pictured her belly button pierced, she pictured a littler ring than the ones he had.

"Most people come in with their own jewelry," he said, and Tessa Lee felt dumb because she wasn't really prepared. "You can start with this one and replace it with another one in a couple of weeks," he suggested.

He told Tessa Lee she'd have to lie down on the couch, but she didn't want to lie down. It seemed wrong, to lie down on a strange man's couch and let him stick a needle in her. She didn't want to hurt his feelings, though, and make him think she was afraid of him.

She knew her granny'd kill her when she saw the ring. It was bigger than she wanted anyway, and when her granny saw her belly like that, she'd have a stroke.

She might even die. It could actually happen. You could get so shocked that your bones just turned into milk, and what good were you then?

So she said, "Can you do it through my nipple instead?"

She wasn't sure why she said it, except that her granny wouldn't see her nipple, while she'd definitely see her belly button.

"Nipple's fine," the guy said. "I'll put it wherever you want it."

"Can I sit up?" she asked.

"If you want to," he said. "Most people do better lying down, though." He pointed her to a chair close to the window, where the light was good.

There was a big aquarium not far from where she sat, on a table against a wall, with a python on one side. The snake didn't move. It just sat there, thick and still, and while the guy set up his equipment, Tessa Lee kept moving the snake in her mind, wishing it was spread out across the aquarium instead of coiled up at one end.

Once, a man had come to the recreation center with a bunch of snakes that he kept in pillowcases. He had a traveling snake show, and he set up a display, and all the kids who lived in Hully Sanders's Mobile City came to see it.

Some of the big boys were scared of the snakes, backed away, didn't want to touch them. But not Travis. Travis held a yellow corn snake for half the afternoon. The snake slid through his fingers, back and forth between his hands. Travis draped it around his neck and laughed when it tried to go down his shirt. Most times other kids made fun of Travis, but not that day.

Tessa Lee'd left the center and rounded up all the kids who weren't there yet. She'd run all the way back to the trailer to get her granny and Rosie Jo, so they could see Travis assisting the snake man. She wanted everybody to see how brave he was.

"This your first piercing?" the guy said.

"Yeah," Tessa Lee told him. "Except my ears."

"Those are different," he said, and Tessa Lee felt stupid.

"I'll use a hollow needle," he said. "Push that through first to make the hole. Then we'll put the jewelry through."

"Okay," she said.

She looked out the window. She didn't want to see the needle, and she didn't want to see the snake.

But she didn't want to be rude or act like she was scared. Amber would be scared, but not her. She'd hitchhiked by herself. She'd slept on the beach. She could do this.

"Do you have any piercings?" she asked him.

"A few," he said.

But there were none on his face or ears, none through his nipples or belly button. Tessa Lee blushed and asked, "How long you been doing this?"

"Been tattooing about ten years," he said. "Just got into piercings not long ago."

"Oh," she said.

"Don't worry," he told her. "I got an autoclave."

She wasn't sure what an autoclave was, but she thought it might have something to do with sex.

The apartment was too hot, and Tessa Lee was sweating. She felt a little faint even before he came over to her and said, "You gotta take off your top, sweetheart."

She loosened the sarong and let it drop around her waist. Her nipples clenched up tight and hard.

"Which one?" he asked.

"Whichever," she whispered.

He smiled at her and said, "Let me see," and he put his hands beneath her breasts and rubbed his thumbs over her nipples.

She swallowed hard and closed her eyes. Her breaths came fast then, and it felt like all her blood rushed warm between her legs.

He squeezed her nipples so hard something shot through her, down to her toes, electricity, waves of it. "Either one'll work," he said. "We can do 'em both if you want."

"Just one's fine," she said weakly, in spite of her craving for symmetry.

"Okay then," he said, and he rubbed something cold and tingly on her breast.

"Oh," she said. Her eyes were watering.

"You gotta relax," he said. "It's just alcohol."

"Oh my god," she said and laughed a little. "I'm so nervous."

"You'll be fine," he told her and patted her thigh. "Scoot up to the edge of the chair and lean back a little for me. Good."

She wasn't sure what he did after that because she was looking up. She could feel his breath on her skin as he worked. His hands were warm, but he gripped her nipple with something cold, maybe some kind of clamp.

"Take a deep breath and let it out," he said, and when she blew out, he pushed.

She closed her eyes to the pressure, to the slow heating sear. The needle popped as it broke through her skin. She could hear the needle carving through, high-pitched.

"Oh my god," she said.

"Okay," he said. "We're under way. Hang on."

But it wasn't fast. It seemed like the needle might be stuck. Then the world got really tiny, as he pushed the needle deeper. Her nipple resisted. It wasn't quick at all. She clenched her muscles tight, her butt muscles and toes. Black fire closed in on her, burned up all her air.

"Halfway," the guy told her. His voice sounded funny, like he was talking to her on the phone from somewhere far away, Russia or China.

Her mouth went dry and turned to iron. It tasted like batteries in her mouth, the flavor filling her mouth, coming up from around her teeth. It seemed never-ending, a stabbing in slow motion. Her eyes were closed, but she could feel the blackness telescoping anyway, blackness all around, and she was tiny like a star, way out in space and burning up.

"It's through," he said, from Russia or China.

"Am I done?" she pleaded. She opened her eyes but kept her chin up high so she wouldn't see it. Her mouth was watering.

The guy laughed. "No, the needle's through. We'll put the jewelry in in a minute."

"I gotta go to the bathroom," she said.

"You can't right now," he told her. But she was already up, staggering out of the chair.

FIRST SHE HAD diarrhea, and as soon as she flushed the toilet, the blackness came on her again.

So she stretched out on the floor on a gray bathmat. She didn't care that it was filthy. She closed her eyes and breathed and tried not to move too much because there was a big needle through her nipple.

"You all right?" the guy called.

"Yeah," she said. "Just give me a minute."

"You want me to get your boyfriend?" he asked.

"No," she said. "I just gotta be still."

In a little while, she could open her eyes. She kept her head turned away so she wouldn't see the needle much. She looked at the dust and hairs at the edges of the floor and at an empty toilet-paper roll someone had meant to throw into the trashcan. It had rolled up beside the trashcan and now a spider had built a web connecting the two.

WHEN SHE WENT back out, he gave her a Coke. It was very cold and very good.

"You okay?" he asked.

"Yeah," she told him.

"You're doing fine," he said. "The first time always hurts a little."

"A little?" she said.

He smiled at her and said, "Soon you'll be back to get the other one done."

"I doubt it," she said.

"Oh yeah," he told her. "It's addictive."

It didn't hurt as much to put the jewelry through. And the nipple ring was pretty, really pretty. Half of her wished she had one on the other side to match.

He handed her a mirror. "You like it?" he asked.

"Yeah," she said.

"I knew you would," he told her and winked.

"Thanks," she said. She wished her momma could see it. She wondered what her momma would think.

He adjusted the ring, and it took her breath again, but not from the pain.

"Anything else I can do for you today?"

She wasn't sure what he meant by that. "I gotta go," she said. She had her money in a little cloth bag, and she pulled it out, started counting.

"I'm gonna throw in an old T-shirt for free," he said, and he went into another room, which Tessa Lee figured was his bedroom, and he came out with an army-green shirt with a band she'd never heard of advertised on the front. "You don't want anything tight to touch it."

Tessa Lee pulled on his T-shirt. It smelled faintly of underarms, and she couldn't help thinking about the long hair under his arms and how soft it looked.

"Don't let your boyfriend pull on that ring for a week or two," he said.

"I won't," Tessa Lee promised.

SHE WAS QUEASY and pale, but they still had a long way to walk.

"I can't believe it," Rash said. "I've always wanted a nipple done, but I never had the nerve!"

"Don't do it," she told him. Her arm was tingling all the way down to her fingers. Maybe the needle had hit a nerve or something. She opened and closed her hand, to make the tingles go away.

"You're so brave!" he continued. He went on and on, until Tessa Lee felt better. They stopped and got ice cream, and they were laughing by the time they got back to the craft stand, where Frieda and Tabitha were waiting.

"You won't believe what Firefly did!" Rash called as they approached.

"Let's see it!" they said, but Tessa Lee was modest.

"You gotta show us," Tabitha insisted, and they made a tent with the second sarong, and Tessa Lee stood inside it and lifted her shirt.

"Wow!" Rash said.

"Looks nice," Frieda told her, and Tessa Lee was proud

then and didn't mind the pins and needles in her arm so much.

"Be sure to put peroxide on it for the next few days," Rash told her.

"He cleaned it for me," Tessa Lee said and blushed.

Then she noticed that all around them, people were breaking down their stands and loading up what they hadn't sold. It was ten minutes until seven. She was late.

But there was one more thing she had to find out. "Do I look like a lesbian to you?" she asked Frieda and Tabitha.

"No way," Tabitha said.

"Who knows?" Frieda disagreed. "What does a lesbian look like?"

"You don't look like a lesbian to me," Rash said.

"My granny thinks I'm a lesbian," Tessa Lee said. "I never really thought about it before."

"When you figure out if you are or not, send me an e-mail and let me know," Rash said. He wrote down his address, drew a sandspur next to it, and gave it to Tessa Lee.

The trashman swallowed back a burp. "I didn't used to be this way," he said.

"Me, neither," Sheila told him. She straightened the creases in her pillowcase skirt. The flowered print went swimming behind her eyes.

They were sitting on the trashman's concrete doorsteps, at the very back of Hully Sanders's Mobile City. His beat-up trailer was parked next to another one with a blanket for a door. There was an old warehouse off to the side, the trash truck parked beside it, a tractor, a pile of clamshells, a couple of Dumpsters stinking ripe.

The sun hadn't gone down completely, but it was sinking fast. They'd bought a twelve-pack when they left the bar, but it was gone already. They'd bought another and were making a good dent in that one, too. Sheila knew she wasn't going back to The House of Possibility. Not then. Not ever.

The trashman crushed the cans with his hands and threw them at a light pole. "No, really," he said. "I didn't drink a bit before the accident."

"What happened?"

"Don't wanna talk about it," he said.

"Come on," Sheila prodded. "Tell me. What turned you into the sorry drunk you are?" She laughed.

"We were getting the trash one day," the trashman said. "And I was riding on the back, where I always stand. We turned the corner around Cheyenne Lake. Maybe we were going a little fast. Tommy—he was the driver—he was always trying to throw me off the back when we went around corners. But there was this little kid, run over the hill and right out in front of us. Bam.

"Wasn't even Tommy's fault, but he quit anyway. Used to live right there," and he pointed to the trailer next door.

"Whoa," Sheila said.

"Now he's in Alaska, working at a fishery. Couldn't stand it."

"That's bad," Sheila said.

"Didn't feel like much," the trashman said. "Felt like we'd hit a cat or something."

"Huh."

"Felt like maybe we hit a big bump in the road, like where the road washed out. You ever hit anything with a car?"

"No," Sheila told him.

"Made a big sound, like a popping sound. You ever step on maypops when you were a kid? That's what it sounded like, times ten."

Sheila leaned over him and got another beer from the cooler. They didn't have any ice in the cooler, so the beer was warm.

"'Member how when you step on a maypop, it busts under your foot? Like it's solid at first, and then it just gives? That's kind of how it felt, when Tommy hit that little boy."

"I can see why you don't like to think about it," Sheila said.

"I didn't even know he'd hit a kid, to tell the truth, 'cause I was on the back of the truck. I thought we'd hit a cat or something."

"Coulda been a cat," Sheila said. "Probably more likely to be a cat."

"It was bad," the trashman told her. "The grill on the front of the truck had stuff all in it, scalp and stuff." The trashman sniffed hard and pushed himself up from the doorsteps, shook his head. "I can't talk about it," he said.

Sheila's eyes had misted up. She wasn't sure why. Maybe because she was so relieved to finally have some beer, and somebody to talk to, somebody who understood how troubles could change you in the most elemental ways.

"I know a man with seventeen locks on his door," she said, but the trashman didn't hear her. He'd stumbled around the corner of the trailer to pee.

A firefly kept her company while he was gone. Just one. She wondered if fireflies had families. You never saw them swarming, but maybe that was because all the firefly families broke apart.

Maybe there was always only one, glowing in lots of different places to disguise the fact that it was traveling solo.

The cigarette between Sheila's fingers burned down to the filter. She didn't throw it out because she didn't know at first that what she smelled was her own skin, scorching black beneath the embers.

It wasn't very Christian of her, to think such things about the preacher, but Lil was sure that if he'd really been ordained by God, God would have given him more interesting things to say.

Lil sat in the choir loft next to Rosie Jo and tried to pay attention, but it was hard. Hard because she couldn't even see the preacher's face, just his backside as he stood there in the pulpit and talked about Amos. Again. She'd never known anybody to get so excited about Amos and something he called "liberation theology," whatever that was. Lil could care less. She stifled a yawn and took a deep breath and tried not to rattle the paper on her peppermint as she unwrapped it.

This preacher liked Amos better than Jesus. He didn't know a good story when he heard one. How hard was it to figure out that crucifixions meant more than sermons to Israelites? Didn't everybody warn the Israelites that if they didn't straighten up, God was gonna smite 'em? Amos wasn't the first one to figure that out.

She read her church bulletin, a little poem on the back written by one of the teenagers who had aspirations of going into the ministry.

She wished Tessa Lee had God on her mind instead of Lord knows what. When Lil'd tried to wake her up for church that morning, she'd snapped something ugly and put her pillow over her face.

Maybe she had multiple-personality syndrome. All day at the craft fair, they'd gotten along just fine. Lil had even let her run around with her strange-looking friends. She'd gone out of her way to make Tessa Lee happy, and then Tessa Lee'd ignored her only request.

Lil'd been worried. What if somebody got her, pulled her into a car, and drove away? Tessa Lee was still just a child. She was all Lil had left in the world. Six thirty passed, and then six forty. What if she'd run away again? Gone off with the lesbians? Lil took down the sun tarp and put the stools back into the van. Six forty-five and six fifty. The crowds thinned down to nothing. What if somebody'd dragged her into an alley and raped her? Lil folded her tablecloth, kicked in the legs of her table, and dragged it to the van by herself.

Tessa Lee came dawdling in after seven and didn't even apologize. She had on some boy's shirt, a shirt Lil had certainly never seen before, and then when Lil asked her where it came from, Tessa Lee said it was none of her business.

None of her business!

She shouldn't have slapped her, though. She wouldn't have slapped her if Tessa Lee hadn't sassed, and she didn't slap her hard. Certainly not as hard as she'd have been slapped if she'd talked that way when she was a girl.

Then Tessa Lee started crying, wouldn't speak all the way home. When Lil asked if she wanted to stop at the Golden Corral, no answer. When Lil asked if she wanted to drive, no answer. Just the quiet snubbing, her back turned to Lil.

How could anybody cry that much over a little slap? She hardly touched her.

The preacher said something about women and cows, and Lil leaned over to Rosie Jo and whispered, "Did Amos call women cows?" and Rosie Jo elbowed her in the side.

She wished she hadn't slapped Tessa Lee, but it wasn't fair for her to be in this position, having to raise another teenager, and one who lied!

It wasn't like Tessa Lee to lie. But Lil'd seen Tessa Lee's friend before Sunday School—the clean-cut boy who played the violin—and she'd asked him how the concert went. He hadn't played at the boardwalk art show at all. He'd spent his Saturday volunteering for Habitat for Humanity.

Now why would Tessa Lee make up such a thing? And why had she started tying herself up in scarves? And hanging around with hoodlums?

Lil wasn't good with girls. She never had been. So why did God give her another one to raise? Forget Amos. She needed sermons on Job.

She knew she should get Tessa Lee some counseling, but what if she got in there and told the therapist that Lil slapped her? Then they might take her away.

It was a lot easier when Lewis was alive. Then when Lil got fed up, Lewis could just take over. Sometimes she wanted to stomp Lewis for leaving her when he did—with two little children and a car payment—and one of the children about to be a teenager. It was easier when Tessa Lee was little, before she needed Tampax and bras.

She hoped Tessa Lee *never* got her driver's license. She hoped she failed five times in a row. How could she let that girl drive off in the van by herself? She was liable to never come back.

Rosie Jo leaned over and pointed out that the preacher's wife was snoozing on the front pew, and Lil shook her head. Rosie Jo must have learned to whisper in a sawmill. She needed some Clorets.

Lil took another deep breath, tried to settle herself, and apologized to God for her sins toward Tessa Lee. She said a quiet prayer asking for more patience and understanding, and she added a line about helping Tessa Lee get her driver's license. Of course she wanted her to pass the test. She wanted her to grow up and become an upstanding citizen and a good Christian wife to a good Christian man, maybe a deacon in the church, maybe the violin player who volunteered to build houses for poor people.

Why didn't preachers preach about practical things—like how to get teenagers out of bed and into the house of God?

Amos was full of gloom and doom, tragedy and plague and infection. Who needed to hear about that? You get away from the lion and bump into the bear. You make it inside your house and get bit by a snake when you're just reaching to turn on the light switch.

Wasn't that the story of her life?

Lil took up her hymnal, turned it to the right page and got ready to sing as the preacher gave the altar call.

The preacher said, "People, why is it so hard to understand? Like the Israelites, you can choose who and what you serve. But you can't escape the consequences of your choices."

Maybe Lil was just living the consequences, being punished for her iniquities. God was the lion and the bear and the snake.

Maybe God was trying to tell her something.

What had she done to herself?

Her nipple hurt. Her arm tingled all the way down to her fingers. She'd let a complete stranger touch her breast, stick a needle through it, and now something bad was wrong. She had nerve damage. She almost spilled her orange juice when she tried to grip the glass. Her hand wasn't working quite right, and it had to be the nipple ring. Why else wouldn't her hand work?

She couldn't stop crying. Nobody'd ever touched her

breast before, and the first guy who did stuck a needle through it and gave her nerve damage.

And she'd paid him fifty dollars to do it!

She was a bad person, a really bad person. But she didn't want to take the ring out. It looked so pretty, dangling there, with the little ball connecting the two sides of the hoop.

She stood before the mirror and tugged at the hoop, just lightly, stretching her hole a little, and it hurt. But it almost felt good, too. It hurt between her legs a little, a pulling, a throbbing there.

If she'd let him, that man would have touched her down there. She was supposed to be a virgin when she got married, but that man would have touched her.

He had hoops in his penis. Tessa Lee was sure. There was nowhere else for him to pierce, and she wondered what that would feel like, to have a penis inside her, one with silver jewelry through it. It would have to hurt a lot. It left her aching in a private way, just thinking about it.

Her granny was at church, and so she went into the bathroom and got a hand mirror and sat on it, looking at herself between her legs. But she couldn't stand it. It made her feel sick. It made her feel like she was looking at her own insides, so she washed the mirror and put it away again and went back to her room and locked the door.

She'd seen a penis before, lots of times, really, because she'd changed Travis's diaper. But she'd seen a grown one, too. Her momma had a boyfriend who went around naked. He took showers with Tessa Lee sometimes and told her not to be afraid, that she could touch it and rub it with soap. He held his hand over hers, and they rubbed it together until it stood up and pulsed and sprayed on the shower wall. But then later, when he wanted her to kiss it, Tessa Lee said no, and told her momma, and that same night they left on a bus. They left even though her momma had a good job then.

She couldn't remember where they went, just being on the bus with her momma and Travis, the smell of exhaust, driving at night, then being in a bus station and trying not to fall asleep while they waited for the next bus to come. Her momma was on the pay phone, talking, and she had to watch Travis, who was sleeping on a pillowcase stuffed full of clothes that kept falling out.

That was all she remembered. There was a black hole in her memory after that. There were a lot of black holes in her memory.

Tessa Lee took off her pajamas and underwear and put on the firefly cloak. Her Granny was at church so she pulled down her shades and turned off the light.

Nobody had put a penis between her legs before and she didn't want a man to do that to her.

She crawled back into her bed and cried into her pillow because her arm tingled and her nipple hurt, and it was all her fault. It was her fault that she had nerve damage and her fault that Travis got killed and her fault that her momma had left them. If Travis still lived with her momma, he wouldn't have been in Hully Sanders's Mobile City on the day that he got killed. If she hadn't told her momma about the boyfriend and the shower, they might all still be together in Mississippi. They might be happy.

She deserved to hurt and be hurt.

The trashman was still snoring when Sheila got up. She found his coffee, made a pot. She ate his cereal dry, because his milk had already clabbered, and then she found his wallet on the end table next to the couch.

His name was Michael Evan Floyd, and he was only twenty-four. A Scorpio. An organ donor. A member of AAA and Ducks Unlimited. She found his fishing license, his Visa card, a blank check, and thirty-four dollars cash.

Something scratched against the door, and when she opened it, a dog came in, a short white dog with just one eye. It looked at her suspiciously, then jumped up on the couch and fell asleep.

She took a shower in his tub. Used his toothbrush, used his comb. She checked her shingles in his mirror, then used his bite-and-itch cream to numb what was left of her rash.

He'd left his keys in the ignition of his truck, so she took the truck to the grocery store and picked up eggs and bacon and bread and beer. On the way out, she picked up the August schedule of events and a map of Hully Sanders's Mobile City.

When she went back to bed to wake him, he looked like a little boy sleeping there. It was almost two in the afternoon, but it could have been morning. He could have been her little boy, or she could have been young, like him.

She pretended it was morning and she was young. She climbed up on the bed and tried to steal a little sheet. She wiggled up behind him and pretended she knew his body, knew his sighs and farts and snores, his habits and ways.

"Michael," she said finally. "Hey, Michael?"

He rolled over and looked at her. He seemed surprised to see her there.

"I'm Evan," he said and rubbed his eyes. He drank some water from a cup beside the bed. "Mike's my dad."

"Oh," she said and laughed. "Well, whoever you are, it's time to rise and shine."

"Is that clock right?" he asked her.

"Yeah."

"What's your name again?"

She told him.

"You're shining," he said. "But I'm not about to let you rise."

He ran his hand across her belly, and when she didn't stop him, he kept right on going.

Sheila pretended she loved him. She pretended he loved her back.

There was a balloon in Tessa Lee's bedroom, floating up toward the ceiling. It'd been there awhile. Amber's momma had brought it by on the day Tessa Lee returned to Hully Sanders's Mobile City. It was a helium balloon, supposedly from Amber, with WELCOME HOME in black calligraphy against a bright green background.

It seemed strange to Tessa Lee that she'd get a balloon like that. Like she'd been in the hospital, like she'd been off to war and returned again. It didn't look right, bobbing around up there, welcoming her home, its ribbon dangling down.

In the night, when she woke up suddenly, remembering that something was wrong but not remembering exactly *what*, she thought that the balloon was somebody's head, and she thought that Travis had come back from the dead. She almost ran to her granny's room, over and over, but she was a bad person and she didn't deserve a granny. It served her right to be scared.

As the helium leaked out a little, the balloon came closer to the ground. It looked more and more like Travis in the dark late at night. It kept coming close to Tessa Lee's head, and she'd wake up scared and bat it away.

She should have been nicer to Travis.

Finally she put the balloon in her closet. She couldn't pop it, but she couldn't stand to look at it anymore, either. It seemed like it wanted something from her, but she wasn't sure what.

The next morning, Evan got up early and went to work. Sheila stayed home with the dog, Baby Cakes, and she scrubbed the bathroom and rested, and then cleaned the kitchen and rested. She watched TV awhile, then found some trash bags and picked up the crushed beer cans from all around the yard. She found a rake and got up the trash that had blown into the bushes.

She sat on the doorsteps and smoked cigarettes and hoped he'd let her stay—for a while, anyway, until she figured out what to do next.

At lunchtime, she waved to the other trash boys who came back to the warehouse to have their sandwiches. They nudged Evan in the shoulder and whistled her way.

She didn't look that bad for her age, not really. Not from a distance. She had the remnants of a good tan, and Reggie always said she had great legs.

She drove Evan's pickup to the laundry and washed all his clothes and towels and sheets. He hadn't done laundry in a while, and being a trashman, he really needed to.

There was a bulletin board in the Laundromat, covered with rental advertisements and business cards. Over to one side there was a poster—HAVE YOU SEEN THIS CHILD?—with her daughter's xeroxed face. It'd been half-covered up with a yard sale announcement, but Sheila took that down.

The picture gave her the creeps. It seemed like Tessa Lee was watching her. For a while, she just stared back, daring the girl to accuse her of anything else. The whole time she moved the clothes from the washers to the dryers, she kept checking the picture to make sure the eyes weren't moving.

In black and white Tessa Lee looked younger than she'd seemed at Fantasies.

From her conch shell back at Fantasies, from inside her closet of mirrors, Sheila really couldn't see that well, especially during the day. At night, without a glare, she could see a lot better. It was all done with mirrors and cameras. They weren't seeing face-to-face. But Tessa Lee had come in the daytime, and the glare made her look older and hard. Maybe the camera'd reflected her wrong.

After a while, Sheila pulled down the poster, folded it up like a washrag, and hid it at the bottom of her basket.

While her clothes were drying, she went to the grocery and bought nail polish, an eye pencil, and mascara. She decided to color her hair and bought some dye, and since there was nobody around her in the checkout line, she asked the clerk, "Did they ever find that girl they were looking for? What was her name? Tessa Lee Birch?"

And the grocery clerk said, "Yeah, she come back. She'd just run away."

Sheila's fingers faltered as she counted out her change. So she was back at home, not with Reggie after all. Not in the conch shell dressed as the mermaid.

"Doesn't she live with her grandparents?" she chanced, and the clerk hollered out, "Hey Roger, does that girl who run away, Tessa Birch, does she live with her grandparents?" and a man who was stocking cans on the soup aisle said, "Lives with her grandma. Her granddaddy's dead. Why?"

"I just wondered," Sheila said quickly, quietly, and she took her bag and went back to fold the laundry.

She folded it all, even Evan's underwear. That must have been the bad thing that had happened. Her daddy'd died. Tessa Lee'd come to tell her. She stacked the laundry on top of Tessa Lee's picture.

Her daddy was dead. She counted in her mind. He wouldn't have been but sixty-five or sixty-six. She'd expected him to live at least ten more years, maybe twenty.

Her daddy'd been careful. Made her wear a life jacket on

the river, even though she knew how to swim. Made her stand back when he lit the grill in case the propane exploded. He wouldn't have died in an accident. It must have been his health.

She'd intended to wait until five to start drinking, but her daddy'd died, so she started at three.

Just one beer while she dyed her hair, another while she made a new skirt out of a pillowcase she found in the linen closet when she went to put away the towels. This one was trimmed in ducks.

Her daddy'd always liked ducks, and she could remember being a little girl and sitting with him in a boat and watching the ducks fly in when he called them with a special whistle. They landed like airplanes, skidded on the water before settling.

Then it was time for Evan, so she got a fresh beer and lit up the grill.

He looked surprised when he came in and found her there with her new brown hair pulled back in clips, with her eye makeup and her duck skirt.

"Are you wearing—?" he stopped and laughed. "Is that my—?"

She went to him and hugged him, pecked him on the cheek. He smelled like week-old shrimp.

She had the hamburgers ready by the time he got out of the shower.

He said he didn't recognize his house or her either one, and when she pouted, he said they both looked great, better than ever.

She didn't tell him that her daddy had died. She didn't want to seem needy. She hoped he'd let her stay awhile. It was their two-day anniversary, and she didn't want to be a buzz kill, so she didn't mention her daddy. Not at all.

Tessa Lee's nipple was crusty and red. When she put peroxide on it, it bubbled all around. Just watching it foam up made her feel sicker.

So she tried not to think about it.

She took the peroxide back to her room and kept it on her desk, along with the cotton balls. She cleaned her nipple every hour or two, to keep her infection from getting bad.

If the infection got bad, she could die, and then the undertaker might tell her granny that she had a nipple ring. Then her granny would think that she wasn't a virgin.

So she cleaned her nipple a lot.

The models of the fireflies sat on her desk and watched her whenever she put peroxide on her nipple. One of them plain, and one of them glowing. Like her nipples. One naked, one adorned.

She liked being adorned. She liked glowing. But she didn't think she liked it enough to die for it. She'd pierced the nipple right over her heart, and now when her heart beat, it stung.

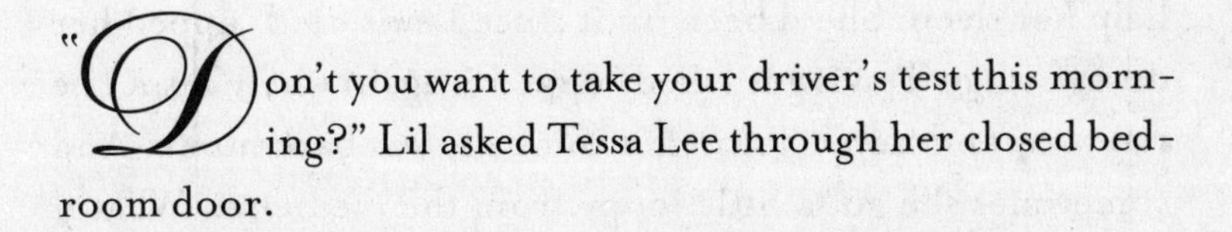

"Don't you want to take your driver's test this morning?" Lil asked Tessa Lee through her closed bedroom door.

"No thanks," Tessa Lee called back.

She'd been hiding in that bedroom for days. Sulking because Lil'd slapped her. Now she was punishing Lil, making her pay. She only came out to use the bathroom or to get something to eat or drink. Then she went right back in and closed the door.

"I'm sorry I hit you," Lil said. "I shouldn't have done that. Why don't you come on out here and let's talk?"

"I don't wanna talk right now," Tessa Lee said softly.

She didn't sound mad. She sounded like she'd been crying.

"You've only got a month 'til school starts back," Lil tried. "Don't you want to just run up there to the highway department and get that test behind you?"

"No ma'am," Tessa Lee said.

"What are you doing in there?"

"Nothing," Tessa Lee said.

"You sound stuffy. Do you have a cold?" Lil asked.

"No ma'am."

"I thought you wanted to drive a rickshaw this summer."

"I did," Tessa Lee whispered.

"Baby, what's wrong?" Lil asked.

"I'm a bad person," Tessa Lee said.

SHE KNEW Tessa Lee needed counseling, but what if she told the counselor about Lil's depressions? They didn't happen much, but Lil took medication to ease her nerves and help her sleep. She'd been on it since Lewis died, upped her dosage when Travis got killed, upped it again when Tessa Lee ran away and never downed it once she was back home. And sometimes she got a little loopy from the medicine. What if

Tessa Lee told the counselor about the time she missed her mouth with her fork? Or the time she sat down in the Cool-Whip bowl?

Lil was jittery, it was true, but she didn't think she was unfit to take care of Tessa Lee.

If Tessa Lee was suicidal, it'd be worth the risk. If she wasn't suicidal, then maybe not. She had to weigh out the risks and figure out what to do.

Tessa Lee had seen the accident. She'd seen Travis, after he'd been hit. Not up close, but from a distance. The mailman had grabbed her and pulled her away, held her kicking and screaming, wouldn't let her loose until the paramedics had taken his body and gone.

Lil hadn't been there. She'd been working that morning at the rec center, but it was almost time for her to get off. She'd promised Tessa Lee she'd take her for her driver's test, but Travis had gone off fishing, and she'd sent Tessa Lee to find him.

Tessa Lee'd been in a terrible mood. She'd been impossible to live with those last weeks of school and didn't even know it was because she couldn't stand for Amber to leave for the summer. Lil knew that, but not Tessa Lee. She'd snapped at Lil that morning and snapped at Travis, and according to all the witnesses, she was hollering for him long before she reached the lake, calling his name so loud all the witnesses had heard: the woman and her children who were on their way to feed the ducks, the jogger, the mailman, the trash boys. She was still across the street from the lake when Travis came running.

He ran right over the hill, straight for Tessa Lee, and never stopped to look for traffic. He ran across the street at the same time the trash truck passed. Who knows why he didn't stop and look? He knew better.

Like Tessa Lee stopping at a green light and going when it turned red. Those things just happened sometimes. Brains blinked out. Tessa Lee'd been lucky. There were no serious consequences when it happened to her.

Travis had caught a fish, still had it hanging from the fishing pole line. He had his little cup of worms in one hand, his pole in the other, the fish still attached, and he was running to show Tessa Lee when the trash truck hit him.

The cup of worms sprayed all over the sidewalk, the dark earth they'd been burrowing in tossed fine like coffee grounds, sown like seeds. That's what the witnesses said.

The fishing pole with the fish still attached went flying like a spear, and after the mailman let go of Tessa Lee, when they wouldn't let her close to Travis's body, she went to that fish, some twenty feet down the road and off by the ditch. That's where Hully said he found her, kneeling over a dead trout. He went to her as soon as he saw there was nothing he could do for Travis.

Now Tessa Lee thought she was a bad person. Lil knew better. Tessa Lee had a good heart.

When Lil was a girl, growing up with her aunt and uncle, she'd suffered her own tragedies. Her aunt had told her that God wouldn't give her anything she couldn't handle.

She'd remembered that, all through the years, and when times were hard, she prayed hard. Technically, she'd handled it all. She sure had.

But Tessa Lee didn't have her faith. Maybe God created counselors to help people like Tessa Lee. She had to get her into therapy.

Lil took half a pill and hoped it'd be enough. She creamed her face and went to bed with the yellow pages, looking up Christian counselors.

She was asleep when Tessa Lee came into her bedroom. "Granny," she said. "Wake up."

"What is it?" It was after midnight, pitch black outside, but the light from the hall let her see that Tessa Lee was crying.

"I'm sick," she said.

"Did you throw up?" Lil asked her. She sat up in a hurry, felt her forehead to see if she had a fever.

"No. I did something bad," Tessa Lee choked out.

"What'd you do?"

"Something bad."

"Well, tell me."

"I lied," she said. "When I told you I went to hear the wind ensemble."

"I know that, child." She reached for Tessa Lee, but just at that moment, Tessa Lee pulled up her T-shirt. And what *was* that in her nipple? An earring?

"Lord have mercy," Lil said. And she prayed in her mind, *help me, help me*.

"I'm sorry," Tessa Lee whimpered.

"Did you do it yourself?" Lil asked her.

"No," Tessa Lee admitted. "A professional did it, when I told you I was going to see the wind ensemble."

"Let's get some better light," Lil said.

As they walked to the bathroom together, Lil considered all the things she might say.

"I'm glad you went to a professional," she said.

"You are?"

"Yeah," Lil told her. "I'd hate to know you were stabbing into an apple or a potato," and they both laughed at that. It helped a little, to laugh. "Did Phillip get his pierced, too?"

"No," Tessa Lee said. "He waited outside."

"That's good, I reckon," Lil said, but again, she wasn't sure.

Her eyes were waking up then, seeing things better, and she looked at the ring in Tessa Lee's nipple and tried not to let her emotions get in the way. She tried to concentrate on concrete things: a nipple, an earring, the alcohol, the cotton swabs.

"My arm's all numb," Tessa Lee said.

"Really?" Lil asked. "Can you make a fist?"

Tessa Lee made a fine fist. She moved her fingers all around.

"I think it's probably gonna be okay," Lil said.

"But I'm ready to take it out," Tessa Lee replied and started crying again.

"Okay, then. Okay." Lil sat her down on the toilet. She got out her manicure kit, found tweezers in two different sizes. "How does this thing work?" Lil asked her, and Tessa Lee explained about the tension holding the ball.

"If this doesn't work, I can get my needle-nosed pliers," Lil joked, but Tessa Lee didn't laugh.

When the ball dropped away, it was easy to slip the hoop out. Lil tried not to think of it as Tessa Lee's nipple. She tried not to think of it as a nipple at all.

THE NEXT MORNING, Tessa Lee was up early, and Lil said, "How's it feel?"

And Tessa Lee said, "Fine."

"Fine? Let me see it."

"Granny, it's fine," Tessa Lee repeated. She poured herself some cereal and sat down at the bar to eat it, like nothing had happened at all.

"How's your arm?"

"Fine."

"No tingling?"

"It's better," Tessa Lee said.

Lil opened up the aspirin and handed her two, and Tessa Lee said, "What are these for?"

"Just take 'em and quit complaining," Lil replied.

THEY HADN'T BEEN to the water park all summer. Their season passes had been in Lil's bible all that time, unused.

Every year, Lil bought season passes in March, when they were half-price. She put them in Travis and Tessa Lee's Easter baskets, then collected them again and put them away for safekeeping until it came time to use them.

After Travis died, nobody even thought of going to the water park. But summer was almost over, and it was hot.

"I thought you had a craft class this morning," Tessa Lee said.

"It got canceled," Lil told her.

"When?" Tessa Lee asked.

"Right this minute," said Lil.

LIL HAD NEVER been on the waterslides before. In past summers, she'd always taken Travis and Tessa Lee and waited at the picnic tables while they went down the slides. She wore her bathing suit, of course, so she could get some sun, but she kept on her shorts to cover her thick thighs, and she hardly got wet at all. She took a magazine along, or a book she'd already read and didn't mind losing, and she flipped to the good parts while Travis and Tessa Lee squealed and splashed and whizzed around. She was there for purely practical reasons, handing out towels, rubbing suncreen on shoulders, keeping up with the flip-flops.

Without Travis, Tessa Lee would have to slide alone. So Lil followed her up the steps for the snake slides, and when Tessa Lee said, "You're coming, too?" Lil just nodded.

She'd always thought she'd embarrass the children if she went along with them, but there were plenty of parents and grandparents on the slides, wet and lumpy and laughing, some of them in cutoffs over their bathing suits. At least she hadn't worn cutoffs. She knew better than that, with a fashion-conscious teenager by her side.

Tessa Lee stopped at a stack of foam mats midway up the hill. "You sure you want to do this?" she asked, and Lil yanked the mat from her hand in answer. She led her to the line where people were waiting.

Tessa Lee laughed. Her eyes looked bright again, not dull and red like they had the past several days. She had her hair all pulled back in a thick braid, and Lil tucked a piece that had fallen behind her ear, then stopped herself before she embarrassed Tessa Lee.

"Which one do you wanna do first?" Tessa Lee asked. "The Water Moccasin, the Python, or the Anaconda?"

"Let's try the Python," Lil said, and for some reason Tessa Lee blushed. It was hard to figure the girl out. So off they went.

When Lil asked how to stay on the mat, Tessa Lee demonstrated the proper way to grip it, then said, "You don't have to do this, you know."

But Lil said, "I'm fine." She hoped she wouldn't get stuck. She could just picture them stopping the slide to unwedge her fat behind.

"You can walk back down if you want to, and meet me at the bottom," Tessa Lee offered.

Did she think Lil couldn't do it? Lil stepped right up to the lifeguard, who held down the mat while she sat. She was just turning back to give Tessa Lee a thumbs-up when—

Blast off! She was sliding down the Python, slithering from side to side, speeding with the current, gaining momentum. Faster and faster—she whooped into the curves, whipped up on the side of the slide and almost over!

Lil held onto her mat and cinched her eyes against all that rushing water, until the Python spit her out into a gurgling pool.

She wiped her face, shook the water from her hair, and looked back just in time to see Tessa Lee come whooshing down.

"Did you like it?" Tessa Lee asked when they'd climbed out.

"Yeah," Lil said. "Let's do it again."

They traded their mats for inner tubes and went down The Falls, spinning around, dipping underneath waterfalls, shooting over rapids. Tessa Lee went first that time, but Lil caught up and passed her, left Tessa Lee behind, laughing, calling for help.

At the next dip, Tessa Lee passed her again and grabbed Lil's arm, and they traveled together for a while, until water yanked them apart. They bounced along, and Lil was glad the inner tubes had handles. The inner tubes were easier than the mats.

When they got stuck a third time, spinning around in a current that wouldn't let them free, a man came rushing past, cocky in his blue tube, and without even thinking about it, Lil lunged for his toe. It was wet and hairy, but Lil held on.

"Granny!" Tessa Lee said.

But it was too late. Lil'd already spun the man around, got him stuck in the whirlpool as she freed herself and Tessa Lee. They shot down the next rapids, while the man was left behind.

"I can't believe you did that!" Tessa Lee squealed as they splashed to the next level. "He was a complete stranger!"

"Hurry," Lil said. "Before he catches up and drowns us."

They laughed so hard. Maybe they'd never laughed that hard before.

Sheila and the one-eyed dog walked all around Hully Sanders's Mobile City. They walked all through the woods in the transient section, over by the pool and the recreation center, through the playground, around the Laundromat and store, past the snack bar and the grocery, past the paddleboats, into the permanent sites.

The permanent sites had been there awhile. They were trailer shaped, but with additions. They were framed out like houses, with underpinning and mature shrubs and grassy yards around the lakes.

She was glad her parents hadn't wound up in a regular old trailer park. That's what she'd thought at first, when she learned where they'd retired.

Sheila knew the name of their street, but when she passed the marker, she didn't have the nerve to walk down it. She walked the street in front of it, then down the street behind. She looked at their house through other people's yards, from a distance.

Their trailer was blue, trimmed in gold, with awnings on the front windows that made it look like it had eyelashes. The dog saw some ducks in the yard and took off chasing them, but the ducks flew away.

"Baby Cakes," she called, but she didn't call loud. She didn't want anyone to hear her.

She imagined Tessa Lee coming to the door, looking out to see who was making all that racket, but nobody came. Nobody was home. The house was closed up tight. The lights were off.

A house that stands long enough becomes a body, takes on curves where angles used to be.

Their trailer-house watched Sheila. Maybe it winked at her. Maybe there was someone inside, the ghost of her daddy lifting the shade.

On the Lazy River, Lil and Tessa Lee sat in a double inner tube and meandered along.

Lil's butt filled her end of the tube, so she couldn't move around as easy as Tessa Lee, who had space to curl up on her side.

Tessa Lee closed her eyes and rested in the sun, and Lil watched her face, her pretty little face, thin like a bird's, freckled like a trout's. She watched her bangs go from dark and wet to dry and lighter as they bumped along the Lazy River. Her braid dragged through the water like a horseshoe crab's tail.

It'd have been perfect if Lewis and Travis were with them. Lil could picture them easily, just up ahead, Travis in his red swim trunks, his little brown body that looked like it'd been stuffed, his sweet round face. And Lewis in his pale blue shorts he always wore swimming, no shirt on, his chest hairs turning gray. She could picture him reaching out, pushing them off the wall, around a bend in the Lazy River.

He looked back and motioned for Lil to hurry.

"We're coming," she replied out loud.

Tessa Lee startled, sat up in the tube. "What'd you say?" she asked.

"Nothing," Lil said, checking herself. "I think you fell asleep."

"Nah," Tessa Lee answered. "I'm not asleep. I'm meditating." She closed her eyes again, and instead of getting off the Lazy River when they circled back around, Lil decided to ride once more and let Tessa Lee relax.

It was Lewis's line—he always said he was meditating when everybody knew he was sleeping. Sunday afternoons he'd be snoring in his chair, and Lil'd say, "Honey, go get in your bed," and he'd say, "I'm just meditating."

What she felt then was sweet longing. She wanted to pull Tessa Lee to her, but Tessa Lee was too old for that. She longed for Lewis, who had left her too soon.

His blood pressure had been fine. His cholesterol was in the normal-high range, but they hadn't even put him on medicine for it yet. They'd changed their diet, started baking what they used to fry. They walked every morning, but they stayed active in other ways, too. Having children kept you active. They all rode bikes. Lewis played Wiffle ball with Tessa Lee and Travis, took the floor mats out of his car to make the bases.

You don't have to be in bad shape to die. What better evidence of that than Travis. When your time comes, it just comes.

The time came for Lewis when he was in the very *act*. In the sack. With Lil.

It was the sort of thing that happens in movies, not real life. It was the sort of thing people joke about at wakes. She didn't want that to happen to Lewis.

So she rolled him over and covered him up. She kept a private vigil all that night, stroking his hair, watching him in the moonlight that came through the window. She didn't call the coroner 'til first light of day, didn't wake the children 'til the ambulance had gone.

In retrospect, it didn't seem like a bad way to die. Seemed like a pretty good way, just happened too soon for her tastes. She wished she had that chance, to die with Lewis there loving her as much as she loved him.

There weren't too many times that Lil indulged her

fantasies, let herself picture Lewis and Travis as if they were alive. But while she was at it, imagining them just up ahead, floating along together, she threw in another tube, one for Sheila, a life preserver. In her mind, she put Sheila in the middle, between her and Lewis, between Tessa Lee and Travis. She kept her there, between the dead and the living, kept her afloat.

Sheila rented a paddleboat and coaxed the one-eyed dog aboard. The dog whimpered as they left the shore but eventually settled down.

The paddleboats were made for two to pedal. The rudder was in the middle, and Sheila kept her hand on it and pedaled alone.

There were boys fishing from a boat in the distance. Maybe one of them was Travis. She counted in her mind. He'd be nine. Or was it ten? She pedaled closer so she could see the boys, but neither of them had Travis's coloring.

There was an egret at the murky water's edge, fishing for lunch. Either a cow egret or a snowy egret, she didn't know which. She couldn't remember which was bigger, or how big egrets got.

She pictured her daddy pedaling beside her, sitting with her in the yellow plastic boat. He hadn't been a man of many words, really. He left most of the talking to her momma. He never said much, just agreed with whatever. She hadn't really missed him before, but that felt different now that he was dead.

She pedaled around reeds, around a bend in the lake, and after a time, she broke into a huddle of ducks. Baby Cakes stood up and started barking.

"Go on, then," she teased the dog. "Get in." But this dog was afraid of water. Maybe he couldn't swim. So he stood there barking in the back of the boat, and some of the ducks flew away.

The water was dark and muddy. She couldn't tell what was down there, beneath her yellow plastic boat. Anything could be down there.

She pedaled the boat to the blue trailer with the golden awnings for eyes. She pedaled up behind it where it couldn't see her, pedaled all the way to the bank, slapping at mosquitoes and horseflies. As they got close to land, Baby Cakes jumped off, and his white legs sunk in the mud. The mud sucked against him when he pulled his legs out.

"Baby Cakes," she called, but he dug himself out and took off, and so she jumped off the paddleboat to go get him.

Her legs sunk, too, in the mud. It felt like there was something in the mud holding onto her legs, trying to pull her down. She worked to loosen one foot, and when it slurped free, water rushed up to fill the hole she'd left there.

Each step was a little bit firmer, but she lost her flip-flops beside that lake. She left them in the mud when she crawled out and into her momma's yard, muddy past her knees.

"Baby Cakes," she called as loud as she dared, but the dog was gone.

Sheila didn't get up close to the house. She stayed far back by the property line, but since there was a hose out beside the shed, she used it to wash off her hands and her legs and feet.

"Baby Cakes," she called softly, but the dog didn't come.

From a distance, she looked at the windows of her momma's house, to see what she could see. But the sun made a glare, and she couldn't see inside them from where she stood.

It looked like a nice yard for children, though. There was a swing, and a basketball hoop, some bikes by the deck. Nothing familiar, but why should anything be familiar?

For some reason, she wanted to write her name there, in the wet dirt next to where the hose coiled up. She picked up a stick, wrote the "S" and the "H." But instead of an "E," she made another "H," then another. Shhh. That's what her note said.

Shhh.

Tessa Lee and Lil ate their lunch by the logroll pool and watched children Travis's age try to leap up onto the log and roll each other off. It was Travis's favorite part of the water park. He could spend all day in the logroll pool. He had a hard time climbing up sometimes, because he was plump and the log sat up high. But once he made it on top, he was good. His legs were short, and he had better balance than most children.

One boy reigned supreme over the log. Others came up to challenge him, but again and again, he kept his balance, stayed on when they fell off.

On either end, children lined up to take their turns.

"Travis could beat him," Lil said.

"Travis would've rolled him off a hundred times by now," Tessa Lee agreed.

WHEN THEY'D BEEN through slides and spouts, through six cycles of the wave pool, when they'd eaten their Dippin' Dots, when the sunscreen had washed into the cracks and creases of their arms, they gathered their things for the ride back home.

Tessa Lee drove.

"What was your favorite part of the day?" Lil asked her.

"I don't know," Tessa Lee said. "Maybe the Lazy River."

"Huh," Lil said. "I thought you'd like the faster rides better."

"I like 'em fast, too," Tessa Lee replied.

A song she loved came on the radio, so she turned it up and sang along awhile. Then she turned down the volume and asked, "Did you have a favorite part?"

"Definitely," Lil said. "I was on the Anaconda, sliding on my mat, and then I whooshed up over the side and landed on the Water Moccasin."

"You did?" Tessa Lee exclaimed. "You didn't tell me!"

"Well," Lil said, "it was a little embarrassing because I landed right on the mat with a fellow I didn't know."

"You're kidding!"

"Watch the road, baby," Lil said. "I had to share his mat, 'cause I'd left mine back on the Python."

"I thought you said you were on the Anaconda."

"Technicalities," Lil dismissed.

"Granny!" Tessa Lee said.

"That was definitely my favorite part," Lil teased.

WHEN THEY WERE just a few blocks from the highway department, Lil said, "Don't you want to try for your license before we go home?"

Tessa Lee made up her excuses, of course. It was too late. She was too wet. She hadn't had time to prepare.

"Nonsense," Lil said. "You'll do better if you don't give yourself time to worry. You know how to drive."

Fifty minutes later, Tessa Lee borrowed Lil's compact to get the shine off her face before she posed for her picture. She'd have to carry that picture around until she was twenty-one and legal. She shook her hair out of the braid and let it fall down past her shoulders, so she'd look older.

"Am I okay?" she asked Lil.

"Sure you are," Lil told her.

The first thing anyone would notice when they looked at Tessa Lee's driver's license would be her smile. Or maybe it was just that when Lil looked at it, her smile was the only thing that mattered.

Tessa Lee was queen of the rickshaws. She was a natural. She'd been living in Hully Sanders's Mobile City long enough to know every road, even the dead ends and cross-streets that nobody traveled much unless they lived there.

She was in good shape, and the rickshaws weren't hard to pedal, anyway.

She had a walkie-talkie that clipped onto her shorts, khaki shorts for rickshaw driving. She had a helmet that made her hair all sweaty and flat, but all the drivers had to wear them. It was company policy. She had a nametag to pin to her navy blue polo. On one side the shirt said "Hully Sanders's Mobile City" with the embroidered logo of Hully's face leaning out of a trailer window, and on the other side her nametag read, "Tessaleigh Birch." Hully'd ordered it awhile back and had it ready for her to put on the day she signed her employment agreement. But he'd spelled it wrong.

Tessa Lee didn't care.

The first day she had to prove herself before Hully's daughter-in-law Linda would put her on the schedule. She became Hully's private driver. She drove him from the office to the rec building and waited while he made payroll. Then she drove him to Bathhouse #3 in the transient section, where some plumbers were working on a leak.

She was careful to come to complete stops, and after the first few blocks, she figured out exactly where to center the rickshaw in the lane, so that when she turned, she didn't get too close to the curb or cross the yellow line on the other side.

"You're doing great," Hully told her when she pulled up next to the bathhouse. "This shouldn't take me more than ten or fifteen minutes, but feel free to walk around. I'll call you when I'm done."

She went to the bathroom on the women's side to check on her nipple. It didn't hurt at all, and she could hardly even see the hole anymore. She hoped it didn't go away completely, before she had a chance to show Amber.

She was back on the rickshaw long before Hully was through.

She backpedaled and listened to the gears click, and she fiddled around with the gears. Then she got off and adjusted the canopy that riders could use to keep the sun or the rain off their heads. It clicked to four different settings, from almost totally open to almost totally private.

The next place Hully needed to go was the warehouse back by the trash bins.

"Now you don't have to take me back there, if it'll upset you."

"It's okay," Tessa Lee said.

"That truck from your brother's accident—it's not there."

"Okay," Tessa Lee said, but she wished he hadn't brought it up. She didn't like to think about it.

She wished Travis could see her on the rickshaw, though. She wished she could give him a ride.

When they got back to the warehouse, Tessa Lee kept her head down. It wasn't the trash truck she didn't want to see. It was the men who rode it, the men who'd been there when it happened.

So she pulled the rickshaw back behind a big hill of crushed up clamshells, and she kept her head down until a dog came up, a white dog with just one eye. It licked her hand and went trotting off, and then Hully came back and patted her shoulder and asked to be driven to the office.

When they got to the office, he talked to Tessa Lee about tire pressure, about lubricating the chains, about day-to-day maintenance for rickshaws.

"You did real good," he said. "And I'm pleased to have you as an employee." He shook her hand in front of all the women working in the office.

"Put her on for bingo," he told Linda. "Or the square dance or wherever you need her. She's ready to roll."

Lil's class had just started. It was a day for decorating baskets. She supplied the bare baskets and all the ribbon and trimmings anyone could imagine. She had a heap of suggestions ready for them. If they wanted to make going-away baskets for college students, she had ribbons for all the universities in the nearby states. She had ribbons with flowers and ribbons with paisleys for wedding gifts or birthdays, ribbons with tiny handprints or the characters from Pooh Bear if they wanted to decorate a basket for a baby shower. She even had rainbow ribbons, which reminded her of summer days and hot air balloons. But she'd found out the rainbow was a symbol of gay and lesbian liberation, and

Lord have mercy, if somebody wanted to liberate them with a basket, she had a ribbon for that, too.

The women were sifting through ribbons while the hot-glue guns heated. They were looking at Lil's demos and exchanging ideas when someone peeked in, stuck her head through the classroom door in the back.

Lil puzzled over her sign-up sheet. She had the right number of people there, but she could always fit one more. She had an extra basket back in the van, and her own glue gun for someone to use.

"Are you here for the basket class?" she called. She smiled at the woman, who was wearing a baseball cap pulled down hard on her head. Her short brown hair curled from beneath it. "Come on in, if you want to make one."

But the woman shook her head, gave a quick wave, backed away. There was something about her. Something strange.

Lil went to the window and watched her walking off, down the street, past the pool. Something about the way she walked.

She didn't want to think it could be Sheila. She was scared to death she might be right, and what would she do then?

During her first week on the job, Tessa Lee pedaled a hundred miles, at least a hundred miles. The second week, she pedaled even more. Her legs felt almost robotic. The muscles in her thighs were tight as coils.

The dispatcher, who was really just Hully's daughter-in-law, would call her up on the walkie-talkie and tell her to go to 1803 Snapper Lane and pick up the Johnson twins and take them to the arcade. And when Tessa Lee got them there, she'd just wait until someone at the arcade came out and asked to be taken to the rec center, or until Linda called again and sent her to the restaurant.

Some of the house numbers were big and gold and shiny. Others were little black stickers glued right to the vinyl on the side. She went to one trailer where the house number was written in Magic Marker on the back of a paper plate, just nailed up like that. At that house, six people tried to fit into her rickshaw. They sat in one another's laps and weighed down the back so that Tessa Lee had to go very slow. But they were singing gospel songs and didn't even notice.

One woman from over in the transient section had a colicky baby who cried all the time. But the baby hushed when he rode on the rickshaw, and so Tessa Lee would pick them up every day and take them for a ride so the baby could sleep.

Sometimes when people didn't need rides, the staff at Hully Sanders's Mobile City used the rickshaw drivers to do their errands. Once she was dispatched to the pool house to pick up some stabilizer and take it back to the lifeguard, who'd run out. Once she pedaled ten bags of mulch from the greenhouse to the flowerbeds next to the snack bar, where the gardeners unloaded it.

She was on the clock, so she couldn't complain too much. But the gardeners and lifeguards didn't tip. Neither did the gospel singers or the kids who went to the arcade.

She never minded picking up the take-out orders from the restaurant and delivering them. She almost always got good tips when she delivered food. Sometimes she got 10 percent of the bill, just like she'd been their waitress.

Of all the regular rickshaw riders, the square dancers tipped the best. So she liked working Thursday and Saturday nights. She liked the old men in their checkered shirts and the old women in their ruffly skirts. Before he'd died, her Pop-Pop had called the square dances, and she and Travis had always do-si-doed together because they were usually the only kids there.

The best and worst thing about driving a rickshaw was having so much private time in her head. She often thought about her momma, especially when she was pedaling the colicky baby around.

She thought a lot about the man who pierced her, too. Sometimes when thoughts of her momma made her sad, she'd switch to thoughts of that man, let herself remember how he rubbed her nipples with his thumbs. The memory gave her chills, made the wind catch in her throat.

And when she couldn't stand to think of that, either, she thought about geometry.

It'd been her favorite subject in school the year before.

She thought about the lines she made, riding on her rickshaw, how she pedaled a triangle, intersected it with a rhombus. She thought about curves and angles and degrees. She tried to picture in her mind what sort of shape she'd pedaled, moving from place to place.

It made a difference, whether she returned along the path she'd already taken or whether she swung out wide and took a different route. It made a difference if it was shady or sunny when she passed a place, because that darkened or lit up her pattern.

She'd had a Spirograph once, when she was seven. It'd been left behind in South Hibiscus the day before she lost her momma. She'd gotten it for her birthday, and her momma had shown her how to use it, how to put the plastic disks inside the larger circle, put the tip of her pen inside a tiny hole in the disk, and trace it around, making shapes in all colors.

Her favorite part was Spirographing on top of shapes she'd already made, making bigger shapes, more intricate shapes, more colorful shapes that touched one another, then went off in their own directions.

She drove her rickshaw everywhere, in service to geometry. There was no place she wouldn't go, because every destination made a new line in that day's shape.

The pictures were so complicated, like pictures of the solar system.

Sometimes she thought about everyone else's geometry, too, how the woman and her colicky baby had a whole different picture. The square dancers intersected her picture for only ten minutes a week, but then when they got home, the man took a bath, while the woman went out for a walk with the dog, and their two shapes exploded in different directions and met back in their bed each night.

Tessa Lee didn't even know them, not really, but they were still connected. And it mattered. It was really the only thing that mattered, the connections, and some of them you couldn't even see.

She thought of Amber's geometry, out there in West Virginia, farther away than the clouds. Amber was making her own Spirographs, but one day soon, she'd make a straight line for Tessa Lee, and then they'd intersect again, until next summer.

She thought of Travis and Pop-Pop in their caskets underground and hoped they were really dead and not trapped there, making little underground scribbles, not able to get out of their containers.

She thought of her tiny momma in her tiny conch shell, making tiny circles in her tiny little place. Even though she knew her momma wasn't in the conch shell, Tessa Lee kept her there in her mind.

There was nowhere else to put her.

It was almost too much to think about—the geometry of whole lives. If she drew her lines in colors, hers in blue, her momma's in orange, Travis's in green, then her beginning was blue and orange and green. But then the orange went away, and the yellow and red came in. And then there was no more yellow, and then there was no more green. Now her colors were all red and blue, except for one day when she had a tiny dot of orange, so quick it almost didn't count. But it had happened, the orange blip.

Like with fireflies. Each night, as she pedaled home, she watched the fireflies flicker and glow. They crossed the road in front of her, flashing their taillights every once in a while. They had a geometry, too, like a dot-to-dot coloring book. You could plot them on graph paper and draw the line of their lives, but you couldn't account for their mystery, why in some moments they burned and in some moments they went dark.

They got drunk at the restaurant, too drunk to drive back home. Evan's truck had a Breathalyzer in it and wouldn't crank unless you breathed into it. Most times they could find somebody sober, one of Evan's friends or coworkers, to come breathe in it and crank the truck. Most times they weren't so drunk they couldn't make it home, and everybody knew how picky those Breathalyzers were, anyway. It didn't necessarily mean you were drunk. You could trip it if you'd just gargled with mouthwash.

But that night, there were only strangers around, strait-laced people who looked like they'd call the cops on you, so Evan said they'd have to walk, and then Sheila suggested they wave down one of those little bicycle carriages.

They stood out by the road for five minutes and were just about to start walking when a carriage came by, and Sheila whooped and waved her arms around, and Evan hollered, "Hey taxi, hey taxi!"

It turned out that the boy who was driving knew Evan.

"This is my little cousin Leo," Evan said. He tried to get Leo to blow into his Breathalyzer so they could drive home, but Sheila said no, she wanted to ride in the carriage.

"Ride us awhile," Evan agreed, "and then we'll come back and crank my truck."

First, Leo took them to the store to get some strawberry wine. As they were leaving, they pulled out the canopy, even though it wasn't raining, and Evan said, "Take us down the darkest roads you know."

Leo grinned, and off they went, drinking strawberry wine and making out in the back. Evan had his hand under Sheila's top when the carriage slowed down, then stopped.

"What's up?" Evan said, and when Sheila peeked out, she could see another bicycle carriage, with a girl driving, a face she recognized.

She turned into Evan's collar and busied herself kissing him there. It was dark and she'd dyed her hair, and the girl didn't know she'd followed her home. She didn't want her to know, not yet.

"Linda's trying to find you," the girl said to Leo. "She's got people waiting for a ride home from bingo."

"Can you go get 'em for me?" Leo asked. "I've got a couple. They're busy, if you know what I mean . . ."

"God," the girl said and laughed. "I hope they give you a good tip."

"Please?" Leo asked.

"I'm supposed to be off now," she complained. "But okay."

"I owe you one," Leo said, and then he started pedaling again, slow at first, then faster.

LEO DROPPED them off later at Evan's truck. There were people around, so they acted at first like Leo was going to drive. He sat behind the wheel, with Evan in the middle and Sheila beside him. He breathed into the Breathalyzer and cranked the truck, then opened the door and stepped down.

"Thank you, man," Evan said.

"No problem," Leo replied.

"See here," Evan continued. "Don't tell nobody . . ."

"I won't," Leo said quickly.

"'Cause they wouldn't understand, if they knew," Evan said.

"Wouldn't understand what?" Sheila asked.

"That's for sure," Leo said.

"Wouldn't understand what?" Sheila repeated.

"Nothing, honey," Evan replied, and he reached over and patted her thigh, and he and Leo both laughed.

Evan was ripped. They were lucky it was late. They were lucky they didn't have far to go. He weaved his way to the back of the mobile home park and drove his truck right up to the door. He put out one of his headlights on the edge of the doorsteps.

Sheila wouldn't drop it. "What were you talking with that boy about?"

"Nothing. Shut up," he said. "I'm ready to go to bed."

"You ashamed of me?" she asked.

"No, I'm not ashamed of you."

She had the strawberry wine in her hand, and she drained it.

"Don't tell me you're not ashamed of me," she said.

"It ain't about you," Evan insisted. "It's just that my wife, she's been telling people she might want to give it another chance, and if people knew . . ."

"Your wife?"

"She left me," Evan said, "A few months back. But she wants to give it another try."

The bottle in Sheila's hand was cool and smooth. She imagined what it would feel like cracking against Evan's skull. There'd be blood everywhere and glass to sweep up. She didn't want the dog to step in the glass, embed it in his paws.

"She went back to Wisconsin," he said. "But it gets cold there in the winter."

Sheila put down the bottle before she swung it by accident.

"Well, I guess there won't be room for me. When your *wife* comes home."

"No," Evan said. "But sooner or later, you'd have to go, anyway."

"How come?" Sheila asked. She dared him to say it.

Evan laughed and shook his head. "It wouldn't work out for us," Evan said. "I mean, I love you and everything, but you're, like, you're only a couple years younger than my mom."

SHE'D INTENDED TO leave that very same night. She didn't want to sleep with him. But since he passed out in the yard, anyway, she slept in the bed, with the one-eyed dog she'd grown so fond of.

She didn't leave the next day, either, because when she woke up, Evan had gone to work on the trash truck, and her head hurt so much that she just kept drinking.

She could call Reggie, tell him she'd been sick. It was worth a try. If he was a jerk, she didn't have to tell him where she was.

She knew she could get hired dancing at a go-go club if she had to.

She might even hitch a ride out to Vegas. Had she ever been to Vegas? She wasn't sure, but she thought she might have been once, a long time ago.

When the beer was gone, she found a bottle in the cabinet underneath the kitchen sink.

It wasn't that she didn't want to strip. She just didn't want to be the low man down. That's why she'd stayed with Reggie so long, 'cause she was the diva at Fantasies. She didn't want to go back to being on the bottom. She was too old to put up with attitudes.

Evan didn't return until late. He'd been out drinking with the trash truck boys, and when he saw her on the couch, he turned around and left again. He slammed the door hard, and Sheila sat there watching the chain swing for a long time before it stopped.

When he came back, he said, "I'm sorry, but you're gonna have to go somewhere else."

"I'm going," Sheila said. "Can you give me a lift?"

"Where to?" Evan asked.

"That bar where you found me?" Sheila suggested.

He said he would, but they couldn't crank the truck. So Sheila left on foot.

IT WAS LATE at night, and the lights were out all around Hully Sanders's Mobile City. The lights were out in her momma's house, so she didn't ring the doorbell.

She went out to the shed behind the house. The door wasn't locked, and she cracked it just enough to squeeze through. Then she passed out on a trash bag full of cattails.

Lil had kept a few of Sheila's things—not out in the open, because she didn't want to be forced to think of her. But she had a drawer in her bureau where she kept the cards Sheila'd made her for Mother's Day, faded construction paper laced together with yarn. She'd kept the story she wrote about the frog who befriended the fly and then went on a food strike. She'd kept her gym outfit from middle school, for some reason, and the dance costume she wore the year they dressed up like kittens. She had her school pictures still in their frames. Her report cards. Her old retainer from right after she got her braces off.

And she'd kept the two-room tent.

It was a good thing.

"You can't stay here," Lil said to her. "It'll just confuse Tessa Lee."

"I didn't want—" Sheila said. "I didn't expect—"

"I'll call Hully," Lil said. "We'll put that tent up in the transient section 'til we figure out what to do."

She couldn't have predicted what it would be like, to see Sheila up close, to touch her again. She was more of a stranger than Lil could have imagined, and she smelled terrible, like vomit and cigarette butts. Her eyes were bloodshot, and those teeth that Lil and Lewis had spent thousands of dollars straightening were gone completely, replaced with a set George Washington would've been ashamed to wear. She was a bag of bones, and Lil couldn't have anticipated how the sorrow would wash through her when she wrapped her arms around the negligence that was her daughter.

"Are you sick or just drunk?" Lil asked.

"Sick and drunk both," Sheila slurred.

She was a stranger, and at the same time, it was like no time had passed at all.

"High, too?"

"Just drunk," Sheila said.

"That's good, I reckon," Lil said. "Let's start with a shower, and I'll fix you something to eat." She led her down the hallway, where pictures of Travis and Tessa Lee lined the walls.

Sheila didn't even look at them, and it made Lil want to shake her. How could she not even look? Drunk, sick, high—it didn't matter. You'd think she'd turn her head to look at the pictures.

There was that old saying going through her head again: "God won't give you anything you can't handle." Her aunt had said that all the time. God had given her aunt eleven children of her own, plus four or five nieces and nephews to raise, and it was true she'd handled them, but *how,* Lil couldn't say. Surely her aunt had had troubles with one or two—out of eleven. One of them must have turned out to be a drunk or a drug addict. And her aunt survived.

Help me, she prayed. *Help me now.*

She always prayed when she needed help. Less often when things were easy. More "Help me's" than "Thank you's." So she said "Thank you," too. *Thank you, Lord, for this chance to see Sheila again. Thank you, Lord, for sending Tessa Lee to work early today.*

What if Tessa Lee'd been home? What if she'd found her? She could strangle Sheila, for jeopardizing everything, again.

Lil turned on the water, got it hot, got a clean towel from the linen closet.

Thank you, Lord, for helping me not strangle Sheila.

It looked like Sheila'd already been strangled a time or two. She undressed there on the bathroom rug, dropped her nasty clothes and stepped right out of them like she had no modesty at all.

Seeing her body softened Lil's aggression. Her body

looked worn out. In worse shape than Lil's. If they went to the water park, Lil'd be embarrassed to be seen with her. There were bruises and scars, too many ribs, and bones down low too private to stick out like that. More imperfections than anybody could keep up with.

And there was a rash streaked around her side.

"You got shingles," Lil said.

"Yeah, God."

"I know a trick for that," Lil said. "Your aunt Pat had 'em. When you get out of the shower, splash 'em with Listerine. It'll make the hurting go away. It's in the cabinet."

While Sheila was cleaning up, Lil made her some grits, buttery and thick like always. She swallowed her pride and called Hully, who said there were nice wooded sites available in the part of the mobile city where Tessa Lee had little reason to go, and he'd be over in a little bit.

"Momma," Sheila said when she was clean. "You got anything I can wear?" and for whatever reason, instead of loaning her something of her own, Lil went into Tessa Lee's bedroom and got that lightning bug housecoat.

Sheila held it up and shook her head. "I don't think I can wear this," she said.

"Put it on," Lil replied. "You got no choice."

THE TENT HAD belonged to Travis. He didn't know it for many years because Lil had put the tent away. She didn't remember it herself until the summer after Lewis died, and Travis was silent, hidden in the maze of his grief.

That was the summer Tessa Lee helped the oil painter.

She left on her bike and spent whole days away, and Lil was alone with Travis.

At some point that summer, when Lil was clearing out Lewis's belongings, giving his shoes and trousers to Goodwill, packing his shirts for Rosie Jo's son who had the same neck size, she'd found the tent in the back of a closet.

She'd almost thrown it out, but instead, she and Travis went into the backyard and set it up together.

The tent had little pockets along the edges for storing small things. Lil had found the wrapper from a rubber in there. Not the rubber itself, thank the Lord, just the paper it'd come in. It made her furious with Sheila all over again, to think she'd be doing that in the tent with her children nearby, two-room tent or not.

Then Travis found a piece of gum in a pocket and opened it up and started chewing. But it was nicotine gum, and he made a face and spit it out. It tickled Lil and helped her forgive Sheila a little. She was trying to quit smoking. That told her something she hadn't known about Sheila, something positive.

Travis loved the tent and played inside it, went there to read and take his naps each afternoon. He didn't remember being left in that tent, but Tessa Lee wouldn't get near it. She wouldn't even walk in the backyard until they took it down that fall when a tropical storm blew through.

IF LIL WAS giving the tent back to Sheila, it seemed right to return the lightning bug housecoat, too. It was the only other thing she'd left—besides her children.

Sheila looked confused as she put it on. She sat at the table and stirred around in her grits. She looked like a drowned woman, watery and pale, like she'd just crawled out of the lake. "I'm sorry 'bout Daddy," she said.

"I wanted to tell you," Lil replied. "But I didn't have a way—"

"What happened?"

"Heart attack," Lil told her, looking out the window, making sure Tessa Lee didn't stop back by the house. Sometimes she came in to use the bathroom or to get a glass of juice.

"You always said he'd go that way," Sheila replied. "Remember?"

"It wasn't how I thought," Lil said. "I wasn't right about everything." She poured herself a cup of coffee, though caffeine was probably the last thing she needed. "He didn't suffer," she said.

"That's good," Sheila replied. "They doing okay? The kids?"

And Lil realized she didn't know.

What was she doing there, if she didn't know?

"Travis's dead," Lil said, before she had a chance to say it different. She said it loud, like Sheila'd killed him herself.

HULLY PICKED a spot not far from a bathhouse, a wooded site where the shade would help with the heat. He and Lil pitched the tent together while Sheila fiddled with the tarp, then flopped down at a picnic table and cried into her hands.

"See here," Hully said. "It's too late for all them tears. What's done is done."

Sheila nodded, but she didn't get up.

"You come from good people," he said. "I've known your momma a long time. Knew your daddy, too. You sober up, and I'll give you a job."

Sheila kept on crying, but she nodded her head.

"Thank you, Hully," Lil said.

"If you don't sober up, you'll have to go," Hully told her. Then he turned to Lil and said, "What else do you need?"

Lil couldn't think of anything. She couldn't think at all. He patted Lil's back and let his hand sit on her shoulder for a long moment.

"I got a little propane stove," he said to Sheila. "I'll bring it out here after awhile, and you can use it."

WHEN HULLY was gone, Lil sat with Sheila at the picnic table. They didn't talk for the longest time. Lil didn't know what to say. She wanted to go get her some things for her campsite—a pillow and sleeping bag, a fan and a cooler, but she was scared that when she returned, Sheila wouldn't be there. What if twenty more years passed before she saw her again? One of them might be dead by then. This could be the very last time.

So she sat there with her beneath a big oak tree. Sheila's hands were so thin, but the veins beneath the skin looked huge and blue. They looked older than her own hands, with bigger knuckles. Or maybe the knuckles just seemed more pronounced on those bony hands. They reminded her of her own momma's hands. Her momma had died when she was five or six. She hadn't thought of her hands since.

She watched Sheila flatten her long fingers against the wooden picnic table, trying to keep them from trembling. Lil made a note to herself to bring back her fingernail polish remover, her file, and fresh nail color. It would help Sheila's feelings, to have her nails done nice, like when she was a little girl and hadn't practiced enough to keep the tiny brush from bumping into her cuticles.

Sheila kept sniffing, then crying quietly. She didn't ask the questions Lil expected, and Lil was glad, in a way, because she felt overrun by feelings already.

She tried to use her old tactics to handle all her feelings, to concentrate on concrete things: a daughter, her fingers, an acorn, a breeze. But nothing was clear-cut, and nothing was simple. She was like an untended garden inside, with onions overtaken by watermelons, peppers crowded out by tomatoes, cucumbers buried beneath squash, rotting on the vines. She was a jumble—messy and wet, decomposing and blooming at the same instant.

After a while, Sheila got up and walked off to the bathhouse. Lil watched that crazy housecoat disappear through the door and thought for sure she'd never see it again. Sheila would leave out the back. Lil would sit there forever, on a wooden bench that needed to be sanded, just waiting.

But in a little bit, she returned, with some toilet paper in her hands, and she sat again with Lil, this time on the same side of the table instead of across.

"I'm sorry, Momma," she said.

"I'm sorry, too."

"I shouldn't have left 'em," she said and sucked her lips inside her mouth.

"No," Lil said. "You shouldn't have."

It was all entirely obvious. Then Lil added, "But what you did to them wasn't all that different from what I did to you, I reckon."

Sheila looked up quickly, stricken, said "Don't say that, Momma. You never left me. You took good care of me."

"What?" Lil said and laughed. "Now you wanna give me the good-mother award?" and Sheila smiled shyly at her. "I took good care of your body," Lil said. "But too many times I left your heart stranded. I know that now." Her voice choked out.

Sheila dissolved then, into loud cries, louder than any sound Lil would expect to come from that brittle body. She let Lil hug her, and it seemed to Lil that she warmed up some, there in her arms, that her skin and muscles resuscitated a little.

Lil held her as long as she could stand it. Then she had to get home. She had to concentrate on concrete things. Tessa Lee'd be back for lunch, and she didn't want her to use the toilet until she'd scrubbed it down with bleach. The bathtub, too. Who knew where Sheila'd been or what diseases she'd picked up?

HULLY FOUND Tessa Lee outside the snack bar where she was waiting for two old ladies to get their scoops of minty ice cream. She'd taken them for ice cream before, and wiped up the drips from the rickshaw floorboards after she'd deposited them at their mobile home.

"You go on home to your granny," Hully told her. "I'll drive the Ambrose sisters back."

Tessa Lee knew something bad had happened for Hully to offer such a thing. He couldn't drive a rickshaw. He had corroded knees. He'd already had surgery on them both, and they were always stiff. Whenever he got out of his truck, he walked like the Tin Man until his knees loosened up. It looked like his knees didn't know how to bend.

"What's wrong?" she asked Hully. "Is Granny sick?"

"No," he said.

But she could feel panic rising up from her belly, hot in her belly, like she'd swallowed a fist and now it wanted to fight. "Is she hurt? Where is she?" Tessa Lee asked.

"She's back home by now, I reckon," he said. "Go see about her. She's just having a hard day. Don't need to be alone."

Tessa Lee took off running fast. She was halfway there before she noticed that she still had on her helmet. She unbuckled it and pulled it from her head and kept on running without even stopping to fluff out her hair.

Hully hadn't looked her in the eyes the whole time. Something bad had happened.

She was panting, and her spit thickened in the back of her throat, clabbered there, and her legs burned, but she didn't stop. She passed Leo's rickshaw and some kids she knew who worked at the paddleboats, but she didn't even slow down. She tried to comfort herself with reasonable thoughts: if her granny was dead, Hully'd have driven her to the funeral home. If her granny was sick, he'd have taken her to the doctor.

When she got to the trailer, nobody was home. The door was left wide open, but her granny's van was gone. She hollered out to nobody at all. Then she ran to Rosie Jo's.

"I don't know a thing," Rosie Jo said. "She went somewhere with Hully and some woman an hour or two ago. I watched 'em out my kitchen window, but I don't know where they went."

"Can I borrow your car?" Tessa Lee asked her, and Rosie Jo looked worried, and Tessa Lee said, "I got my license!" and pulled it out to show her.

But Rosie Jo was already trading her yard shoes for sandals. "I'll drive you," she said. "Where to?"

Tessa Lee didn't know. "The hospital, I guess."

"If she was sick, she would've called me," Rosie Jo insisted. "Maybe they just went to the grocery store."

"What did the woman look like?" Tessa Lee asked.

"I didn't see her too good," Rosie Jo replied and put the car in drive.

They hadn't made it to the stop sign at the end of the street when Lil pulled in. She came around the corner doing forty.

Tessa Lee jumped out of the car before Rosie Jo had even stopped, running behind the white van, hollering "Granny! Granny! What's the matter?"

Sheila crawled into the two-room tent. It was roomy for a tent, but still cramped. Sitting up, her head almost touched the ceiling, so she stretched out on the ground there and wondered why her momma and Hully Sanders had set up the tent on top of tree roots.

She crossed her arms over her chest, the folds from the sleeves of the firefly cloak gathered over her belly. She rested in the burial position.

Her boy was dead. The last time she'd seen him, he'd

been sleeping in that tent, huddled next to his sister beneath that same cloak. Now he was gone.

She couldn't think about it. She kept herself still. She kept her eyes closed and let her tears run into her ears and puddle there.

She'd meant to come back and get them. She'd always planned to, when she made enough money, got a good job, got settled down in a good school district, got cleaned up.

Her nose was running and she sniffed it back in. Hold it all in. Keep it all in. She didn't even want to know how Travis had died. She could only handle just this much.

She wiped her face with the sleeves of the cloak, pushed the wetness away and let her face tighten beneath the lingering salt.

The cloak had been a gift. There'd been a man she'd loved, and with him, things had been different. She'd felt different when she was with him.

Before him and after him, sex was sex. Not hard, but not easy, either, like vacuuming or cleaning the toilet, a chore, a bore, just something that had to be done. She'd made money from sex, sure, but then it was a job. Mundane. Like filing.

But once, she'd been in love. It was completely different then.

One night after they'd made love, she told him he made her feel like she was full of fireflies, lighting up and blinking in the dark. Before it'd seemed dark all the time inside her. And then there was a glowing.

He held her close, after that, and they made love again. Every flicker was a tiny explosion, magical, sensational.

When he gave her the firefly cloak, he apologized for it.

He thought it was hideous, but he wanted her to have something with fireflies on it, and it was all he could find. There were no firefly bathrobes in any of the local stores, and so he'd picked out the fabric and had his cousin, who was a seamstress, make it.

Sheila loved that firefly cloak, and she kept it even after he was gone. It reminded her of what was possible, out there in the dark.

"She was *here*?" Tessa Lee asked. "Here in this house?" It was true there was a bowl and a juice glass on the table. Her granny never left dirty dishes behind, especially not with grits inside to harden and turn to glue.

"You made her *grits*?" she asked, because she loved grits, but most days, she just got cereal because grits took too much work for early in the morning and instant grits were full of chemicals that she didn't want in her body.

"She was hungry," Lil said. "Looked like she hadn't eaten in a long while." Rosie Jo, who had followed them inside, took the dishes over to the sink and was about to add water when Tessa Lee stopped her.

"Don't you wash that!" Tessa Lee said, pointing her finger at Rosie Jo, and Rosie Jo froze. "It's evidence," Tessa Lee said. "You'll get your fingerprints all over it."

"She's not a criminal!" Lil said.

"Oh yes, she is!" Tessa Lee insisted. "Child abandonment's a crime. And what about the drugs?"

"You straighten up," Lil said. "She's not on drugs anymore. And Rosie Jo can wash whatever dishes she wants." So Rosie Jo went back to work as Tessa Lee tore down the hall.

"She used our *shower*?" she exclaimed, and Lil just followed her into the bathroom. When Tessa Lee pushed back the shower door, the walls were still beaded wet, and a washrag tossed over the faucet dripped obscenely onto the drain.

"Oh my *God*," Tessa Lee said. "Are those her *clothes*?" Sheila's dirty clothes were kicked into a small pile between the vanity and the scales.

"Yeah," Lil said. "I'll wash 'em for her. She's wearing that lightning bug housecoat for the time being."

"You gave her my cloak?" Tessa Lee shoved past Lil and ran down the hall to her bedroom to look for it.

"It used to be hers, didn't it?" Lil said from behind, rushing to keep up as Tessa Lee flung open her bedroom door.

"You gave her my cloak?" she hollered again and threw out her arms.

"Well, honey, when you first got here, you said you were keeping it for her to wear when she came back."

"But I was only eight then!"

"I didn't know you'd care so much."

"It's *mine*!" Tessa Lee said. "You came in my *room* and got it?"

"I didn't go plundering," Lil said. "It was there on the hook. I just picked it up and handed it to her. She didn't have nothing to wear."

"Granny, how could you!" Tessa Lee shouted. "It was all I had to remember her by." She was crying by then, big outraged tears.

"Baby, she's back now," Lil said. "Things might be different."

"That doesn't mean they'll be *better*!" Tessa Lee replied.

She stormed out of her bedroom, past her granny, past the kitchen where Rosie Jo washed dishes. She was heading for Travis's bedroom, which was once a laundry-closet at the far end of the trailer. But when she swung the door open, there was no one there—just the twin bed with a sailboat comforter, pushed against the wall, the bookshelf headboard that Pop-Pop had built. Her momma wasn't in there, and neither was Travis. There was no closet in that room where anybody could hide. She couldn't hide under the bed, either, because it was a space-saver bed, with drawers for Travis's clothes beneath the mattress.

Lil came up behind her and stared into the empty room, too. "Wasn't but just a month ago you were trying so hard to find her. I thought you'd be glad to have her back."

"It was more than a month," Tessa Lee said, quieter now. "Where's she at?"

"Out by Cheyenne Lake, at a campsite under one of them big oaks."

"Wearing my firefly cloak?" Tessa Lee said.

"Yep."

"I'm going to get it," Tessa Lee said, and she took off out the door.

Sheila closed her eyes. She'd sleep off her hangover, and when she felt better, she'd find out what had happened to Travis. As soon as her hangover passed, she'd go to Hully Sanders and see about getting a job. She could stay there in the tent for a while, for the rest of the summer and into the fall. By the time it got cold, she'd have saved up some money. She'd have a plan, as soon as her hangover went away.

Maybe Tessa Lee would go with her, wherever she went next. They could go to Vegas, get an apartment. Her momma could visit at Christmastime, and they could all go see the Rockettes.

The flaps on the tent were open so a breeze could push through, but it was still warm. Warm and uncomfortable. Like in the conch shell.

There was one day in the conch shell when a man came up to the window and stared at her for a long while. He looked at her the way people look at aquariums. He talked to her and told her he thought living in a seashell seemed like a good idea.

Most people who came to her window talked dirty, told her exactly what they'd do if they could get inside the shell. But this man just asked if she could hear the ocean all the time and if her shell spiraled around inside like the broken conch shells he found on the beach. Soon, she realized he wasn't teasing. He thought she was a real mermaid, captured by pirates.

He looked wild-eyed and greasy, but he seemed sweet

enough. Sheila was almost sorry to mislead him when she told him to buy his ticket at the booth to his left.

He said, "If I do that, buy a ticket, can I get to you?"

"Sure," Sheila said.

"I'm coming," he said.

"I'm waiting," Sheila replied, and then she just forgot about him, because she said that to everybody. It was part of the job description.

But this man was persistent. He came back out to the street, back to her window, and he said, "You lied to me, little mermaid. You aren't inside that wax museum at all."

"Sure I am," Sheila teased. "You just missed me."

"I looked for you everywhere," he said.

"No," she said. "You couldn't have, or you'd have found me."

"I want to get to where you are," he said.

"Then buy a ticket at the booth to your left."

She couldn't believe he did it again, but he did—went back through the museum, and by then Sheila felt guilty for leading him on. But was it her fault he was soft in the head? She was just doing her job.

When he came back a third time, he said, "You tricked me!"

"Oh, honey," Sheila told him. "I'm made outta wax."

"Wax don't talk," he said.

"I'm not even real. There's no such thing as a mermaid."

And then she heard the glass breaking, and the camera that let her see what was happening outside her picture window went haywire and then dark. She could hear the commotion, the shattered glass and the people outside yelling and sirens blaring.

She wasn't in the picture window, of course. She was in a little closet just beside it. She wasn't in a conch shell at all. She was in a bed, in a fish tail corset, surrounded by mirrors tilted in a thousand directions. But if the window was broken, there was no reflection, anyway. So she clicked off the light and started to pull herself out.

Reggie stopped her. He opened the door and told her to get back to work.

"What happened?" she asked.

"Some psycho punched his hand through," Reggie told her.

"I might as well clock out, then," Sheila said.

"I run this place," he said. "Not you. Get back to work."

So she spent the next hours in the conch shell that no one could see, just sitting there, waiting for nothing, without a plan.

In the two-room tent, she waited that way again. There was no reason for her to stay, but she couldn't go. Someone else was running her show.

She pictured Tessa Lee outside the picture window, reflected back to her in the firefly cloak.

"I'm just an illusion, honey," she'd said to the paranoid man.

She was never sure if he'd broken the glass to get in, or to get her out.

The campsites were across the mobile city, on the other side of the pool and recreation center. And Tessa Lee was on foot, but Lil had a car. So she took the time to gather a pillow and a blanket. She rummaged through her own drawers and found a few things for Sheila to wear, in case Tessa Lee made her strip.

She picked up random things, a radio that would run on batteries, a few hard candies from the candy dish as she passed it, the Listerine for her shingles, the fingernail polish remover. She tucked things in her pockets and gathered them in her arms. A box of Frosted Mini-Wheats—her own cereal, not Tessa Lee's.

"I'll stay here and make a pie, I reckon," Rosie Jo offered, and Lil just thanked her as she tore out the door.

She drove the van back to Sheila's campsite in a hurry, half expecting to pass Tessa Lee along the way. She wondered if she should stop and offer her a ride, if she passed her. But she didn't see her anywhere.

When she got to the campsite, she didn't see anyone. Just the rust-colored tent with a dome-shaped top. There was no sign of Tessa Lee, and no sign of Sheila, no sound coming from inside that tent. It was good that Hully'd put them in a quiet place, with no other campers nearby, because Lil knew that if she looked inside and the tent was empty, the cry she let out would scare the Canadians right back to Quebec. It'd travel a long, long way.

She pushed past the flap on the tent and found Sheila there sleeping. She crawled in beside her, wedged a pillow beneath her head, and began to rub her back.

Sheila jerked, and Lil said, "It's okay. It's just me."

Her voice was gravelly when she said, "Hey, Momma," and she cleared her throat.

"Shhh," Lil said, "just rest," and she put her hand on Sheila's back again, but Sheila winced, and Lil remembered the shingles and rubbed her arm instead.

She sat there a long time, running her hand over the faded robe, but easy. She didn't want to hurt her.

Sheila was so hard and soft at once, beneath Lil's hand, and Lil closed her eyes and pretended she was touching clay, softening it up to mold. The tent was warm, very warm, and even the breeze that blew through sometimes was warm.

After a while, Lil lay down beside her and watched the shadows of the tree limbs wave and sway in the ceiling of the tent. She prayed, "Thank you," and she prayed, "Help me." And she also prayed, "Forgive me." So many times she'd prayed for Sheila—or she'd thought she'd prayed for Sheila—when really, she'd already written Sheila off. She'd been too mad and disillusioned to believe in the possibility of what she prayed for. What she really wanted was relief. She'd prayed for Sheila because she wanted to feel better herself.

She was so tired. And she was so sorry.

Lil didn't know that Sheila was awake—or maybe she wasn't awake. Maybe she was dreaming when she whispered, "I used to live in a swaybacked house."

Lil rolled over, curled against her in spite of the heat. "You still do," she said.

Tessa Lee didn't go to her momma's campsite for a long time. She intended to go there, but then she passed the recreation center and saw her rickshaw parked right outside, and for some reason, she climbed up on it. Her walkie-talkie was in the basket, where Hully must have left it, and so she called to the dispatcher, who said, "Hully told me you were taking the afternoon off," and Tessa Lee said, "I'm back now," and the dispatcher said, "I'll clock you in. Can you go pick up an order from the restaurant and take it to 2525 Starfish Way?"

She drove her rickshaw around all that afternoon, pedaling as hard as she could, standing up on the pedals and not even using her seat, taking the long way everywhere. She didn't think about anything but geometry and the burning in her calves. She saw Hully once, and he tried to wave her over, but she never even slowed down.

And once she saw her granny and her momma in the van. They were at the store, putting ice into a cooler in the back, and her granny shouted out her name, but Tessa Lee ignored her. She had two men in the back of her rickshaw, eager to get to the gazebo bar, so she pretended not to know her granny at all.

Technically, she was supposed to get off work at six, but she didn't leave. She didn't know what to do, or where to go, so she just kept working.

The sun was going down when Hully Sanders called her from the dispatcher's walkie-talkie: "I need one last order picked up and delivered, and then you're off, sweetheart."

"Okay," Tessa Lee said.

"This one's prepaid," Hully told her. "Don't come back

now. I mean it." And Tessa Lee knew right then who'd ordered it and where she was headed.

The pizza smelled good. As she pedaled toward Cheyenne Lake, she knew already that it'd have extra cheese and mushrooms and peppers and onions. But she didn't know if she'd be able to swallow it.

WHEN SHE GOT there, they were waiting. They'd hung a lantern from a tree. The two-room tent was right beneath it.

Tessa Lee's legs went weak when she saw them. Suddenly it seemed like she couldn't pedal another inch, like the rickshaw just wouldn't go.

She sat there on the rickshaw seat till her granny came to her. Her granny came and got her and hugged her. Then her momma came up, and Tessa Lee was scared she might try to hug her, too. But her momma was no dummy. She got the pizza off the backseat of the rickshaw instead.

"Hey, Tessa Lee," she said.

And Tessa Lee said, "Hey."

Her momma smiled, and so Tessa Lee smiled, but she knew better than to trust a smile. Her momma didn't have any teeth in the front and tried to hide it with her lips. She might not even be smiling at all, so Tessa Lee only gave her as much of a smile as she'd be able to deny later, if she needed to.

Her momma was tall, even taller than Tessa Lee. She'd seemed so shrunken in the conch shell that Tessa Lee'd assumed she was shorter. Her skinny ankles and long brown feet protruded from beneath the firefly cloak, and her toenails were painted thundering plum, her granny's favorite color.

The firefly cloak wasn't long enough for her, really. Tessa

Lee'd meant to steal it back, rip it right off her momma's hide. She'd pictured herself pushing her momma down and shaking her out of the firefly cloak. She'd be the female firefly. Her momma'd be the male of another species. She'd trick her. She'd pounce.

But she didn't.

She hadn't seen anyone else wear it in so long. It looked different on her momma. The fireflies weren't even fireflies anymore. They were so tiny, and so faded, and it made Tessa Lee so sad.

"I hear you want your robe back," her momma said.

"It's a cloak. You know that."

"Okay then," her momma replied, and Tessa Lee wasn't sure about her tone. She didn't know whether her momma was making fun.

"If you know I want it back, why are you still wearing it?" Tessa Lee asked. She wasn't sure about her own tone, either. Her voice echoed inside her ears, like she was hollow.

"Just wanted to hear you ask for it," her momma said.

"Give it to me," Tessa Lee demanded.

Her momma unhooked the clasp at the throat, the big pin that had once been in Rash's ear, and she unhooked the smaller clasps down the front, one at a time with her big knuckled hands. She held Tessa Lee's eyes the whole time, and Tessa Lee didn't look away. She wanted to, but she didn't look away.

Her momma pulled off the firefly cloak and tossed it at Tessa Lee.

But Tessa Lee didn't catch it. Her momma was naked. Right there in Hully Sanders's Mobile City. Naked and unapologetic.

Her granny ducked into the tent and grabbed a blanket and put it around her. "There's no sense in that," her granny scolded. "You know better than that!"

Tessa Lee couldn't believe it. She laughed and picked up the firefly cloak, shook it out, and put it on. Her momma shrugged, went inside the tent, and came out wearing one of her granny's craft smocks.

The firefly cloak felt different. It felt warm already, like a nest, or like it must feel beneath the leaves where fireflies sleep.

LATER THAT NIGHT, when it was dark, when she and her Granny had eaten the pizza, and her momma had eaten the inside of the fruit pie that Rosie Jo had made, they took a ride on the rickshaw.

Tessa Lee was glad to be driving, up front and separate from her granny and her momma. She pulled the firefly cloak up over her knees and knotted it so that it wouldn't get hung up in the chain.

"Where to?" she asked.

"Anywhere," her granny said.

"Circle the city and wrap it up tight," her momma added. "Tie a knot so it can't get loose."

So Tessa Lee made Spirographs. She could hear her granny talking to her momma behind her, but she didn't know what they were saying. She thought her momma might be crying, or maybe it was her granny. Or maybe they were laughing. Tessa Lee kept pedaling and didn't look back.

The wind caught the hood of her cloak and blew it out behind her. The wind caught her sleeves and made them into wings. She leaned into her handlebars and pedaled as hard as she could.

It was a dark night, without a moon, though there were faint stars up above. They looked more like glowing eggs than stars. Like something very far away was about to be born.

She drove them all around Hully Sanders's Mobile City, and then she drove them around Cheyenne Lake, circling it on the rickshaw. As long as her legs could hold up, she could ride them, and they could make a geometry that would never go away, even if nobody else could see it.

She knew the roads so well that she could pedal with her eyes closed. With her eyes closed and the wind blowing her cloak, it almost seemed like she was swimming. She was a mermaid, too, but not a captive. She pretended that her momma and her granny were mermaids swimming behind her, pulling a net, catching everything she'd ever left behind and forgotten. She was seining through water, then seining through air. If she could just pedal fast enough, she could seine through time; she could back up and catch Travis, rescue his soul before it flew off.

But her legs were tired. Her granny and her momma grew heavier and heavier. Even standing up on the pedals, her legs gave out. She slowed down the rickshaw and gradually pulled off the road.

When Travis had been killed, the fish he'd caught flew away. It streaked through the air, still hooked to his fishing pole line, and landed beside the bank of the lake in a clump of weeds. But the earthworm he'd used to catch the fish was alive. Tessa Lee had found it in the fish's mouth, squirmed-up and twisting.

She hadn't talked to her granny about all that had happened on the day Travis died. Suddenly, it seemed important.

But when she turned around on the rickshaw, her granny's face was buried in her momma's chest, and her momma was holding her granny close, with her nose in the part of her granny's frizzy hair. They were folded into each other and wrapped around like wings.

Her momma looked up at Tessa Lee, and Tessa Lee felt very far from them both. Her granny and her momma were curved together, but she was pointy, the high tip of a teardrop. The night was so dark, not a firefly anywhere, and Tessa Lee's voice hooked on itself in her throat.

"How'd you get away from those pirates?" she asked. It was almost a whisper, but her momma heard.

Her momma shook her head and said, "I don't know. I guess all the pirates drowned." She looked off over Cheyenne Lake, dreamy, and it seemed to Tessa Lee that she might see something out there in the night, maybe the sails of a pirate ship in the distance. "Oh honey," her momma said at last. "I was the only pirate."

Tessa Lee nodded and walked over to the water. She stood by the reeds and grasses that grew up around the edges, at the place where water turned into land.

That day when Travis died, she'd freed the hook from the fish's lip, slipped the frantic worm off, and dropped it into the grass. The worm fought for a while, flipping and dancing around in a panic. Then it unknotted and wiggled toward dampness and shade.

How could something speared like that keep on living?

Maybe the worm died anyway. Maybe a firefly ate it. Or maybe it was still out there somewhere, sleeping beneath a rotting leaf or burrowing into the soil, going deeper and deeper into the peaceful darkness, and all the while moving toward the glow at the Earth's warm core.

Origins of Firefly Cloak

Back seven or eight years ago, I first tried to write the story of two little children, a girl and her younger brother, who'd been abandoned by their mother and were being raised by their grandparents in a trailer park called Hully Sanders' Mobile City. The little girl (named Lacie in that version) was about eight years old. The little boy (Gary in that version) was four or five. I chronicled their adventures in vignettes, writing mostly from Lacie's point of view, and I dealt with the story of the mother who'd abandoned them and the space between their fantasy of who she was and the rumors they heard about her around the trailer park. I worked on that book for a year or two. While the story itself compelled me, the sections read more like prose poems than a novel. There was no clear plot, no dramatic arc, and after a while, I put the project aside.

Then a few years ago, a boy from my neighborhood was killed very suddenly. He was the younger brother of the teenage girl who sometimes cut my grass. He visited me on my porch and drank grape juice and played with the dog while his sister worked. After he died, the family moved away. I found myself thinking of his sister a lot and wondering how his death had changed her world.

Though the characters of Tessa Lee and Travis have very little in common with those two children from my neighborhood, that real-life event served as a catalyst for *Firefly Cloak*. I realized that the two fictional children I'd written so much about years before needed to grow up–and in fact, if the girl's brother died, then she'd have an excellent reason to go off looking for her mother. With Travis's death, I came up with Tessa Lee's motivation to find her momma. Allowing her to run away set into motion all the events that make up the structure of the book.

And that's how *Firefly Cloak* was born.

One of the things I've learned from my writing is that I sometimes have to be patient with stories. Sometimes the characters are right, the circumstances are right, but the timing is all wrong. Sometimes characters need to grow up in order for their stories to assume meaning. Sometimes *I* need to grow up in order to understand what's significant about a story I'm inclined to tell.

Sheri Reynolds
June 7, 2006

Firefly Cloak

Readers' Group Guide

ABOUT THIS GUIDE

A heartrending tale of loss and reconciliation, Sheri Reynolds's *Firefly Cloak* is a novel full of depth and wisdom. Seven years ago, Tessa Lee and her little brother, Travis were abandoned by their mother. While Sheila tried to outrun her numerous—and dangerous—personal demons, her young children were raised by their loving and over-protective maternal grandparents. But after Travis's sudden death, Tessa Lee finds herself unmoored again, and goes in search of her mother. What she finds is the truth—and perhaps, finally, a family.

This guide is designed to help you direct your reading group's discussion of Sheri Reynolds's atmospheric and touching novel *Firefly Cloak*.

QUESTIONS FOR DISCUSSION

1. Sheri Reynolds's characters are vibrant and so fully realized that they have a way of taking up residence in your heart. Who is your favorite, and why?
2. Hully Sanders's Mobile City is clearly in the South and on the coast, but it could be in any number of states. Why do you think the specific location is never mentioned? Do you think this was a deliberate choice the author made?
3. Tessa Lee is part adult and part child, with one foot in imaginary lands and the other in a life of trauma. Do you think, despite this, she will flourish in life?
4. Why do you believe Tessa Lee latched on so strongly to the cloak—and to fireflies—as a talisman and an obsession? What do fireflies have in common with Sheila and Tessa Lee?
5. The novel interweaves many full and lovely themes. Which ones—motherhood, magic, loss, redemption, symmetry and geometry, and flight, to name a few—resonated most with you personally, and why?
6. As readers, we never actually meet Lewis/Pop-Pop or Travis; we only see them through other character's memories. Were they any less real to you because of this?
7. Sheila's killing of the baby birds is a dramatic, tense, almost unbearable scene. Did you feel, while reading it, that Sheila was doing to the baby birds what she couldn't bring herself to do to her children? In her mind, was Sheila murdering them or freeing them?

8. Was Sheila's stay at the house with seventeen locks real or a hallucination? Was the old man an actual person or a metaphor?

9. Was the incident at the Cock-a-doodle-doo, when Lil slapped the black men at the bar, shocking to you? Did you feel it was out-of-character, or particularly revealing?

10. "All [Lil had] ever wanted was to give Sheila the life she hadn't had herself. Mostly she'd wanted to keep her safe, pass along strong values, not let her be mistreated or experience adult things too soon" (p. 172). Lil gave Sheila and Tessa Lee very similar upbringings. Had Lil not softened and grown herself, would Tessa Lee have headed down the same destructive path as her mother? Why or why not?

11. Rash is an unexpectedly complex character. Do you think he pitied Tessa Lee? Did he see himself in her? Did he admire her? Do you think his life was better for having met and helped her?

12. Why do you think Tessa Lee got her nipple pierced? Were you shocked that she went through with it? What do you think it revealed about her innermost strengths and weaknesses?

13. Do you believe Sheila, Lil and/or Tessa Lee achieved redemption in the novel's final pages? Why or why not? Who do you believe was most in need of it?

14. Will Sheila stay with Tessa Lee and Lil? Or is the better question, will Tessa Lee stay with Sheila and Lil?